LADIES' BANE

Miss Silver looked thoughtfully across her rapidly moving needles.

'Are you sure that you really wish to engage my services?'

'I shouldn't have come if I didn't! I want the village talk, the village gossip. I want the Falconer angle. Elizabeth Moore says you're a wonder at getting people to talk. Well, that's what I want. Villages can be as tight as clams. I sent a man down to snoop around and didn't get a thing, and he wouldn't if he'd stayed there a year instead of a day. But one of Miss Falconer's p.g.'s pottering round with her, buying oddments, and going to church on Sundays – well, that's different. Especially if you could carry on a spot of knitting.'

Miss Silver smiled indulgently and remarked that she never went anywhere without her knitting.

**Also by the same author,
and available in Coronet Books:**

Ladies' Bane

Patricia Wentworth

CORONET BOOKS
Hodder and Stoughton

First published in Great Britain 1954 by
Hodder and Stoughton Limited

Coronet edition 1979
Third impression 1981

British Library C.I.P.

Wentworth, Patricia
  Ladies' Bane.
  I. Title
  823'.9'1F   PR6045.E66L/

  ISBN 0-340-25057-7

Printed and bound in Great Britain for
Hodder and Stoughton Paperbacks, a
division of Hodder and Stoughton Ltd.,
Mill Road, Dunton Green, Sevenoaks,
Kent (Editorial Office: 47 Bedford
Square, London, WC1 3DP) by
Hunt Barnard Printing Ltd.,
Aylesbury, Bucks.

CHAPTER I

Looking back, Ione Muir was to wonder what would have happened if she had chosen any other day to go up to town. With all the days of the week to choose from, she had picked a Tuesday, and that particular Tuesday. Suppose she had chosen some other day. Suppose she had gone a week earlier or a week later. Suppose she had not gone at all. Just how much difference would it have made? Would she have met Jim Severn in some other way? Would it all have been the same in the end? Or would it have been different – perhaps dreadfully different? Did certain people, certain events, certain crimes, produce as it were a vortex into which you must inevitably have been drawn? Or did it all just turn on the choice of a day or a train? She was never quite sure.

She took the 9.45 to town. Any other train, and she would not have run into Fenella Caldecott as she emerged from the Knightsbridge Tube.

'Ione! I haven't seen you since – when was it – Celia's wedding? What a lovely bride she made! Fortunately one didn't have to look at the bridegroom – one never does at a wedding – but Celia was going to have to live with him, and honestly, I don't know how she could! One oughtn't to say things like that, but it's only to you, and I'm sure I hope they are very happy indeed. Curious how some girls just seem to disappear after they are married. Cornwall, wasn't it? Too remote! And that reminds me – what about Allegra? She's another of the vanished ones. Why on earth do girls marry the sort of people who carry them off to the ends of the earth?' She bent a long, slim neck to glance at her wristwatch and gave a faint scream. 'Darling, I'm going to be late for my fitting! And André just crosses you off if you're even half a minute behind your time, though he doesn't mind how

5

many hours he keeps you waiting himself!' She waved a hand, called over her shoulder, 'Meet me for lunch at the club,' and was gone.

Ione watched her go. Fenella hadn't changed in the least, and she probably never would. Even at school she had possessed a long, slim elegance which triumphed over such garments as a gym tunic and the quite hideous St. Griselda uniform. Now, clothed by the great André, she was a most decorative creature. Not really her friend, but Allegra's.

She had not said she would meet Fenella for lunch, but she supposed that she would. What really decided her was that there hadn't been time to ask whether she had heard from Allegra. They had been such very close friends.

She went about her shopping with rather an abstracted mind. Allegra had always been a bad correspondent. Anyone may be a bad correspondent without there being anything wrong. It is when people are busy and happy that they don't bother to write. If there is anything wrong you hear. Or do you? Perhaps Fenella had heard –

Taking one o'clock as the starting-point, she had to wait three-quarters of an hour for Fenella at the club, and then she had to hear all about the fitting, and why Fenella had left Mirabelle whom she had always previously declared to be the only really imaginative dressmaker on this side of the Channel.

'But, darling, a complete *devil*! You won't believe it, but she sent me to the Crayshaw wedding in an absolute duplicate of Pippa Casabianca's going-away dress! In Paris, you know, and a whole month before! I might never have known, only Yvonne de Crassac sent me the photographs! Well, that really was the *end*! And I'm terribly lucky to get in with André, because he has a waiting-list about a mile long!'

There was a good deal more of this before Ione had a chance to mention Allegra.

'Have I heard from her lately? Darling, we don't *correspond*! The old school tie rather fades out after a year or two, don't you think? But I did like your charming brother-in-law – quite sinfully goodlooking, as Elizabeth Tremayne said! I said no one ever looked at the bridegroom, but when

6

Allegra was married we all *did*! Funny how those very handsome men don't seem to care so much about looks in a girl, and you know, I did think that dead white was a mistake for Allegra. So *cold*, if you know what I mean!'

There was no unkindness in Fenella. Dress was her one real interest in life, and she took it seriously. When her mind turned to Allegra Muir's wedding she could not only pass over the two-year gap and visualise every detail, but she could no more help re-dressing and re-grouping the bride and her attendants than she could stop the even flow of her breath. And the worst of it was that she was right. Nothing could have been less becoming to Allegra than all that icy white which had made her look pinched and grey, like something lost in a snowstorm. Ione was ruefully aware that she hadn't looked any too good in it herself. And that awful lumpy girl Margot – could anything have been worse! She laughed and said,

'It's the last time I'm going to be a bridesmaid anyhow. You have to when it's your sister, but never again! The idea of herding a lot of girls together and putting them into something which is bound to be the last thing on earth that most of them ought to wear – well, it's simply barbaric!'

Fenella did not laugh – she hardly ever did. She said earnestly,

'You're too right, darling. Let me see – there was you – and Elizabeth Tremayne – and the Miller twins with all that red hair – and that frightful lumpy schoolgirl – what was her name?'

'Margot Trent. She's a relation of Geoffrey's, and he is her guardian. We had to have her. She looked terrible.'

Fenella shook her head sadly.

'Schoolgirls always do in white. They're either much too fat like this Margot girl, or else they've got sharp red elbows and bones sticking out all over them. She still lives with them, doesn't she? I don't know how Allegra could! Has she fined down at all?'

'I don't know.'

'But you've seen her, haven't you?'

'Well, not very lately.'

7

'But you've seen Allegra. I'm simply counting on your giving me all her news. You must have seen Allegra!'

Ione felt that her colour was rising. She said,

'Well, I was in America.'

'America! What on earth were you doing there?'

'We have relations in New Jersey. I went to visit them, and stayed on longer than I meant to. As a matter of fact, I tumbled into a job.'

Fenella had a remembering look.

'Yes – now don't tell me! I did hear about it – it was Sylvia Scott! She sent me an American magazine with a picture of you doing one of those monologues you used to be dragged in for at school concerts. It said you were having quite a success.'

Ione laughed.

'They seemed to like them. A friend of my cousins got me to do one or two at a big party, and then other people asked me, and in the end I had a very good professional offer, so I thought I had better take it and bring some dollars home.'

'Well, I don't know how you do it!' Fenella's attention wavered. She came back to Allegra. 'What is her house like? Are they able to get any staff?'

'I expect so – I don't know.'

'You haven't been there? *Ione!*'

'I had to go and look after my old cousin who was ill.'

'Do you mean to say you haven't seen Allegra since the wedding?'

'No, of course not. I saw her when she came back from her honeymoon.'

'You've never been to stay with her?'

'I couldn't leave Cousin Eleanor.'

Fenella shook her head.

'It's quite fatal to go and look after an old lady. They never die, and you never get away.'

Ione laughed.

'I'm going to stay with Allegra next week,' she said.

In her mind something said insistently, 'If they don't put you off again.'

CHAPTER II

The dining-room at Fenella's club was one of those rooms where you don't notice very much what the weather is like outside. At lunchtime in the middle of January the lights would be on anyhow, so it was not until they had lingered over their coffee and Fenella remembered that she had an appointment to try an absolutely new hair-do that either of them noticed the fog.

'And if I really can't drop you, darling, I'd better fly, or goodness knows if I'll get there!'

Ione's 'No – quite the wrong direction' was gathered up in the rush of departure. She stood for a moment on the pavement outside the club before deciding that it was no use trying to do any more shopping, and that she had better just walk round to the nearest Tube station and go home. At the time it seemed not only a sensible thing to do, but a perfectly easy one. She knew this part of London like the back of her hand, and the station was not more than five minutes walk. Yet before the five minutes were up she was lost.

She had somehow missed a turning which she ought to have taken. Well, that was quite simple – she must go back and find it. She turned, walked for another five minutes, and knew that she had got right off the track. And what was worse, she had walked into a much denser patch of fog. If it had been like this in front of the club, she would never have started out. As it was, she had no idea of how far she had come, or in what direction. She found that she had no ideas about anything. No amount of darkness is so bewildering as fog, since it not only baffles, but confuses every sense. The eye still sees, but what it sees bears no relation to reality. The ear still hears, but it can no longer decide what is near and what is far. Everything is unnatural, distorted.

Well, she must keep on walking. These London fogs vary

9

very much in density. She might at any time emerge from the worst of it, or at the very least come out upon some thoroughfare where she could ask her way. If it was as thick as this, it would be too much to hope that the buses would be running, or that there would be a taxi, but someone would be able to tell her the way to the Tube. Someone? It came over her that it was a good many minutes now since she had so much as heard a passing footstep.

She began to walk again without the least idea of where she was going. She found it extremely difficult to keep a straight line. Her left foot would slip from the kerb with a jerk, and a minute or two later her right, groping, would bruise itself against the wall in front of a house. The street-lamps really made everything worse. They showed only as dim orange cocoons which lighted nothing except the fog.

It was when she was passing one of them that she made her first contact with another human being. A step sounded – somewhere beside her, behind her, she didn't know which – and a hand came out of the fog to snatch at her bag. It missed, because she stepped sideways into the road and ran for it, her heart thudding against her side. When she pulled up, there was no other sound but her own labouring breath. Stupid to have been so startled. It was only some petty thief who wanted her bag, and would have had it, his eyes being probably better at this kind of thing than hers, if she hadn't swerved almost before the snatching hand shot out.

She came after this to a more frequented place. People went by, singly for the most part and at fairly long intervals. It must be about four o'clock, and of course no one who could help it would be out. After the attempt to snatch her bag she no longer thought of asking the way. You hear a footstep, and it tells you hardly anything at all. Or does it? She found herself getting interested in the footsteps. The slow, heavy one which might belong to an elderly tradesman full of solid worth or to the mother of six. Or perhaps to a prosperous burglar out to do a little quiet housebreaking in the fog. The light hurrying step of someone who would probably scream if you spoke to her. The hesitating step of someone who was probably as lost as herself, but who could be by chance another lurking thief.

She thought afterwards that she must have turned a corner without knowing it, because there were no more footsteps. The street seemed narrow, and the lamps a good deal farther apart. She pictured it as one of those quiet backwaters set with neat narrow-fronted houses all alike. She knew that the fronts were narrow, because there was a balustrade – so many dumpy stone pillars and three or four steps up to the front door. That the balustrade was there to guard an area upon which the basement windows looked out, she was to learn in rather a painful manner. Under the pressure of that odd disposition to bear either to one side or to the other a right hand swerve brought her up against an area gate. She hit it hard with her knee, and it gave and let her through. Half stumbling, half falling, she came down quite a lot of steps and finished up on her hands and knees upon damp stone.

It was painful enough, but she was all in one piece. Her hat hung over an ear, her stockings were certainly laddered, and her gloves were slimy. She took them off, straightened her hat, and groped about for the bag which had flown out of her hand. She had just found it, when there was a sound. It came from over her head. A key had been turned in a lock and a bolt drawn back. The front door of the house was opening.

Her first thought was that someone had heard her fall down the area steps. Anyone in one of the front rooms could hardly have helped doing so. She was just thinking that it would look better if she were on her feet, when a voice said,

'I'm a dependable man – I can't put it any stronger than that. My word is my bond. There's not a man living that can say I ever let him down. A sure friend in trouble and a dependable man – that's me.'

Three things were borne in upon Ione. The gentleman who was speaking hailed at one time or another from the far side of the Scottish border. He had fortified himself against the fog by recourse to his native beverage. And neither he nor the person whom he was addressing had the slightest idea that anyone had just made a crash landing in the area.

11

The steps that ran up from the street to the front door were almost over her head. If she stayed where she was she would neither be seen nor heard. There was no reason at all why she should not disclose herself, find out where she was, and ask to be set upon her way. The dependable gentleman might even prove to be a dependable guide.

There was no reason – but there was an instinct. If she had told her tongue to speak it would not have obeyed her. But she did not tell it to speak. She stayed as still as a hare stays in its form, and for the same reason. Over her head someone was whispering. She could not tell whether it was man or woman. Then the Scot again:

'Oh, I'm on my way, I'm on my way, and I'll take my foot from the door when I'm ready. And a nice sort of an afternoon to go out in – as black as the Earl o' Hell's waistcoat! If ye'd a heart in ye, ye'd not be sending me out in it.'

The whispering voice said something, and the Scot laughed.

'Oh, ye're a prudent pairson, and I've nothing against prudence – in reason. And if ye think it's reasonable to turn a man out in a fog like this, ye can just consider, if I'm run over, who'll do your dirty work for ye then? Ye can just think about that . . . All right, all right, I'm going! And I haven't said I'll do it yet, but I'll give it my careful consideration and let ye know. But mind, ye'll have to think again – about the remuneration. I'll not do it for any less than two thousand, and I'm of the opinion that I'd be a fool to do it for that. It's my neck I'll be risking, and I'll not risk it for a penny less than two thousand.'

He came rolling down the steps, and the door banged to above him. She heard the key turn and the bolt go home. The rolling steps went past her and down the street to the lilt of a tune. The gentleman who was considering if he would risk his neck was whistling as he went.

'For ye'll tak the high road,
And I'll tak the low road,
And I'll be in Scotland afore ye – [2]

12

The words sprang up in Ione's mind to meet the tune, and with them the impulse to get out of this place into which she had fallen and away from the house where someone whispered, and someone haggled about the price of his neck. It was one of those impulses which take hold of you. She didn't think about it, she didn't even know that she was going to obey it. She just found herself running up the area steps and out into the road. It was the sheer blank wall of the fog that stopped her. The moment that she was away from the area and the steps, her sense of direction was gone. She couldn't see the street-lamp. So far as she was concerned, it was just blotted out. All that remained in the blind world of fog were the failing strains of *Loch Lomond*. When they were gone she would be all alone.

She began to run, but almost at once she checked herself. If she was to follow him, he mustn't hear her. She mustn't run. As long as he went on whistling, she thought she could follow the sound. But she mustn't let him get far ahead. The fog muffled everything. It would be dreadfully easy to lose the sound, and once it was lost there would be nothing to guide her.

When she thought about it afterwards she found it extremely difficult to understand why she should have had any desire to follow the rolling Scot. He had certainly had too much to drink, and she had heard him discussing the remuneration he would require for what sounded uncommonly like one of the major crimes. Against this there was nothing reasonable to advance. He seemed to know where he was going – and it might quite easily be the last place on earth in which she would wish to find herself. He sounded confident, and he whistled melodiously. It was, of course, his confidence which was the lure. He had a stick in his hand, and he went along at a cheerful pace, now tapping with it on the pavement, now rattling it with noisy gusto along the line of a stone balustrade. And all the time he whistled. When he had finished with *Loch Lomond* he did tricky things with the *Bluebells of Scotland*, and then rather let himself go on the *Road to the Isles*. If he hadn't made so much noise he might have heard her. By and bye she became more confident and came up as close as she dared. He seemed to know where he was going, for he turned twice – once to the left, and once, after crossing the road, to the right.

After a little while she began to make a plan. He mustn't know that she had been following him. He mustn't connect her in any way with the house or with the street, which were now at quite a safe distance behind them. But if she could pass him in the fog, get a little way ahead, and then turn and come back, it would look like a perfectly chance encounter, and she could ask him whether he knew where they were. The more she thought about this plan, the more she liked it. Curiously enough, she had no fear of speaking to him. He might be going to engage in high-ranking crime, but she felt perfectly sure that he wouldn't snatch her bag or hit her over the head in the street. She passed him, running lightly, whilst he was giving a spirited rendering of *Bonnie Dundee*, and was just going to slow up and turn, when she ran slap into someone else. Her outstretched hands touched a rough coat, and a moment later her face was hard against it and her mouth full of muffler. By the time she had gasped and spat it out a man's voice was saying over the top of her head, 'I say, I am awfully sorry! Are you hurt?' and *Bonnie Dundee* was breaking off. The voice was a nice one. She gave the arm which was holding her a frantic pinch, stood on tiptoe to get as near as possible to where she thought there might be an ear, and whispered,

'Say I ran into you – a little way back.'

He said, 'All right.'

Her whispered 'Thank you' reached him, and then a clear and charming voice, 'Oh, here's someone! Perhaps he knows where we are! Do ask him!'

The fog became permeated with an aroma of whisky. The voice that had rolled out its demand for two thousand pounds now enquired in a genial manner,

'And where would ye be wanting to be?' There seemed to be at least three r's in the 'where'.

Ione had turned. She was still holding the arm which she had pinched. There was a sharp pain in her ankle. She said just a little breathlessly,

14

'I'm afraid I am quite lost. I don't know if you can help us at all.'

There was the sound of a laugh.

'If ye had asked me that same thing just about ten minutes ago, I'd have told ye, but I'm beginning to think that I might have been mistaken. It's a bad fog that would baffle me, but I'll admit that I'm not just so sure of my surroundings as I'd like to be. I have an idea where I went wrong, but I'm far from saying I could find my way back to it. No, no – it's "Keep right on to the end of the road, keep right on to the end – " ' He passed easily into song, but pulled up before the end of the verse. 'Ye take my meaning? If ye keep right on ye'll aye get somewhere. If ye stay where ye are ye might just as well be dead and buried, and a grand saving of trouble to all concerned.'

The voice which belonged to the arm that Ione was holding said quietly,

'I can tell you where we are, for what it is worth. Not very much, I'm afraid, because I can't see the slightest chance of getting anywhere else until the fog lifts.'

Ione pinched again hard.

'Oh, why didn't you say so before?'

There was a trace of laughter in his voice as he said,

'You didn't give me time,' Then, in an explanatory manner in the direction of the aroma of whisky, 'This lady and I collided a little way back. I think she must have been coming out of a side road.'

'And who's to tell which is which?' demanded the Scot very reasonably. 'But if ye find yourself in a position to tell us where we are, I'll be obliged for the information.'

'We're in Bicklesbury Road, if that means anything to you. My name is Severn. I'm an architect, and I came here to look at some houses which a client has bought and wants to have turned into flats. By the time I got here the fog was coming down fast, and I was a perfect fool not to go home. I thought I'd just take a quick look round, but when I got in it was really too dark to do anything. I pottered a bit, using a torch and hoping the fog would lift. Then my battery failed, and I came out into this. I'm afraid it's not too good.'

15

It was all in the middle of the Scot endeavouring to place the exact whereabouts of Bicklesbury Road and introducing himself as Professor MacPhail that Ione became aware that whatever happened to the two men, she wasn't going to be able to walk any farther. The ankle was becoming very insistent. She might have twisted it when she fell down all those steps. She might have given it a wrench just now when she bumped into Mr. Severn – she didn't really know, and it didn't really matter. All she did know was that it wouldn't take her any farther. She said so, breaking in upon an itinerary proposed by the Professor.

'I'm afraid it's no good to me even if we could find the way, and I'm quite sure we couldn't. I'm afraid I've sprained my ankle.'

It might have been the whole weight of the day, or it might have been the way things have of invading you and suddenly taking over, but as she spoke she felt the fog begin to flicker. Her weight came on Jim Severn's arm, and if he hadn't been quick she would have gone down. After that everything was pretty hazy, and she just let go. There were voices, and she was being carried. It was rather like a slow motion picture. That was the fog of course. Nothing could really move in a fog like this. The buses would be stopped – and the cars – and the people who were abroad would crawl like beetles and wish to be at home again – and the watches and clocks would all slow down and time too –

She came to herself with the feeling that she had been a long way off. She was lying on something very hard, and there was at least one thing that had not stopped. Professor Macphail was still talking.

'And we could be very comfortable here till the fog lifts if there was so much as a chair to sit on, or a candle-end to give us a glint of light. It's wonderful how little ye can be doing with. There was my old grandfather, and well I remember him, brought up on a small farm, and the only light they had was the tallow dips they made themselves, and they had to be saving of those, so for the most part he would just study his lessons by the light of the kitchen fire. And his eyesight perrfect at eighty-seven years of age!'

Ione struggled up on her elbow. The place was dark enough, but not so thick with fog. It was a horrid yellowish darkness, but it was easier to breathe than it had been out in the street. The floor under her was wood. The palm of her hand as she leaned on it was aware of dust and grit. She said in the best tradition of the fainting heroine,

'Where are we?'

'Are you better?'

'Oh, yes – I'm all right. I don't know what happened – everything just slipped. Where have we got to?'

'One of the houses I was looking over. I really don't think there's a chance of getting anywhere until the fog lifts, and it's better here than outside. I'm afraid everything's been cut off, and there isn't a stick of furniture in the place. But you can't walk on a sprained ankle, and we shouldn't get anywhere if you could. Look here, I laid you down flat because you had gone off, but now you have come round I think the best way would be to sit on the stairs. After all, one does it at a dance.'

They sat on the stairs, and time went slowly by. Ione had a step to herself to begin with, but after an interval when she must have drifted into an uneasy sleep she found that there was a shoulder under her head and an arm that steadied her. It wasn't the Professor's arm, because the whisky seemed to be some way off . . . She slid back into sleep again . . .

It was the kind of sleep in which you keep on coming to the surface and drifting off. Whenever she did come back, the Professor seemed to be talking, the sound of his rolling r's like the drum-beat in a dance rhythm. Presently he was saying,

'There's that old chestnut about the mandarin in China. Ye'll have heard it *ad nauseam*, but it raises a very interesting moral problem. If by pressing a button which would cause the death of this totally unknown person, ye could benefit three-quarters of the human race, would ye, or would ye not, be justified in pressing the button?'

Mr. Severn's voice was much nearer as he said,

'How do you know it's going to benefit three-quarters of

the human race?' The tone had a touch of boredom, a touch of amusement.

'That,' said the Professor, 'ye will just have to hypothesize.'

The word rolled grandly off his tongue. Ione considered it with awe. She could not believe that it really existed, but at a more convenient time, when she was able to have recourse to a dictionary, she discovered that it did. At the moment it just floated away and became part of a general state of mind in which dream and reality kept on changing place. The floor was hard, but her ankle had stopped hurting. She heard Mr. Severn say,

'Well, three-quarters of the human race is a fairly large order, and if you get down to brass tacks, I feel pretty sure that the button-pusher is really only interested in one member of it – himself. Is he going to do himself a bit of good, or isn't he? And if he does his button-pushing, is he going to get away with it? That's a really very much better problem than the other, you know.'

Professor MacPhail was understood to dissent from this. He used the word sordid with more r's than the dictionary provides. He was saying that in order to arrive at a philosophic conclusion it was necessary to 'impairsonalise' the problem, when Ione drifted away again. There was something about the rise and fall of his periods and the drumming of those Scottish r's that was very soporific.

When she really woke there was a feeling of time having passed. She sat up, and was aware of stiffness, and of an arm about her. When she moved it had tightened, but now it relaxed. The voice that had talked with the Professor said,

'Are you awake?'

She drew a long breath.

'Yes – I am. You've been holding me – how very kind. I don't know when I've slept like that – I might have been drugged – '

She became aware of several things simultaneously. The air was clearer to breathe, there was light coming in through the fanlight over the door, and there was enough of it to show that there was no longer a third occupant of the stair.

'Where is the Professor?'

18

'He went when the fog lifted – about half an hour ago.'

'But why didn't you wake me? We ought to have gone too.'

'Well, I think on the whole he preferred to fade away on his own.'

The light which lay in a yellow oblong across the treads of the stairs was not daylight. It came from a street-lamp which couldn't be very far away. The fog had lifted, but it was still dark.

She said, 'What time is it?'

'It must be nearly three o'clock. If you don't mind being left, I think the best plan will be for me to go and get my car. It's in a lock-up garage about a quarter of a mile from here. Is there anywhere I can take you?'

Well, was there? After that fall down the area steps she didn't feel so sure about an hotel. Three o'clock in the morning is a bit tricky anyway, and if her clothes were in a mess and there was green slime on her face – no, it didn't really seem to be a very good plan. She said frankly,

'I was thinking about an hotel, but I don't know that it would do. You see, I had a fall down some area steps – that was when I must have twisted my ankle. I don't really feel that I can confront a respectable night porter.'

'You don't live in town?'

'No – just up for the day. My name is Ione Muir.'

'I think I said mine was Jim Severn.'

'Yes. Well, about where I'm to go to – I suppose I could knock up Elizabeth Tremayne or Jessica Thorne, but I'd much rather not. Elizabeth would make a good story out of it, and Jessica would go round saying how dreadful it was for weeks. They don't keep the waiting-room open at a railway station, do they? No, I'm practically sure they don't. I'm afraid it will just have to be an hotel.'

He said in rather a hesitating manner,

'I've got a flat, and my old nurse keeps house for me. She's the most respectable person I ever met.'

Iona broke into laughter.

'And just what, do you suppose, she'll say when you come home with a strange female at three o'clock in the morning!'

CHAPTER III

There is something strange about being alone in an empty house. Ione sat on the second step from the bottom of the stair and did what she could to her face and her hair. She had a pocket-comb in her bag, and a compact, and some cleansing-tissue, but what the face really wanted was hot water and soap, and the fact that there was green slime on her hands didn't make things any easier. She used all the cleansing-tissue, but the result as viewed in a three-inch mirror by the light which was coming through the transom was discouraging. The smudges under her eyes were because of being lost in the fog and falling down steps, but the general greenish tinge was probably due to the fact that the tissue had merely spread the slime instead of removing it. She combed her hair, and thought she looked like one of the plainer ghosts.

She put on her hat, and took it off again. She couldn't have believed that anything could have made her look worse, but it did. She had rather fancied herself in it, but it was one of those bits of nonsense which depend on everything else being just so – a tilt here, a twist there, and exactly the right hair-do and make-up. Rather snappy when she started out, but now all it did was to make her look like a ghost the worse for drink. She crammed it into the pocket of her coat and sat back to wait for Jim Severn.

The empty silence of the house began to close in upon her. The little sounds which she had been making were at an end. They had gone into the silence and the emptiness and been swallowed up. She began to think of all the times she had been alone in a house without minding it in the least. Why on earth should she mind now? The fact that the house was empty was neither here nor there. Sofas and tables and chairs, and a carpet on the floor – there is really nothing about these to make you feel safe. If there were a carpet on this stair, it would be a little less hard to sit on, but that was all. If she knew that she had only to cross the hall, open a door, and come into a comfortable furnished room, she would not be any more secure than she was at this moment. She was, of course, perfectly secure. The door was locked, and no one could get in without the key which was on Jim Severn's ring. There was no one but herself in the house.

There was silence, and emptiness, and cold. And now the silence began fantastically to quiver, as if there was a pressure upon it and it might be going to break. Ione pulled her thought up sharply. This, at least, she knew for what it was, a thing out of nursery days when she would lie awake at the top of a tall old house and wait for the everydayness about her to splinter and let through all the terrors of a child's imagination – thin sliding shadows and broad rolling ones – things that bounced and were suddenly not there any more – things that lurked and made faces at you just out of sight.

The imagination was still a very lively one, but she had it under much better control. She could tell it now quite firmly that it was playing tricks and switch it over to devising a new monologue. *Not* one about an empty house! That was the sort you could do more comfortably in a lighted room in front of a nice warm fire. This one might be about a girl who got into the wrong house and stumbled on something she wasn't meant to know. Quite effective if she could hit on just the right vein . . . When Jim Severn's key turned in the lock she was a long way off.

The air outside was cold. She could see all the street-lamps. Even at the end of the road there was only a little mist to blur them. As long as she was careful with her ankle it felt all right. In fact everything in the garden was lovely. She looked at Jim Severn, and he looked at her. She had known that he was tall because of where his voice came from when she ran into him. She saw now that he held himself well, and that he was goodlooking in a pleasant, unobtrusive sort of way. It seemed a pity that she couldn't have done a better job of her face. First impressions –

What Jim Severn saw was a girl in a torn fur coat with dark hair falling rather straight on either side of a very pale face. He knew already that she had a voice that was not like any other. When it spoke to him out of the fog his ear had been charmed and his imagination captured. It was that kind of voice. Now that he looked at her, he could only think how pale she was and hope that she wasn't going to faint again. Then he noticed that she had rather amusing eyebrows like little slanting wings. In the lamplight her eyes looked dark.

After that blind groping through the fog the smooth motion of the car was like a beautiful dream. To be able to see across the street and away to the end of it, to be carried along without having to force reluctant feet to carry her, not to have to bother about what was going to happen next – all this was part of the dream. There was also the thought that there might be hot coffee and a bath.

It wasn't until they were out of the car and half way to the second floor in an automatic lift that she remembered Jim Severn's old nurse. She ought to have been relying firmly on her, but she had just let her drift into the background of her mind. She couldn't – no she couldn't really pretend that anybody's old nurse was going to be pleased when her Mr. Jim turned up in the middle of the night with a strange girl.

His key turned in the lock and they came into a small pleasant hall with a light burning. She found herself hoping passionately that Nannie was one of those people who could sleep through anything.

The hope failed before she had time to nourish it. From a door on the left there emerged a figure in a quilted dressing-gown of navy blue silk with a good deal of white hair disposed for the night under a strong brown net. There were firm rosy cheeks, and the sort of bright blue eyes that give you the impression that you are being gone over with a magnifying-glass.

Jim Severn hastened to say his piece.

'Nannie, this is Miss Muir. We've been held up in the fog, and I'm afraid she has hurt herself. Barbara's room is ready, isn't it?'

The blue eyes transferred their gaze to him.

'It's never been otherwise since we come here.' They returned to Ione. 'Good-evening, Miss Muir,' The air fairly crisped with frost.

Ione said in a lovely piteous voice,

'Oh, Nannie, I know it looks dreadful, but I fell down some area steps – and Mr. Severn has been so *kind*. Do you think – oh, do you think I could possibly have a wash?'

It might have been one thing, or it might have been another. It might have been the quality of the voice or the quiver in it, or just the drawn fatigue of the face out of which two candid eyes looked into hers, but the temperature underwent a marked improvement. Nannie knew a lady when she saw and heard one, green slime or no green slime, and she knew when what was wanted was a hot bath and a hot drink, and a nice warm bed.

It was while she was laying down the law on these lines that Jim Severn was understood to say that he must go and put away the car.

Nannie threw open the bathroom door.

'Constant hot water is what we have, and it's not everyone can say that. Now, miss, here's your towel, and I'll just go and get you one of Miss Barbara's nightgowns, and the dressing-gown she keeps here, and some slippers. Eh, dear, but you've laddered your stockings – past doing anything to by the look of them! And a tear in your coat – but that will mend. Fur tears easy, and it mends easy too.'

She bustled away, and came back again with an amusing flowered dressing-gown, scarlet slippers, and an extremely decorative nightdress.

'Now, my dear, you just have a nice hot bath. And you needn't spare the water – it does two easy. But you'd better not be too long, for Mr. Jim will be wanting his. There's some of Miss Barbara's bath-salts in that jar.'

It was a heavenly bath, and when it was over there was a heavenly hot drink and a soft, delicious bed. By the time Nannie had tucked her in, opened the window, and put out the light she might have been ordering her about since she was three years old. She didn't go to sleep. She plunged into it. Dreamless depths closed over her.

CHAPTER IV

The ice never formed again. Nannie brought her a cup of tea at eight, and told her all about Barbara whilst she was drinking it. It appeared that she ceased to be Miss Barbara to anyone except Nannie for the last ten years or so. She was Lady Carradyne.

'And Sir Humphrey is a very nice gentleman. Wonderful interested in everything to do with the land like a gentleman ought to be, and does very well at it too, so Miss Barbara says. They've got a boy of eight and a half, and a little girl of five – a real little love. But of course I couldn't leave Mr. Jim, so I recommended my niece. And if Miss Barbara has a mind to come up to town and stay over, well, there's her room always ready, and no need to let us know. She's got her key and can just walk in.'

Ione checked the thought that it was just as well that Barbara hadn't walked in at, say, four o'clock in the morning to find a strange girl in her bed.

Nannie went on talking. By the time Ione was dressed, with a pair of Barbara's stockings to take the place of her ruined ones, she knew what an old and distinguished firm of architects Jim Severn belonged to. There were two uncles in it, and one of them wouldn't be very long before he retired, and then Mr. Jim would go up a step.

'His father died when the children were still in the nursery – him and Miss Barbara – and their mother married again. But she didn't live long either, so you may say they never had anyone but each other, Mr. Jim and Miss Barbara.'

Ione listened, but she had to think as well. The first thing to be done was to ring up Wanetree and placate Norris, who would certainly be feeling fierce about her failure either to return or to let them know that she was not coming back

24

last night. She ought to have done it before really – not in the middle of the night, but more or less at crack of dawn, which at this time of year would be getting on for a quarter to eight.

Norris was Cousin Eleanor's maid, and a domestic tyrant of forty years standing. She answered the call in a very bad temper indeed and scolded Ione as if she were five years old.

'Staying out all night, and not so much as troubling to give us a ring! I'm sure I don't know what things are coming to! And if Miss Eleanor isn't downright ill, thinking something might have happened – well, it's no thanks to those that should know better, and that I will say, and nobody is going to get me from it!'

Ione took a deep patient breath. She really had known Norris since she was five, and the only thing you could do with her when she was in a mood was just to go on saying whatever you had to say until some of it got in.

'Listen, Norrie – '

'And don't you Norrie me, Miss Ione! There's those that can have dust thrown in their eyes, and those that can't *nor* won't!'

'Norris, do just *listen! There was a fog* – F, O, G – fog.'

'Nor I don't want things spelled at me neither!'

'Look in the morning papers! It was the worst fog ever. I fell down some area steps, and I never got near a telephone till half past three, and then I thought I'd better let it alone.'

'I should think so indeed – waking the whole house in the middle of the night!'

'Norrie – you didn't tell Cousin Eleanor, did you? . . . No, I thought you wouldn't. It's so bad for her to worry.'

There was a portentous sniff at the other end of the line.

'And whose fault would it be if she did? Only for me she'd be half off her head by now, but I'm not so short of trouble that I'd go telling her what there's no need for her to fret about! She doesn't know but what I'm taking you in a cup of tea at this identical moment.'

Ione rang off with relief and got dressed. She put in some good work on the face. Nobody wants to be remembered as a green wraith floating in a fog. Barbara seemed to have brought Nannie very well up to date, for she actually approved the result, commenting favourably on Ione's choice of lipstick. She had mended the tear in the fur coat and sponged and pressed the skirt of the brown suit. The hat went on nicely. Altogether quite a pleasant transformation scene.

Men hadn't to bother of course. Jim Severn looked exactly the same at breakfast as he had done the night before under a street-lamp. There was a moment when this breakfast-table meeting seemed stranger than anything that had happened last night. This time yesterday neither of them knew that the other existed. Only six hours ago neither of them had the faintest idea what the other looked like. And now here they were, sitting down to breakfast together in his flat. If only Norrie knew! But even Norrie would be satisfied with Nannie as a chaperon. She began to laugh, and he saw how quick and sensitive her face was, and that her eyes were not really dark, but grey with brown flecks in them.

Well, you can't just laugh in a man's face and not tell him why, so she told him about Norris and Cousin Eleanor. And from there they seemed to get on to her American visit, she didn't quite know how or why, and she told him about the monologues.

'Of course you have just the right voice. I should think you could make it express anything you wanted it to. Are you going on with them over here?'

'I've had some offers – but I told you Cousin Eleanor has been ill. And she's not just an ordinary cousin, she brought us up.'

'Us?'

'I have a sister – Allegra. She is married to a man called Geoffrey Trent. I'm going to stay with them next week, and after that I shall have to make some plans. Cousin Eleanor is much better.'

Jim Severn was frowning.

'Now where did I come across that name? . . . Of course – how stupid!'

He got up, went out of the room, and came back again with a crumpled piece of paper in his hand.

'I was quite puzzled for the moment. But of course you

26

must have dropped it last night. I picked it up on the stairs in the house we were in.'

Ione took the paper and smoothed it out. It was a bit torn irregularly off the edge of a newspaper. It was rather dirty and very much creased. The words pencilled upon the blank margin were well on their way to being illegible. If they had not been familiar to Ione she would probably have been unable to read them. As it was, she stared at them in surprise. There was a name, and the name was Geoffrey Trent. And there was an address.

She stared at it. Faint as the words were, she could not mistake them:

The Ladies' House,
Bleake.

It was Geoffrey Trent's address, but how in the world could Jim Severn have come by it? Her voice dragged a little as she said,

'I've never seen it before.'

CHAPTER V

As Ione walked into Mr. Sanderson's office she had the faintly regretful feeling that she was passing from adventure to the commonplace. At the time some of the adventure had been very unpleasant, but in retrospect it merely provided a thrill. It is always amusing to stand on the threshold of a new friendship and speculate as to its possibilities. Jim Severn quite obviously wanted to be friends. She had promised to lunch with him when she came back from her visit to Allegra. They had begun tentatively to explore one another's minds. Rather like going into a house that you have never been in before and trying to find out what the owner is like, what sort of things are prized, and what rejected. Is it a warm, welcoming, livable house, or is it the narrow kind which is shut up with its own thoughts and has no friends? You look, you touch, you guess, you explore. There are some locked doors. Not so good if there are too many of them. As far as she had gone, Jim Severn's house felt clean and airy. She hoped he thought the same of hers. Of course everyone had their cellars and their attics.

These attractive speculations were at once dispelled by the atmosphere of Mr. Sanderson's office. It was warm, and it was handsomely furnished, but there lingered upon it a suggestion of mould, and mice, and a rather pungent kind of furniture-polish. It was always the same, and so was Mr. Sanderson, tall and grey and formal in his City clothes and a collar that had been out of fashion for so long that it was just beginning to come back again. Since he had worn folding glasses with steel rims ever since he had first taken his place in the firm which was Sanderson, Sanderson, Hildred and Sanderson, he saw no reason why he should discard them for the up-to-date horn-rimmed variety. They hung always a little crooked upon a nose rather meagrely equipped to sustain them, and they were apt to fall off when he bent forward to examine anything at all closely. He peered through them at Ione now and said that it was always a pleasure to see her.

'And your sister too of course – but I did not think her looking very well.'

Ione stopped herself saying all the things she wanted to say – such as, when had he seen Allegra, and why there should have been any mystery about her visit to town. They could have met, they could have lunched together, and they could have settled about her visit by word of mouth instead of having a long niggling correspondence.

She pushed all this away into the back of her mind and said,

'She always finds London rather tiring, I think. I am going to stay with her next week, and I hope to find her better.'

Mr. Sanderson brightened.

'That will be very nice for you both – very nice indeed.

28

And you will be able to talk the whole business over thoroughly. As I told her, it requires careful consideration.'

Ione had not the slightest idea what he was talking about, but she meant to find out. She turned a limpid gaze upon him and said,

'Yes, I'm sure it does. The trouble is, I'm not at all clear about it. Legal things are always so difficult. I thought perhaps you would be able to explain.'

Mr. Sanderson was gratified. He had just had an interview with a couple of masterful ladies who insisted on laying down the law to him, and Ione's modest desire for instruction appeared to him in a most pleasing light.

'You will remember that under your father's will the property was divided between you and your sister. But certain unforeseen circumstances have arisen. There has been a very sharp drop in the value of the shares allotted to your sister, so that what appeared at the time to be a substantial fortune has undergone a considerable reduction – in point of fact a very considerable reduction.'

Ione experienced some unusual emotions. There was a strong rush of feeling that was strongly, even violently checked. She felt as you do when you run downstairs in the dark and find at the bottom that there is a step which you have not allowed for. There was a sensation of surprise and shock. She did not know that her colour had suddenly flamed, and she certainly would not have expected Mr. Sanderson to be aware of it. He said in his best legal manner,

'Your sister's visit was for the purpose of finding out whether the trustees would consent to the sale of these shares. There is, of course, something to be said for cutting your losses. She suggests that it would be a good thing if she could buy the house for which they are at present paying a somewhat exorbitant rent. It would, of course, be quite possible for the trustees to authorise the purchase of a suitable house, but, as I told her, the matter requires very careful consideration.'

Ione's colour was very bright. She said,

'Mr. Sanderson, it's a dreadful position for me. Of course I had no idea. I've been away – and Allegra is the worst

29

correspondent. I must think what I can do – '

Mr. Sanderson gazed at her with pleasure and approbation. That heightened colour was very becoming, and so was this generous concern about her sister. But she must not be allowed to do anything in a hurry. There was, in fact, not very much that could be done. He took off his glasses, polished them with a stiff white linen handkerchief, and put them back crooked.

'My dear Miss Ione, I am afraid there is not very much that you can do about it. The division was fair enough at the time, but it is now nearly twenty years since your father's death, and I do not need to point out to you that there have been very great changes, especially in the last few years. I am afraid I took it for granted that your sister had talked the matter over with you.'

Ione shook her head.

'There has been no opportunity, and Allegra wouldn't write about anything like that. I am going to stay with her next week. I shall hear all about it then.'

He was frowning slightly as he said,

'Yes – yes. But pray do not allow a generous impulse to carry you away. As you are aware, you have no control over your capital, and your trustees would not allow any transfer. It would not, in fact, be within their power to do so. And really there is no need for you to distress yourself. Mrs. Trent is still in the enjoyment of a very fair income.' The frown had passed. He beamed at her through the tilted glasses. 'So you are going to stay at the Ladies' House next week. A curious name – but I understand from your sister that it was the dower house of the Falconer family. The last male heir having been killed in the war, most of the property has been sold already, and now Mrs. Trent tells me that they would have an opportunity of acquiring the Ladies' House at a reasonable figure. Of course, as I told her, the whole thing would have to be gone into very thoroughly. These old houses' – he shook his head in a worried manner – 'you never know what the dilapidations may amount to. If, for instance, the roof is unsound, the property might become a serious liability. Then there is the plumbing to be considered. In my experience this is often very far from satisfactory. Mrs. Trent tells me that they have electric light, but there again many disastrous fires in country mansions are traceable to insufficient care in the matter of wiring. I really could not advise my fellow trustees to authorise the expenditure of any part of Mrs. Trent's capital unless I felt perfectly satisfied upon these points.'

Ione said, 'No, I suppose not.' She had begun to feel that she really could not go on talking to Mr. Sanderson any longer. The sense of shock persisted. She wanted time to think. There was a horrid feeling at the back of her mind that perhaps all this about the money might have something to do with the fact that Allegra's letters had been so few and far between. It was just a feeling – it couldn't possibly be true. But she couldn't deal with it here. Mr. Sanderson was saying something about not committing herself, but she really wasn't sure of what it was. The room seemed to have become uncomfortably hot. She said,

'I won't do anything in a hurry – I promise you I won't.'

He inclined his head, and the glasses dropped to the full length of the cord which sustained them. He blinked at her and said,

'No precipitate action in any direction, Miss Ione. The matter must be given the most careful consideration.'

CHAPTER VI

Ione looked from the window of her taxi. She had been a little disappointed that no one had met her train at Wraydon, but of course there might have been half a dozen good reasons for that – and at least two bad ones. Unlike as they were in most things, she and Allegra had one thing in common, railway timetables just failed to penetrate any intelligence they might be supposed to possess. She did not

31

think that she had given Allegra the wrong time of arrival, but she would not have cared to be dogmatic about it. On the other hand, it was more than likely that Allegra might have read the figures upside-down, or inside-out, or any which way. After all, there was no particular point about being met. She got her luggage into a taxi, learned that it was two and a half miles to Bleake, and gave herself up to an interested survey of the landscape.

The first thing that met her eye was an enormous poster on the hoarding which decorated the station enclosure.

COMING NEXT WEEK
FERRINGTON'S FAMOUS FOLLIES
WITH
THE GREAT PROSPERO
UNIQUE OPPORTUNITY
UNRIVALLED ATTRACTION

The yellow and black of the poster flashed past. She had to lean forward to catch the last of it. They emerged from the station yard upon the ordinary surroundings of a country town, not looking their best in the grey light of a January afternoon. There was an hour of daylight still to come, but it was being economically, not to say parsimoniously, distributed. Sunset and the falling of the dark might have been just round the corner of any one of half a dozen gloomy streets. As the houses grew smaller and thinned out, the surrounding country was seen to be of an agricultural nature, but when presently they took a turn to the right they were in a lane with high hedgerows and the ground began to rise.

After quite a steep climb they crossed a main road, entered another lane, and came down into the village of Bleake. Even under this dull sky it was attractive – the village street wide, with cottages set back amongst gardens which would display a bright patchwork of flowers in spring and summer – the church with a low, squat tower and a high holly hedge broken by standards fancifully clipped. So far from living up to its name of Bleake, the place had a quite sheltered look. The trees grew straight and shapely, with none of that tor-

32

tured straining to get away from the wind which is the unmistakable mark of the place which is really exposed to stormy weather. It lay in the grey light with an air of content.

They drove right through the village past the church and what was obviously the parsonage, and turned in between grey stone pillars. There was a lodge, but the gates were open. The drive rose a little and came out upon a modest sweep. They had arrived.

Standing there ringing the bell, seeing her luggage off the car and paying the driver, Ione was too close to the house to get any real view of it. She had a general impression of grey walls and tangles of creepers. And then the door was opened by a man, and she came into a square hall with a single small light burning at the foot of a stair going up between dark panelled walls. The man was youngish. He had a sharp hatchet face and light eyes.

She had just got as far as this, when a door on the right of the hall was thrown open and a girl ran out. It was Geoffrey's ward, Margot Trent. Ione knew her at once. She had been the unwanted bridesmaid at Allegra's wedding – a lumpy girl in her middle teens with the misplaced sense of humour which runs to practical jokes. She had stuck a drawing-pin through Allegra's train at the wedding, but had fortunately been detected in the act by one of the Miller twins. She was still plump and still hearty. She advanced upon Ione with a boisterous 'Hullo!' and then just stood in the middle of the hall and shouted,

'Geoffrey – Allegra – she's come!'

They emerged from the room out of which Margot had come, in that order.

Ione felt a quick unreasonable resentment. Everyone in that room must have heard the car drive up, but it was left for a servant to open the door. And after the servant Margot, Geoffrey who had to be shouted for, and only at the long last of it Allegra.

What was the matter with Allegra that she couldn't be the first to meet her sister? All the time she was shaking hands with Geoffrey and touching Allegra's cold hand and colder cheek the question repeated itself – what was the matter with

Allegra? She had always been a little creature, small and pale and slight, but now she looked as if any breath of wind might blow her away. The fair hair, thistledown-soft and light, was cut in a square bob to frame the little pointed face. Two years ago there had been a delicate, elusive charm, and the grey-blue eyes had had their moments of being really blue. Now there was a greyness over all the soft pastel tints. Ione told herself that it was the gloomy hall, the sparse lighting, and the stupidly bright lipstick which Allegra had applied to her pallid mouth. But when they came into the drawing-room the greyness was still there, like mould on a sickly plant.

Geoffrey Trent could not have been more charming. If Ione's welcome had been momentarily delayed it could hardly have been warmer now.

'We began to think that you were never coming to see us – weren't we, Allegra? And she has wanted you so much. You know, we are planning to buy the house if the trustees will let us. It really is an opportunity not to be missed. It is the most delightful place. The dower house of the Falconers, you know. Another of our good old families come to an end. They trace their descent from Robert, Head Falconer to Edward III, who gave him these lands. Pity, isn't it, but the last poor chap was killed in the war, and there's no one left but an old spinster aunt. The big house was bombed during the war, and she can't afford to live here, so she is willing to sell. It's a case of one man's misfortune being anothers' opportunity, I'm afraid. But of course we should really be doing her a good turn, because she needs the money. Now don't you call this a perfectly charming room? Put on all the lights, Margot, so that she can see it properly!'

The lights were in the ceiling and in two clusters of candles held by gilt sconces on either side of a white marble mantelpiece. As they all came on, the grey sky outside darkened and receded, and the room sprang into light and faint delicate colour. A lovely room, with its brocaded curtains, its carpet in soft pastel shades, the loose covers upon its chairs and the deep comfortable couch taking up the dim hyacinth and rose and lilac of the curtains. A very charming room, and one which should have been just the right background for Allegra. And it wasn't. Amidst all these lovely gradations of tone she was like a false note in a melody – off the note and out of key where she ought to have been in her own right place.

The impression deepened painfully as Ione listened to Geoffrey talking about the house, and about how much Allegra loved it. When he appealed to her she said, 'Yes' or 'No' in a little flat voice. When Ione spoke to her she answered her with dragging words. Of course she had never been a talker, and Geoffrey talked so much. Ione thought, 'He *is* sinfully good-looking.' It was Elizabeth Tremayne who had said that at the wedding. And a lot more too! 'Darling, I wouldn't marry him for anything in the world! It would be like having to live with the Crown Jewels! I mean, *someone* is simply bound to be trying to snatch him all the time!'

She pushed Elizabeth away with resentment. What a thing to remember! And Fenella had quoted it too – Anyhow it wasn't any good Geoffrey thinking he could get round her by turning on the charm – not while Allegra looked like a little disintegrating ghost.

Margot came bouncing into the room with a plate of hot scones in her hand.

'Cheer up!' she said with her mouth full. 'Tea's coming! And you'd better start on the scones while they're hot. There's real butter in them – I saw Mrs. Flaxman put it in. And here's Fred with the tea!'

Geoffrey Trent turned a little, put his hand on a plump shoulder, and said in a low but quite audible voice,

'I really should prefer you to call him Flaxman.'

She broke into one of her noisy laughs.

'How snob you are, Geoff! And it's no use – I'm just not made that way!' She thrust her plate of scones at Allegra. 'Have one – they're scrumptious!'

Geoffrey turned back to Ione with a very creditable smile.

'She'll grow up some day,' he said indulgently. 'It's a pity she looks older than she really is.'

'She was about fifteen at the time of the wedding, wasn't she?'

'Not so much. She is not seventeen yet.'

Flaxman had come into the room and was setting down the tray which, with the handsome tea-service it supported, had been Cousin Eleanor's present to Allegra. Ione thought she had never seen silver better kept. The rather aloof-looking butler obviously knew his job. She reflected that Allegra was lucky. The word dropped out of her mind like a stone falling through water.

Allegra was pouring out. When she lifted the teapot her hand shook under the weight of it and the tea splashed over on to the tray – even the milk-jug wavered. Ione came forward to take her cup and turned with it to see Jacqueline Delauny come into the room. She knew of course that they had a governess for Margot – just that, and the name, which sounded French. But Geoffrey was introducing her as Miss Delauny, and when she spoke her accent was as English as his. She did not quite know why, but she received a shock. She had, perhaps, expected someone older, but Miss Delauny was not so very young. Her voice when she spoke was deep, the words quiet and measured – nothing in fact to give Ione this feeling of having run into something quite unexpected.

She had black smooth hair breaking into a wave or two over the small, finely proportioned ears. Dark eyes with just the suspicion of a slant – or was it only the eyebrows that slanted? A mobile face without any natural advantages of feature or colouring, but all very ably assisted – the skin creamed and powdered to a magnolia pallor, the wide mouth rendered decorative by a shade of lipstick which was new to Ione. For the rest, a plain dark skirt and jumper.

As the talk about the tea-table went on, Ione began to adjust herself. There was no fault to be found in Jacqueline Delauny's manner. She was pleasant, with just the right amount to say for herself, and she really appeared to exercise a tactful influence upon Margot Trent. If it had not been for Allegra, sitting there like her own ghost with no more to say than an occasional yes or no to a question too direct to be ignored, Ione would have found it all agreeable enough. As it was, she possessed her soul in patience against the moment when they would be alone. Allegra could hardly avoid taking her to her room or going up with her when she went to bed. She did not realise until afterwards that she had used the word *avoid* – not in fact until she was herself alone in her bedroom after the last good-night had been said. She came to it then of necessity, because not for one moment had she and Allegra been alone. It was Jacqueline Delauny who had taken her upstairs into the room whose gay chintz curtains only partly disguised the fact that it was situated in one of the older parts of the house, and it was Jacqueline Delauny who had just left her now.

'The third door on the left is the bathroom. Margot and I are round that corner and along at the end of the passage. This is a very confusing house until you get used to it. Do you know, there are seven staircases, though it is not at all a big house.'

'Seven staircases!'

Jacqueline's wide smile flashed out.

'Terrible, isn't it? Mr. Trent has had two of them shut up. He will want to show you the house tomorrow. It is very interesting. Oh, there is just one thing. Perhaps it would be better if you would lock your door. Margot has improved, but she still thinks practical joking a form of humour, so perhaps – '

Ione turned the key in the lock with vigour. Her first impressions about Jacqueline were gone. She seemed a friendly person with a hard enough job on her hands. She found herself wondering if Margot was really quite normal.

She had a bath. The water boiling, a good deal to her surprise. She wondered if it was Geoffrey, or some previous tenant, whom she had to thank for that. It costs a pretty penny to provide new plumbing and an up-to-date heating system in a house which has started life somewhere back in the fourteenth century. Geoffrey had announced the date with pride at dinner. Now, as her hot bath began to run away, Ione wondered how much of his and how much of Allegra's money had also gone down the drain.

She told herself it wasn't her business, and went back to her room. As she opened the door, a large wet bath sponge fell on her head. Since she was wearing a bath-cap and a towelling robe, the chief damage was a horrid dark patch on the carpet. When she had rubbed it as dry as she could, it still looked rather too much like a bloodstain to be comfortable. You wouldn't think of such a thing in any ordinary room of course, so why think of it now? And the carpet wasn't even red, but a soft brownish pink. It was only where the water had darkened it that it looked as if the stain was blood.

Completely out of temper with these ridiculous fancies, with herself for having them, and with Margot Trent for having provoked them, Ione re-locked the door and got into bed. It was then, with the light turned off, that she became aware of the silence in the room. The country can be anything but quiet, but here in the Ladies' House an extraordinary silence prevailed. The walls were so thick that each room contained its own sounds. You would not hear a step on any of those seven stairs. You would never know whether anyone moved above, or below, or even in the very next room. Each chamber as the sounds within it ceased would become its own deep well of silence in which thought and movement slowly petrified.

It didn't really seem to matter if they did. The tides of sleep flowed in.

CHAPTER VII

Allegra did not appear at breakfast. It transpired that she never did. Remembering Cousin Eleanor's spartan upbringing, Ione found this disquieting. When she suggested taking up Allegra's tray she got a smiling shake of the head from Geoffrey.

'There is no need. We are quite civilised – daily maid from the village to eke out the Flaxmans. And Allegra doesn't really care about talking until she is dressed. She won't be long, and meanwhile I am going to show you the house. It's well worth seeing.'

It was. And there was no mistaking Geoffrey's pride and interest. He had to catch himself up once or twice.

'I expect I sound silly, talking as if it were a kind of ancestral possession, but do you know, that is the way I begin to find myself thinking about it. I've always had a fancy for old houses, and absurd as it may sound, this place has got me. I feel as if I had roots in it, which is of course quite ridiculous.'

It was said in a very disarming way with a rueful sparkle of the blue eyes, a humorous twist of the handsome mouth. Ione had to smile too and agree that it was ridiculous, but that places did get hold of you like that.

Geoffrey laughed.

'Well, as long as you don't mind my getting away on my hobby horse! You see, this is really the original Manor House, built by Robert the Falconer or his son Robert – there seems to be some doubt which. Of course there are modern additions. The drawing-room and Allegra's bedroom over it are only seventeenth-century, but take those away, and you have a compact fourteenth-century manor house with no less than seven staircases – easy access between the floors for purposes of defence – cellars under the house with a well that never runs dry, and a useful dungeon or two. Of course the windows have all been changed and enlarged, and what the house-agents call modern conveniences have been contrived. As a matter of fact we have struck it very lucky indeed. Some wealthy Americans had a lease of the house in the thirties. They wanted to buy, but young Falconer wouldn't sell, though I believe they offered a fabulous price. As a matter of fact, both he and the American were killed in the war, and the widow went back to the States. But before all that happened they had put in some absolutely first-class plumbing, so we've got central heating and a continuous supply of hot water, which is more than you can say about most old houses, and a good few modern ones.'

He went on talking about the house.

'The furniture isn't all period, thank goodness. I should draw the line at fourteenth-century chairs, and besides, don't you think that furnishing to a period is all wrong? No one wants to go back into the dark ages and stay there, but if a family has its beginnings there, and then has the luck to go on living in a place like this for hundreds of years, they would have their old things and go on adding to them and keeping the best of what they added until every period had left its mark.' He spoke with a quick boyish enthusiasm which was very attractive.

Up to now she had neither liked nor disliked Geoffrey Trent. She simply had not known him. He was a stranger whom Allegra had met at a house-party and married within three months of that first meeting. Ione could count on the fingers of one hand the times when he and she had met. There had been a round of visits, and then the rush and scramble of the wedding. Cousin Eleanor had been too ill to have them for more than a brief week-end, but they had gone the rounds of relations of Allegra's – friends of Geoffrey's! Aunt Marion and Aunt Hester, Uncle Henry, and old Cousin Oliver Wayne. But on Geoffrey's side not a single solitary relation except Margot Trent. Masses of friends of course – but a sinfully goodlooking bachelor with money would certainly not lack for friends. Parties for the races, for this, for that, for everything conceivable – they simply never stopped. Allegra had been completely worn out before the wedding day. But she oughtn't to go on looking as if she had just used up the last drop of her strength.

Right in the middle of Geoffrey showing her one of the staircases he kept locked – and a horrid dark, precipitous affair it was – she found herself saying,

'What is the matter with Allegra?'

He stopped halfway through a sentence, appeared to have some difficulty in deflecting his attention from the medieval stair, and repeated his wife's name in a tone tinged with surprise.

'Allegra?'

Ione could have stamped her foot. She restrained the impulse. She had too many impulses, and she was always having to restrain them. It made life varied and interesting, but if you didn't watch out it could land you in a mess. She certainly didn't want to have a row with Geoffrey, and about nothing at all. She looked at him frankly and said,

'Aren't you worried about her? I think you ought to be. She looks dreadful.'

He frowned.

'She was tired last night.'

Ione shook her head.

'Has she seen a doctor? What does he say?'

'She has seen two – one here, and one in town. They both say the same thing – she is not very strong, but there is nothing wrong with her.'

She drew a long breath of relief. She was aware that he was watching her.

'What did you think was wrong?'

'I don't know. I've never seen her like this – no life, no interest. She didn't even seem glad to see me.'

He gave rather a rueful smile.

'Too bad – and I'm afraid it's all my fault. The fact is we had had a bit of a tiff, and you arrived before we had time to make it up. All over now and nothing to worry about, but Allegra is like a child, she can't be happy if she thinks I'm vexed.'

Ione felt herself put in the wrong – very charmingly, kindly, even gaily. She was a maker of mountains out of molehills. She was that immemorial butt of all comedians, the visiting in-law who is determined to find something wrong. She had a very good sketch on those lines herself, and it always went down well. She turned on what she hoped was a friendly smile and said,

'How tactless of me not to come by a later train and give you time to put things right. But I don't see how I was to know.'

He laughed cheerfully.

'No need to worry. Our quarrels never last very long.'

He was locking the little dark stairway as he spoke.

'I think it's better to keep it shut up – don't you? It's of no real use, and it's so near this other one that anyone might make a mistake and perhaps get a nasty fall. Now, you see, this one isn't nearly so steep.'

Like the other it was closed in by its own door and ran

down between dark walls. It was certainly less precipitous, and perhaps – but she was not entirely sure upon this point – it did not smell quite so strongly of mould. It came into her mind that a medieval house might be terribly interesting to visit, but she could think of nothing she would dislike more than to have to live in one. As she followed Geoffrey up and down staircases and along narrow and most bewildering passages, the impression deepened, and she found herself dwelling passionately upon the mental picture of a perfectly modern house full of windows and without a dark corner in it anywhere.

'Now,' said Geoffrey, 'this is the real gem of the place.' He opened a door, not this time upon one of those horrid enclosed stairways, but upon a flight of stone steps going down, a long way down, into a tiny banqueting hall. Barely twenty feet long, it had the height of two floors and a beautiful arched roof, the windows just glass slits in stone walls which were covered in panelling.

The first opening of the door took Ione by surprise. It was like standing on a cliff and looking down. And the place was full of shadows.

And then Geoffrey lifted his hand to a switch and all the lights came on, ten down each side of the hall, candles held in iron sconces set against the panelling, and above them in the middle of the right-hand wall, shining in red, and blue, and gold, the crest and coat-of-arms of the Falconers. The colours were bright and fresh without being garish. Geoffrey was explaining how carefully they had been restored.

'That American knew quite a lot about it. He didn't mind how much trouble he took, or what he spent. What he kept saying was that he'd got to get everything just dead right.'

The stone steps had no railing. Ione came down them carefully. She waited until she had reached the bottom before she said,

'How do you know? About the American, I mean.'

He laughed.

'Nothing mysterious about it – Miss Falconer told me. The last survivor, you know – the one I'm trying to buy the house from. She lives here in the village in one of the cottages.

Rather a come-down after this place, poor old thing, but she says she prefers it.'

Ione had a warm feeling for Miss Falconer. As an alternative to living in the Middle Ages on practically nothing a year, one of the cottages which she had seen as she drove through the village sounded rather cosy. There would at anyrate not be a torture chamber under the kitchen floor. As she was quite determined to be tactful, she kept these thoughts to herself, admired the old fireplace – 'in its original state' – the massive stone slabs which formed the floor, and the long refectory table which with its dozen massive chairs had, so Geoffrey assured her, been here at least since Tudor times.

'We must give a dinner-party whilst you are here, and let you see it in all its glory. There's a serving-hatch in that corner, so the food does get here hot, but those steps down from the second floor are the only way in and out unless the great doors at the end are opened, and apparently there's a heavy tradition that that is only done for the marriage of the heir or at his funeral feast. As I told you, the last poor chap was killed in France and buried there. But Miss Falconer kept to the old custom. She had a memorial service for him in the village church, and after it the big doors were opened and all the villagers came trooping up for bread and ale, just as they had always done when the lord of the manor died.'

Ione felt a shiver go over her. The place was as cold as a well. But the rest of the house was warm.

'Doesn't the central heating get as far as this?'

'I'm afraid it doesn't. Miss Falconer absolutely refused to let anyone touch this room, and I must say I think she was right. It's the perfect fourteenth-century banqueting hall in miniature, and it would be sacrilege to lay a finger on it. It's a case of piling up the old Yule log on that enormous stone hearth when we throw a party. We must get some people in whilst you are with us. But I needn't keep you here if you're cold. Come along up the steps again, and we'll just go down one of our many staircases and have a look at the cellars.'

The cellars were really not so bad. The American had had them whitewashed, a triumph of common sense over the historical variety, and as the furnace which supplied the hot water system was right in the middle of them, they were neither cold nor damp. Doors stood open to allow the warm air to circulate, and there was plenty of bright electric light.

But with the opening of an arched door at the extreme end of the last cellar cheerfulness vanished from the scene. The door itself was immensely old, immensely thick, and in addition to a portentous lock there still hung from rusted staples the two iron bars with which it could be made secure. Geoffrey lifted one of them and showed her how it fitted into the slot on the other side. When the door swung back a breath of appalling cold and damp came up out of the darkness. And then, with a click, there was light striking up from below, making odd shadows on the worn stone steps. They must have been very old, or they must have been very much used.

Ione descended them with reluctance. If she hadn't made up her mind to be tactful at all costs, she would have seen Geoffrey at Jericho or in one of his own dungeons before she would have abandoned the American's warm and white-washed cellars. If it hadn't been for Allegra, she would just have stamped on one of the stone flags and said no. As it was, she went down, and it was quite the horridest place she had ever been in. Walls and floor were of stone, and they ran with a cold sweat. There were slimy trails on the stone. There was air to breathe, but it was heavy and unwholesome. Two doors stood open to the space into which the steps came down. Prison and torture chamber, as Geoffrey informed her in a robustly cheerful voice. But when he proposed to conduct her into these revolting apartments her tact gave out and she assured him with some warmth that she would take his word for what they were, and that she absolutely refused to set foot in either of them. As this appeared to amuse him, there was no harm done, and she consented to let him show her the well.

And then wished she hadn't.

It was at the far end, and the mouth of it was covered by a heavy oak lid, but when Geoffrey drew this aside, there was no parapet, no defence against a sheer black drop. It just went straight down to its own deep hidden spring.

44

Geoffrey was telling her how deep it was.

'A hundred and eighty feet, and it never runs dry. That would be why Robert the Falconer built his house over it. Nobody knew when they might have to stand a siege in those days, and if you hadn't got an unfailing spring inside your defences you just couldn't stay the course. Here – listen!'

He pushed a hand into his pocket, came up with a penny, and leaned forward over the middle of the well to drop it in. It was a long, dizzy time before Ione heard the faint, the very faint, sound it made when it touched the water. She said with conviction,

'Horrible! Geoffrey, I'm sorry, but I can't do any more wells or cellars. I've never liked underground places, and you make it all much too vivid. So if you don't want me to begin to scream for help –'

'Nobody would hear you if you did, my dear girl,' he said. But he was laughing and he looked pleased, so she hadn't put her foot in it. And whether she had, or whether she hadn't, she couldn't have endured another five minutes in this frightful place.

From half-way up the steps she looked back to see Geoffrey pushing the heavy oak cover into position. She was glad to know that she need not think of the well with its black mouth gaping in the darkness when they were gone.

Geoffrey stood up, took out a handkerchief, and rubbed his hands. He came running after her, still with that laughing look on his face.

CHAPTER VIII

'So you think I make a good guide?'

'Much too good. You made me feel as if I was back in the fourteenth century.'

'And you didn't like it?'

His tone was light and teasing. She let her own answer it.

'Not a bit.'

They came up into the daylight, and she exclaimed.

'I've got some of that horrible slime on my hands! I must wash!'

He held up his own, which were a good deal worse.

'I ought to have warned you not to touch anything. Look here, I'll get clean, and then I'll go along and see if Allegra is dressed. She ought to be by now.'

When Ione had washed and been thankful that the water was just as hot this morning as it had been last night, she went to her room. It had been done and left in perfect order, but to her annoyed surprise it was not empty. Margot Trent was there, standing just inside the door and looking down at the damp patch on the carpet. She giggled as Ione came in,

'Did you get the sponge on your head?'

'I did.'

'It's a gorgeous big one, isn't it? The place on the carpet shows quite a lot! Looks like a blood stain! I say, it would be a joke if someone thought it really was one! It would have been better if I had filled the sponge with red ink, wouldn't it? Oh, what a pity I didn't – then it would never have come out!'

'The carpet would have been spoilt, to say nothing of anything I happened to have been wearing. But I suppose that wouldn't matter.'

It was obvious that sarcasm meant nothing to Margot. She stared at Ione out of the bright blue eyes which were rather like Geoffrey Trent's and said,

'Oh, well, I could have got them another carpet if they were stuffy enough to want to bother about it. I've got plenty of money.'

'Have you?'

'*Oodles!* I dare say I could buy a hundred carpets if I wanted to, only I don't suppose Geoffrey would let me. He is supposed to look after my money until I'm twenty-one. And he really is the limit! He knows perfectly well that I've simply set my heart on having a racing car! There's some stupid fuss about not getting a licence until you're seventeen, but I'm going to be soon and I've got it all planned. And

Geoffrey says he won't give me a single penny of my own money to buy one! What's spoiling a carpet or two to that?'

Ione had an inward shudder at the thought of Margot at the wheel of a racing car. She said,

'Well, you know, if you had an accident, they might take away your licence for years, and you wouldn't like that.'

'No, I shouldn't, should I?'

The creature was as open and transparent as a child. The angry frown of a moment ago was gone. She beamed and said,

'But he can't expect me not to have any fun at all – now, can he?'

'So you will go on spoiling carpets?'

She got a vigorous shake of the head.

'Oh, no – that would be dull. I'll have to think up something else. As a matter of fact – ' She broke off laughing, and shaking her head. 'No – no – I'm not going to tell you. I'm not going to tell anyone. People can't keep anything to themselves, and it's a lot too good to be spoiled!' She began to laugh immoderately. 'You just – wait – and see!' She caught her breath, choked, went off into a fresh paroxysm, and finally, stuffing a not very clean handkerchief into her mouth, ran out of the room. She very nearly collided with Jacqueline Delauny, and ran away still hooting with laughter.

Miss Delauny hesitated for a moment, and then knocked on the half open door.

'Miss Muir – may I come in? I do hope Margot hasn't been doing anything foolish. I am afraid she laid a booby-trap for you last night.'

'And I walked into it! Fortunately I had on a bath-cap and a towelling robe, so there was no harm done except to the carpet. But Margot has just been lamenting over the fact that she didn't think of filling the sponge with red ink until it was too late.'

Miss Delauny made a small vexed sound.

'Miss Muir, I do apologise. I thought she was safely in bed and asleep by the time you went to your bath. We are doing our best to break her of these tricks. And they are not malicious. She is the most good-tempered girl. It is just that she thinks this sort of thing amusing. It is her idea of fun, and she just can't see why other people are not amused by it.'

Ione sat down on the edge of her bed.

'Of course she wants fun. Every girl does. She is a healthy creature and simply bursting with vitality. Why on earth doesn't Geoffrey send her to school? She wants gym, and games, and dancing. Hockey or lacrosse a couple of times a week would do more to stop her practical joking than any amount of scolding.'

Jacqueline Delauny looked offended.

'Margot is never scolded. The appeal is always to her reason.'

'Has she got any reason to appeal to? I shouldn't have thought she had. Of course it's not my business, except in so far as it affects Allegra – and I don't think anyone would say that she is in a fit state of health for rough practical joking. But to come back to where I started – why doesn't Geoffrey send her to school?'

Jacqueline Delauny had gone over to the window. Standing there with her back to Ione, she said in an expressionless voice,

'They won't keep her.'

CHAPTER IX

Geoffrey Trent came whistling along the passage. 'Are you ready? Allegra has just gone down, and there's a fire in the drawing-room. I hope you won't find it too warm, but she feels the cold a good deal.'

Allegra had been like any other country girl, in and out of the house all day and healthily impervious to the weather. Ione had the thought in her mind as she followed Geoffrey to the drawing-room where some winter sunshine straggled in and quite a large wood fire smouldered upon the hearth.

At the first glance Ione found herself convicted of worrying about nothing. Allegra had colour in her cheeks and brightness in her eyes. She ran to kiss Ione, and keeping hold of her hand, took her to the big sofa beside the fire, talking all the time.

'You slept all right? I was simply dead, or I'd have come to see you. I get so tired at night. Not always, you know, but just sometimes, and then there's nothing for it but to go to bed and sleep. The beds themselves are all terribly old, but those Americans who were here had the most lovely spring mattresses put in everywhere. After all, you couldn't expect mattresses to go for hundreds of years, even if they were made from the best goose feathers like Miss Falconer says they were. Did Geoffrey tell you about her? He wants to buy the house, you know, but she won't make up her mind. And nor will Mr. Sanderson – I can't think why. Anyone would imagine that it wasn't my own money! And it's really quite insulting the way he goes on making difficulties – as if I was a perfect fool and Geoffrey couldn't be trusted to look after my interests!' She took a quick shallow breath, and Ione managed to say,

'Lawyers are like that. They don't mean to be insulting – it's just their way.'

Allegra was off again. Nothing could be less like the silent shadowy girl of yesterday. But Ione's initial relief was passing into an even more acute anxiety. The colour in the thin cheeks was too bright. Allegra's tongue had never raced at this unnatural speed. And those glances going here and there, but never resting, never meeting Ione's –

Then quite suddenly their eyes did meet, accidentally as it seemed, and so briefly that for the moment Ione merely knew that she had received a tingling shock. There was no time for thought before the lashes came down and the head was turned. The realisation of what she had seen came unwillingly and slowly. The pupils in those over bright eyes were too small. They were much, much, much too small.

Allegra went on with that rapid talk. Ione was grateful for it – there was no need for her to say anything. She had disturbing thoughts. The sofa on which they were sitting stood with its back to the windows through which those gleams of sunlight brightened only to fade again. There was a fire-screen between Allegra and the not very brightly burning logs upon the hearth. There was, in fact, no natural cause for those contracted pupils. But there was an unnatural and most frightening one. One of Ione's impulses came surging up, and no matter what she said to herself about it after-wards, you don't begin to be tactful with your own only sister just because she has got married and you haven't seen her for the best part of two years – at least not all in a moment, and when you have just had a most horrid shock. The impulse took charge. She leaned forward, caught both Allegra's hands in hers, and said in her most arresting voice,

'Ally, what have you been taking?'

The hands were cold. They tugged feebly to get away, and were held in a strong, warm clasp. The eyelashes fluttered and came down over the telltale eyes. When the question had been repeated even more firmly, Allegra moved her head in protest.

'Taking?'

'You heard me.'

'I don't know what you mean. Io, you're hurting me!'

'No, I'm not! I said, "What have you been taking?" and you are going to tell me! When I got here last night you were like a dead fish. Now you're like someone in a fever, and the pupils of your eyes have gone away to practically nothing at all. One of the things that does that is morphia. Why are you taking morphia?'

Allegra shook back her hair and gave a little tinkling laugh.

'Io, how funny you are! That's just my medicine. I went up to see a doctor in London, and he said I needed a tonic. I feel marvellous after it. But Geoffrey doesn't like me taking it. That is why I was so flat last night – he took away the bottle and locked it up. We had quite a quarrel about it, and of course that upset me too. I just can't bear it when Geoffrey is angry. And he very seldom is – except just about my medicine. And you know, I do think that is unreasonable – don't you? Because I feel wonderful after I've taken it, and

50

you'd think he'd be pleased about that, wouldn't you?'

She was gazing at Ione now out of those over bright eyes with their effect of being all iris.

'What was your doctor's name, Ally?'

'The one here – or the one in London?'

'Both.'

'The one here is Dr. Whichcote. He's rather old, but very kind. The one in London – no, do you know, I've forgotten. Geoffrey wanted me to go and see him, and Dr. Whichcote fixed it up. I only saw him once, and his name has gone right out of my head, but he gave me my lovely medicine, and he said, just like Dr. Whichcote does, that I'm quite all right, so there's no need for anyone to fuss. And now will you please let go of my hands, Io?'

Ione let them go. She wasn't satisfied – no one could possibly have been satisfied with this shallow empty tale. She would have to take it to Geoffrey and have a show-down. That Allegra was being drugged was apparent. Neither Ally's own denials nor those of anyone else were going to shake Ione about that. And if Geoffrey hadn't a very good explanation, she was prepared to bring the family about his ears. What she could not understand was why he should have let her come here, knowing as he must have done that Allegra's state could hardly pass unnoticed. Her visit had been postponed often enough. There had been excuse after excuse. And then suddenly she was not only invited, but positively urged to come. Was she considered to be such a fool that she couldn't put two and two together? Or had things come to such a point that Geoffrey no longer cared whether she guessed or not?

Allegra's tongue ran on. She had left the subject of her medicine and was talking about the house.

'It's terribly old, isn't it? I expect all these old houses have stories about them. Geoffrey says they are just nonsense – but – I don't know – ' Her voice dragged on the words. She looked over her shoulder and back again. Then she leaned forward and whispered. 'Do you know what they call this house in the village? It was made into a dower house when the eighteenth-century Falconers built the big place which was burnt down in the blitz. They changed the name then from the Manor House to the Ladies' House. But that's not what they call it in the village. They never have, and they never will. Florrie told me about it – she is the daily housemaid, and she is a chattering kind of girl. She didn't want to tell me, but I got it out of her. Her family has lived in Bleake almost as long as the Falconers have, so she *knows*. And she says even when it was the Manor House, hundreds of years before the big place was built, it had another, secret name. And do you know what it was?' She put her lips quite close to Ione's ear and dropped her voice to a thread. 'They called it Ladies' Bane.'

Ione was startled.

'Why?'

'Oh, I don't know – some old story.' She shook back her hair and gave that tinkling laugh. 'Stupid, isn't it? A thing like that couldn't be true.'

'A thing like what? If you don't tell me, I shall ask Geoffrey.'

A fleeting look of terror passed over the little pointed face. Allegra's hands came out and clutched her.

'No – no – you mustn't ever! I'll tell you. But it's all nonsense, and you mustn't think about it or speak about it – especially not to Geoffrey, because it would make him dreadfully angry. I oughtn't to have said a word, but sometimes it frightens me. Oh, Io, it *does*!' She came very close again and whispered as she had done before. 'It's just – they say – that anyone who is mistress here – will lose the thing – she cares for most – in all the world.'

The last words came in a terrified rush. And only just in time, because Geoffrey Trent came into the room. There had been no sound of an opening door. If it had been unlatched, would that frightened whisper have reached him? Ione did not think it possible. Then how much had he seen of the frightened whispering attitude? Allegra had been quick to lean back in her corner of the sofa and to call his name in a tone of pleased surprise. Curiously enough, it was this which made the least agreeable impression. The Allegra

52

of two years ago would not have known how to change her part like that. She had had no need for that or any other art. She had been simple, candid, sincere. She had also been loving and vulnerable. There were obvious changes now.

That bright blue glance of Geoffrey's travelled over the sisters and came to rest upon his wife. She met it with a flush and a smile.

'I was telling Ione about the house. But I really oughtn't to – I told her so. You do it so much better.'

He laughed and came to stand in front of the fire.

'I've just about exhausted her patience, I should think. But' – with a return of his eager manner – 'it is all rather absorbing, isn't it?'

Ione smiled and nodded.

'I feel as if I had been on a personally conducted tour of the fourteenth century.'

'And you didn't like it?'

'Well, not the underground part. But then I've got rather a thing about cellars, so if I scream in the night, you'll know why.'

Allegra's little restless hands were plucking at one another. They stopped for a moment now. She stared at them and said,

'No one would hear you if you did – the walls are too thick.'

If there had been a pause just then it would not have been a pleasant one. But there was no pause, because Geoffrey spoke, still with that pleasant eagerness about him,

'I'm not suggesting anything about the inside of the house, but I did wonder whether you would care to see the outside. Of course there's nothing in the garden at this time of year, but you can see how it's been laid out. There's a really wonderful rock garden in what used to be an old quarry. Those Americans spent hundreds on it, and it's really very hot stuff indeed. Wouldn't you like to see it? And if you come, perhaps Allegra will too. She doesn't get out enough. Dr. Whichcote says she ought to have plenty of fresh air.'

'It's so cold – ' Words and tone were those of a fretful

53

child. She shrank back into her corner as if an attempt might be made to dislodge her by main force.

'You would be much warmer when you came in, my dear.'

Allegra shook her head till the light, fine hair flew up in a cloud.

'No – no – I wouldn't! I just get colder and colder until the last bit of warmness is gone!' Her eyes implored him. The hands were plucking at one another again.

Ione got up.

'All right, darling, we won't make you come this time – will we, Geoffrey? I'll just get a coat.'

CHAPTER X

They went out by a door at the end of one of the narrow stone passages. It brought them into a small enclosed courtyard shut in on three sides by the house, and on the fourth by a wall with an arched doorway in the middle of it. The door was open and showed a glimpse of green. Beyond it lay first a stone terrace with formal trees in tubs, and then three other terraces, of grass, and stone, and grass again, set with rose-beds growing from a carpet of pansy and viola. The effect in summer would be lovely. Even now there was bloom upon the pansies, a bud showing purple, and even an occasional draggled flower. Steps went gently down to a lawn. There was a fine cedar, and a magnificent leafless tree which Geoffrey told her was a copper beech.

She had made up her mind to say nothing of what was weighing upon it until he had had his fill of showmanship. The garden was certainly beautiful. Even the bare bones of it in this winter month were a delight to the eye. After the lawn there were trees – a glade that would be full of blue-bells and primroses in the spring. And then out again on to open ground which began to slope.

'This is what the American spent his money on,' said Geoffrey Trent. 'I said hundreds, but it must have been nearer thousands – a couple at least. It was an old quarry with a derelict pond at the bottom. Most of the tin cans and dead cats of the neighbourhood used to find their way into it, I believe. He got one of the first landscape gardeners in the country to come down, and you can see what he has done. This side there wasn't much drop, and it's all been very carefully laid out with these shallow steps and the right settings and exposures for alpines. Those small rhododendrons are an absolute sheet of colour in the spring. The pond has been made into a magnificent lily pond, and those weeping willows over there are coming along like a house on fire. But the real feature is the steep face of the quarry over there. It has a south exposure, and when everything has had a little more time to grow it will be one of the loveliest things in England – sheets of aubrietia in every shade from lilac to crimson, curtains of white and purple wistaria, and every kind of flowering bush which could be persuaded to root itself. You can't be surprised we are crazy about the place, now can you? The bother is that my capital is all in stuff that is pretty far down now but is bound to recover, and it would be madness for me to sell out. So unless we can persuade those obstinate trustees of yours to let Allegra use some of hers I'm afraid we're in the soup. I shall wear them down, if it's to be done – I'm quite good at going on until I get what I want. As a matter of fact, I believe I really have made some impression at last, because Mr. Sanderson is sending a chap down to vet the place tomorrow.'

Ione had no intention of letting herself be drawn into a discussion as to whether Allegra's money should or should not be used for the purchase of the Ladies' House. The fact that she already had very strong opinions on the subject was a good enough reason for holding her tongue while she was Geoffrey's guest.

And the quarry shook her. It was already beautiful, even in its winter sleep. And what it would be like in the spring – in the summer – Already there was prunus in a pale rosy mist, and witch hazel in a golden cloud. There were winter roses, and iris stylosa. There was yellow jasmine, and the winter-blooming heather. She could turn whole-heartedly to Geoffrey and say,

'What a perfectly marvellous place!'

He was flushed with pleasure.

'Well, it is, isn't it! But you mustn't let me bore you with it. Jacqueline says I do, you know. She says I don't know where to stop. So you'll just have to tell me quite frankly when you've had enough.'

That sounded very downright for Margot's governess. She said,

'You have known Miss Delauny a long time?'

'Oh, not so very long. I'm very grateful to her. Margot is a bit of a problem, and she is good at managing her.'

It was not Margot whom Ione wanted to discuss with Geoffrey Trent. She made a slight gesture with her hand as if to put her aside, and said,

'Geoffrey, I want to talk to you about Allegra. What is she taking?'

A very decided change came over his face. The pleasure went out of it, and he met her look with a very direct one.

'What makes you ask me that?'

'Because I saw Allegra last night, and I've seen her this morning. I'm not quite a fool, and it is perfectly obvious that she is under the influence of a drug – morphia for choice. Besides, she told me about her wonderful medicine.'

'I see. Did she tell you I gave it to her?'

'No. She said the specialist she went to in London gave it to her, but that you were always trying to prevent her taking it.'

He turned aside for a moment, walked a few paces away, and came back again to say rather curtly,

'If you know anything at all about drug cases you must be aware that they all have one thing in common – they are incapable of speaking the truth.'

He saw her colour come with a rush and then fade.

'You mean she wasn't telling the truth – about the medicine?'

'Of course she wasn't! The man I took her to was Blank.'

He mentioned a world-famous name. 'What he wanted her to do was to go into a sanatorium. She has refused, and goes on refusing. Every time the subject is mentioned she cries herself into a state of exhaustion. Frankly, I am at my wits' end.'

'And the medicine she spoke of?'

He threw up a hand.

'A harmless tonic prescribed by Dr. Whichcote.'

'Then where does the drug come in?'

'If we knew that, we could stop it, but I just haven't a clue. She's got some hiding-place – she must have. Mind you, I don't suppose she's got very much of whatever it is. But I'm afraid she did manage to get hold of a fresh stock when she was in town. I went up with her of course, and we lunched together. But I didn't want to butt in on her interview with Sanderson. I didn't want him to think that I was pushing her in any way – about the house, or anything. So I arranged to drop her at his office, and she said she would take a taxi as soon as she had finished her talk with him and meet me at the club for tea. Well, she arrived very late and in one of those excited moods. My heart went down like a stone. Of course she swore she hadn't got anything – turned out her bag and made me feel in her pockets. It was pathetic – ' He broke off suddenly and put a hand on her arm. 'Ione – is this really all news to you? Was there nothing which aroused your suspicion before she was married?'

Nothing could have exceeded the horrified surprise in her voice.

'Before she was married?'

He said in a dreadfully bitter voice,

'I found out that Allegra was a drug addict before we had been married a week.'

The shock was overwhelming. She heard herself say, 'No – no!' But even as she said it her mind was battling with the thought of how little she had seen of Allegra in those crowded weeks before the wedding. She said in an exhausted voice,

'I didn't know – I can't believe it – '

'Do you suppose I wanted to? I took her to a very clever French doctor, and he told me what to do. He said it hadn't

57

been going on very long, and she would be all right. I thought we had got her cured, but six months later it started again. It's been hell.'

Ione steadied herself.

'Has she never told you how she gets the stuff? Can't you get it out of her?'

He said grimly,

'I can get a string of lies. If you really, genuinely don't know anything, then I think it must have been someone at one of the house-parties we went to who induced her to try the stuff. There was a fairly wild crowd at a couple of the places, but I can't even begin to make a guess at who could possibly have done such a damnable thing. Allegra was being run off her legs. That's the way girls begin with that sort of thing – it's just something to pick them up and carry them over a sticky patch.'

As he spoke, there was a loud 'Coo-ee!' from the quarry top. Margot Trent was leaning over and waving. When they looked up, she shouted, 'Watch me!' and began to run along the edge, balancing with an arm out on either side. Geoffrey shouted, 'Get back!' but she only burst out laughing. She had just passed out of sight behind a tall conifer rooted some four feet down, when there was a most appalling scream followed by the sound of a crash.

Geoffrey said, 'Oh, my God!' swung round upon his heel, and ran. Ione followed him, her heart banging, her breath coming short.

A rock garden is no place through which to run a headlong course – steps going up and steps going down – the unexpected pool the sudden sharp descent – the boulder which masks a twist in the path. Looking back afterwards, she could not understand why she had not stumbled and come down. Geoffrey at least knew the way, yet she came up with him almost as he reached the foot of the quarry wall.

And there was nothing there.

He stood staring down at the harmless shrubs and plants which were all that there was to see. And then, very slowly, his glance travelled upwards whilst Ione's followed it. There might be a crumpled, broken body caught somewhere on that irregular rock face. Threequarters of the way up, and nothing yet. The lower branches of the conifer came into view only a matter of four feet from the top. It rose up in a blue-green pillar, very beautiful and shapely, and from behind it there came great gusts and shouts of laughter.

Ione stepped back. She had to see, and she was too nearly under the cliff. She stepped back, and she saw Margot holding to the tree, her face scarlet, her eyes streaming. She bent this way and that in her paroxysms of mirth. In a voice which Ione would hardly have recognised Geoffrey shouted, 'Keep still!'

But this merely provoked her to fresh explosions.

'Didn't I take you in beautifully! Didn't you think I'd come to a sticky end!' She leaned against the tree and shook the tears away. 'That was a stone I pushed over, wrapped up in a bit of sacking! You'll find it behind the thing with the red berries! And didn't I give a lovely scream! I'd got it all thought out, because I've got a rope round my waist, and it's tied to the tree so I couldn't fall if I tried! All right, all right – I'm going up now! Just watch me!'

In a moment she had scrambled, wriggled and jerked herself to the top of the cliff. It was not a graceful performance. One of her suspenders had broken, and the stout pink leg which the fallen stocking exposed was covered with scratches. As she stood there laughing and undoing the rope at her waist, Geoffrey turned with a sound of pure rage and went striding away in the direction of the house.

CHAPTER XI

'Oh, no, we never scold her,' said Jacqueline Delauny. Her tone was that of the civilised person who is addressing a member of some backward tribe.

Ione's reactions were of the simplest. She felt an inward glow of fury, and she said,

'Why?'

Miss Delauny's superiority became a little more pronounced.

'It would not help.'

'Have you tried?'

'Oh, no. Any harshness would only make things worse.'

'Well, I think you should see what a good scolding would do. I quite agree that she doesn't mean any harm, but she ought to be made to realise that this sort of thing isn't funny. I never had such a shock in my life, and I don't suppose Geoffrey had either. Well, that's all right – we can take it. But supposing Allegra had been there – are you going to tell me she is fit to have a shock like that, or that she ought to be in the house with someone who is liable to give her that kind of shock at any moment? Margot probably won't do that particular thing again, but can you, or can Geoffrey, guarantee that the next thing she does may not be equally horrible and even more dangerous? Because that rope might have slipped or broken, you know. The whole thing makes me feel quite sick.'

Jacqueline Delauny maintained the calm level of her voice. 'Miss Muir, I understand your feelings and have every sympathy with them, but you must be aware that I am not the authority in the matter. If you care to speak to Mr. Trent about it, he will, I am sure, be able to satisfy you that we are all doing our best. It has been an unfortunate occurrence, and it has naturally upset you. It has upset Mr. Trent, and I think it would be kinder not to discuss the matter with him for a few days.'

Ione became aware that she was being put in the wrong. All the tolerance, the kindness, the consideration for others, were on Jacqueline Delauny's side. Ione Muir was the visitor who was disturbing the harmony of the household. It was a completely infuriating situation, and she must get herself out of it as best she could. She produced a kind, tolerant smile of her own and said,

'Poor Geoffrey! It's a frightful millstone to have tied round his neck, isn't it?'

By the evening Allegra had relapsed into the little pale

ghost of yesterday. Margot was on her best behaviour. She had changed into a well cut frock of dark blue velvet, her hair had been brushed until it shone, and her hands and nails were spotlessly clean. She giggled to herself every now and then as if her thoughts were pleasurably occupied, but on the whole her manner was more restrained than Ione had seen it yet, and she really wondered whether Geoffrey's temper had not carried him into giving her the dressing-down she had asked for. He was certainly in very much better spirits. She saw him for the first time as the gay and charming host, leading the talk with great skill but never monopolising it. He had been in some unusual places, he had a gift of description, and he could make a story come alive.

Allegra drooped in her sofa corner as the talk flowed round her. If Geoffrey included her in some passing allusion, he did not make the mistake of expecting an answer. It was this which gave Ione her most painful impression. The lifeless apathy, the silence, which were to her so startling and so new, were nothing of the sort to Jacqueline Delauny or to Geoffrey Trent. They were something to which they had become accustomed. With these thoughts in her mind, it said much for the charms of Geoffrey's conversation that the evening passed with so little sense of strain.

At half-past ten the following morning Ione set out to walk into the village. Geoffrey was apologetic over letting her go alone.

'I'd come with you, only I'm expecting this chap about the house. The church is always open, and you can buy picture-postcards at the general shop.' He laughed. 'In fact a perfect riot of entertainment!'

She had not got very far beyond the gate, when the taxi which had brought her from Wraydon came into view at the end of the street. She was looking at it with interest and wondering what the expert was going to say about the Ladies' House, when the car stopped a few yards away and Jim Severn jumped out. Ione was surprised to find how pleased she was to see him. Startled too. Because of all the unexpected things! Or was it?

He held her hand and forgot to let it go.

'Ione! Were you coming to meet me? How extraodinarily nice of you!'

'I'm afraid I wasn't. You see you are a Dreadful Shock – because I hadn't the faintest idea you were coming.'

'Didn't your brother-in-law get my letter?'

She laughed.

'If you are "the chap he was going to see about the house", he did. But that's all I knew. He didn't mention your name.'

'Well, it was put up to our firm, and I thought I'd come myself. It's a very interesting place by all accounts. And you told me you were going to be here on a visit.'

It was at this point that she became aware of the interested scrutiny of a stout woman with a mop of grey hair, an old man with a clay pipe between his teeth, a lumpy boy on a bicycle which he was balancing against a cottage wall, and the taxi driver. Jim Severn was still holding her hand, and the taxi's meter was ticking up. With a fine bright colour in her cheeks, she detached herself and said,

'Hadn't you better pay your taxi? You are just there, and I can show you the way.'

Jim Severn extracted a case from the back of the car and overpaid the driver, watched with the greatest interest by the little knot of sightseers, to whom a woman in a pixie hood and a little girl with her thumb in her mouth had now added themselves.

Just inside the gates of the Ladies' House he stopped.

'Your brother-in-law seems very keen about getting this place. Do you know, we've had it to look over before – in '33. There was an American who wanted to buy it then, and the owner wouldn't sell – couldn't in fact, because the heir was a minor. But the guardian, who was a Miss Falconer, gave the American a seven years' lease with the option of renewal and let him make a lot of improvements – hot water system and all that sort of thing. My Uncle John went down himself, and he has dug out all his notes for me, and the plans. He was very anxious not to spoil the character of the place, and it's no joke working a modern hot water system into one of these old houses, but I gather he made a pretty good job of it.'

'There is *really* hot water!'

They began to move again. The drive was quite a short one. It was too short. They reached the front door before either of them wished to.

Ione walked back to the village and bought picture-postcards.

She returned to find Geoffrey Trent in the highest of good humours. To have an expert to share his enthusiasm for the Ladies' House, to talk about it to his heart's content and to so agreeable a fellow as Jim Severn was an experience in which he was obviously revelling. And when he discovered the elder Mr Severn's previous connection with the house, and the fact that his nephew was a friend of Ione's, nothing would serve him but that Jim make a week-end of it and stay with them.

'It's a sheer impossibility to get the hang of a place like this in an hour or two. You want to live with it, in it – you want to steep yourself in the atmosphere, before you can even begin to think of making a report.'

Jim Severn made no demur. He had, as a matter of fact, intended to put in the week-end in the neighbourhood – at the Station Hotel at Wraydon if nothing better turned up. He could take Ione out to lunch and see whether that strong sense of attraction held. The circumstances of their first meeting had been of the kind to stir the imagination. He found himself thinking about her in a very persistent way, and he wanted to check up on it. Sometimes these curious first impressions held, and sometimes they did not. It was a matter of ten years since he had been so disturbed over a woman, and he wanted to know where he stood. Love at first sight – well, it happened. Or love at the first sound of a voice which was not like any other. If he had only met her under the shroud of the fog and never seen her face, he would have known her anywhere and at any time the moment she opened her lips and spoke.

CHAPTER XII

Miss Maud Silver looked up from the card in her hand to the client whom Emma Meadows was ushering in, a short, broad person in the roughest of tweeds, stoutest of brogues, and the most sensible of country hats. Repeating the name which she had just read, Miss Silver said in a tone of mild enquiry,

'Miss Josepha Bowden?'

Her free hand was warmly grasped and rung.

'How do you do? You have no idea what relief it is to hear my name pronounced correctly. You have no idea of the number of people who just say Joseph and then add some kind of a little grunt. Most infuriating! It is, of course, pronounced as if the "e" were doubled – Joseepha, and I cannot tell you how much pleasure it gave me to hear you say it properly.'

She seated herself in the chair which had been placed for her on the far side of the large writing-table, stripped off a pair of thick leather gloves, and said,

'You are Miss Maud Silver?'

Miss Silver inclined her head.

Miss Bowden's eyes were fixed upon her. They were rather good eyes, grey with a growth of strongly curling lashes. Her hair which was streaked with grey curled too, and quite obviously without any other assistance than that of nature, one glance being enough to dispel the idea that she would ever bother about her appearance for longer than she could possibly help. She was fortunate in possessing what had once been a very fine complexion and was still in spite of the buffetings of all kinds of weather in all quarters of the globe an extraordinarily healthy and colourful affair. With her eyes on Miss Silver's face she said,

'I have come to see you on a – well, I don't know how to put it, and I hate beating about the bush, but it's – well – it's a delicate matter.'

A great many delicate matters had been brought into that room and laid before Miss Silver – in doubt, in perplexity, in dreadful anxiety, or mortal fear. Josepha Bowden went on,

'Elizabeth Moore is a distant connection of mine – she is Elizabeth Robertson now. She tells me you got her young man out of a mess, and what is a great deal more important so far as I am concerned, she says that you can hold your tongue, and *that you actually do*.'

The temperature of the room appeared at this moment to sustain a chill. There was a faint distance in Miss Silver's voice as she replied that the confidences of a client were, of course, inviolate.

'There now – I've offended you, and that's the last thing I meant to do! I can't wrap things up and be tactful about them. All I can do is to tell the truth and hope that everyone else is going to do the same. And, do you know, they very often do. I've got out of quite a lot of tight places that way. I'm a traveller, you know – or perhaps you don't. I go knocking round in odd places, and then I write books about them.'

Miss Silver's memory was seldom at a loss for long. It now connected Miss Josepha Bowden quite firmly with such phrases as 'Intrepid woman explorer,' 'The first European to attempt this dangerous route', and the like. She smiled in her own peculiarly charming manner and said,

'Oh, yes – I have seen accounts of some of your journeys. So very interesting. And now what can I do for you?'

Miss Bowden sat back in her chair and allowed her eyes to travel about the room. It was the pride of Miss Silver's heart, and it never failed to make its own impression upon her clients. They were sometimes wafted back to the home of some old-fashioned relative who had preserved the furnishings and pictures of an earlier date. Miss Bowden perfectly remembered being taken to see an aged great-aunt who possessed chairs in curly walnut frames which could not be distinguished from those on either side of Miss Silver's hearth, and at least two of the pictures which had graced Aunt

Janet's walls looked down at her now from over the mantel-piece and above the bookcase – the *Black Brunswicker's* farewell to his bride and *Bubbles*.

She hastened into speech.

'I've been rude again, but I was admiring your things. My great-aunt Janet had chairs like these, and some of the pictures too.'

Miss Silver beamed.

'They came to me from my grandparents, and I value them highly. Whilst I was engaged in the scholastic profession it seemed improbable that I should ever be in a position to accommodate them in a flat of my own, but when circumstances enabled me to exchange that profession for a more lucrative one I was able to do so.'

Her eye travelled fondly about her little room, so bright, so cosy, with its peacock-blue curtains and carpet, both new since the war but repeating as far as possible the shade and pattern of their predecessors. She came back to Miss Josepha Bowden.

'You think that I can help you in some way?'

'I don't know.'

Miss Silver waited. After a pause Miss Bowden said with a jerk, 'When I said it was delicate – well, it *is*. And most people would say it was none of my business, and I suppose, strictly speaking, it isn't. But if you're going to mind your own business to that extent, people might be murdered right and left under your nose and you wouldn't feel called upon to do anything about it. And if I was one of the people who was going to be murdered I'd rather have someone who didn't mind sticking his fingers into other people's pies.'

Miss Silver gazed at her mildly.

'Do you know of anyone who is going to be murdered?'

'I'm sure I hope *not*!' said Josepha Bowden with considerable force.

Miss Silver continued to gaze at her in an expectant manner.

Miss Bowden pushed back her chair and planted a hand squarely on either knee.

66

'Well, as a matter of fact, I'm worried about my god-daughter Allegra.'

The name meant nothing to Miss Silver. She waited for more. Miss Bowden went on.

'When I said this was delicate, I meant all of it – right from the beginning where I come in. Allegra isn't any relation of mine, but she's the daughter of the woman who got me out of a very nasty mess when I was a girl – about the nastiest mess a girl can get herself into, and you can dot the i's and cross the t's for yourself. She died when Allegra was a child, and if there's ever anything I can do to show that I haven't forgotten what she did for me, well, I'm here to do it whether anyone thinks I'm interfering or not.'

Miss Silver had picked up some soft white knitting. About two inches of a baby's bootee hung down like a little frill from the needles.

'You are in some concern about Miss Allegra?'

Josepha gave a loud vexed laugh.

'That's the bother – she isn't Miss Allegra! She's married, and I want to know a lot more than I do about the man – where he comes from – what he was doing before he married Allegra – whether he really has got any money, and if so, where *that* comes from – and why, ever since her marriage, she doesn't answer anyone's letters, or go and stay with her relations or have them to stay with her.'

Miss Silver shook her head.

'I could not undertake such an enquiry in respect of the husband. It would not be in my line at all.'

'And I wouldn't want you to undertake it. To put it quite bluntly, it's a man's job, and I'll have to get a man working on it. I've just put things clumsily – I always do. What I want you for is this. Look here, I'm taking Elizabeth's word for you, and I'm taking you as I've found you and I'm going to put my cards down on the table. The man's name is Geoffrey Trent, and he's taken Allegra to live in some kind of a medieval house in a village called Bleake. I hear he's trying to buy the place – with Allegra's money. She has quite a lot, and most of it is in trust, thank goodness. But her other god-mother left her enough to buy this place and a good bit over without any strings to it at all. So one of the things I want to know is why that money isn't being used.'

'It is not?'

Miss Bowden shook her head vigorously.

'No. They are trying to get round the trustees to let them use some of the money out of the trust, and I want to know why. There's been some talk about losses.'

Miss Silver coughed.

'You think that the other money may have been spent?'

Josepha Bowden thumped her knee.

'Looks like it to me! If they've still got it, why don't they use it? Then there's this house – I want to know more about it. Old houses don't appeal to me. After all, nobody washed in the middle ages, and I don't fancy living in a place where nobody ever had a bath between the cradle and the grave for hundreds and hundreds of years – it doesn't sound healthy to me! Now what I want you to do is to go down and stay in the village. There's a Miss Falconer who will take an occasional p.g. if she thinks they are all right. She lives in a cottage, but this place Geoffrey Trent wants to buy, the Ladies' House, belongs to her. There hasn't been any money for donkey's years, and the last male Falconer was killed in the war, so she ought to be tumbling over herself to sell. But by all accounts she isn't. That's one of the things I want to know about.'

Miss Silver laid down her knitting, opened a drawer on her left, and looked out what used to be called a copybook with a bright blue cover. Moved by the insatiable curiosity which is one of his besetting sins, Detective Inspector Frank Abbott of Scotland Yard had once explored the source and origin of these survivals from an earlier and more brightly coloured world. It then transpired that a grateful client retiring from the conduct of an old-fashioned stationery business had come across a couple of gross of these books, and had forthwith presented them to Miss Silver. 'And really, my dear Frank, the supply appears to be inexhaustible.'

The bit of bright colour pleased Miss Bowden. She watched Miss Silver write down Miss Falconer's name, the names of the village, the Ladies' House, and of Mr. and Mrs.

Geoffrey Trent, together with the question upon which she had desired to be informed.

Pencil in hand, Miss Silver looked up and said,

'Pray proceed.'

'I want to know why Miss Falconer doesn't jump at selling the place. Have you got that down?'

Miss Silver inclined her head.

'The survivors of an old family are often averse from parting with the last vestiges of former greatness.'

Miss Bowden made the sound which is usually written, 'Humph!'

'That's as may be! I just want to make sure that she hasn't got some kink in her conscience. Geoffrey Trent would be welcome to buy up all the insanitary ruins in England he'd a mind to if he hadn't married my god-daughter. But he has, and that brings me in neck and crop. The person I am concerned about is Allegra, and I don't want her saddled with a mouldy old manor built over a cesspool – if they even had cesspools at the time it was built – or one of these places that has got a curse on it, or some particularly horrid kind of ghost!' She banged her knee even more decidedly than before. 'And we all know that ghosts and curses are just a lot of superstitious nonsense! But I'm not having Allegra subjected to them! There is such a thing as suggestion, and she's not in a state to have unpleasant things suggested to her!'

Miss Silver coughed.

'Without admitting any reality in these phenomena or pronouncing an opinion as to whether they have their origin in trickery or in the vagaries of the human mind, they can at times be extremely unpleasant.'

Miss Bowden nodded vigorously.

'I consider myself a strong-minded woman, and so, I suppose, do you. At this moment, at twenty minutes past eleven in the morning, sitting here in your nice bright room, I have a perfectly healthy and civilised disbelief in ghosts, spectres, apparitions, ghouls, vampires, and curses. But put me in a haunted room at midnight, with doors opening by themselves and the candle guttering and going out, and I don't pretend for a moment that I shouldn't probably scream the house down. It's all atmosphere, and whether the thing can get you to believe in it or not. I've seen a man die of a curse in Africa. He believed in it like mad, and he just lay down and died, like an animal will if it's been too badly frightened. And that brings me back to Allegra. I want to know whether anything is frightening her. She is the kind that would be easy enough to scare. A gentle, timid kind of creature with a soft voice and pretty ways. Not half the pluck and go and spirit of her sister Ione.'

'There is a sister?'

'Yes – unmarried – Ione Muir. I hear she's on a visit to Allegra now. First time for two years, but she's been out in the States. Made rather a hit there with monologues, sketches – you know the sort of thing. I'm told they went quite wild about her. Well, she's been back some time now, but until a few days ago she hadn't so much as laid eyes on Allegra. That's one of the things that's been worrying me. She's been going down there half a dozen times, and they've always put her off. And Allegra's been coming up to meet her in London, but there's always been a telegram or a last minute call to say she couldn't come. I ran into Ione in Bond Street and dragged it all out of her. I just said to her, "Look here, you can make this hard work for me and very irritating for yourself, but I intend to know what is going on about Allegra, and you can't put me off. I shall just go on until I find out, so it will be a whole lot easier if you come across and tell me what you know".'

Miss Silver picked up her knitting again.

'And then she told you?'

Josepha Bowden nodded.

'Told me I was a human battering-ram and I ought to be ashamed of myself! So then we went in and had some coffee, and she told me all about it. Not that there was really anything to tell – only about being put off, and Allegra never turning up when she'd made an appointment. Once we got the ice broken, I think she was glad enough to talk – I could see she was just as worried as I was. So it was a considerable relief to me to hear that her visit to Allegra had actually come off at last.'

Miss Silver looked thoughtfully across her rapidly moving needles.

'Since Miss Muir is now staying at the Ladies' House and will be able to give you a much fuller account of the situation there than I can possibly hope to do, are you sure that you really wish to engage my services?'

She got one of those hearty laughs.

'I shouldn't have come if I didn't! I want the village talk, the village gossip. I want the Falconer angle. Elizabeth Moore says you're a wonder at getting people to talk. Well, that's what I want. Villages can be as tight as clams. I sent a man down to snoop around and didn't get a thing, and he wouldn't if he'd stayed there a year instead of a day. But one of Miss Falconer's p.g.'s pottering round with her, buying oddments, and going to church on Sundays – well, that's different. Especially if you could carry on a spot of knitting.'

Miss Silver, inured by now to Miss Bowden's informal mode of conversation, smiled indulgently and remarked that she never went anywhere without her knitting.

'And your fees?'

Miss Silver named a sum which only a few years before she would have considered alarming. It was accepted with a careless,

'That's all right. I've got plenty of money – a lot more than I shall ever use. When you spend most of your time with all your worldly goods in a couple of saddlebags you don't get cluttered up with possessions like the stay-at-homes do. I shall probably settle down, if I ever do, in a tent on a bit of ground that I overlooked when I was selling the rest of the land my forebears managed to hang round my neck. It's got a nice spring on it, and if I find a tent too cold I can always make it a caravan.' She got up out of her chair and held out a strong brown hand. 'I think you'll do the job all right, and I'd like you to go down as soon as you can. Miss Falconer is on the telephone, and I suggest you ring her up and say something on the lines of a friend of yours had met someone who had stayed with her in the summer, and would she by any chance be prepared to take you in? You had better mention references, because she won't take anyone without them.'

Miss Silver smiled. She would be able to offer some quite unexceptionable references which could be verified on the telephone. Having taken down a few more particulars, she suffered a hearty handshake from Miss Bowden, who thereupon departed with every appearance of being very well satisfied with her morning's work.

As soon as the front door had closed upon her Miss Silver drew the table-telephone towards her and dialled Trunks.

CHAPTER XIII

The dining-room of the George Hotel at Wraydon is very strictly in the tradition of its many Georgian and Victorian counterparts. It has a row of tall windows curtained in olive green and rather heavily screened by yellowing net. The tables – it does have separate tables – are solidly constructed, and shrouded to within an inch or two of the floor. The tablecloths have seen better days. Sometimes there is a vase containing a couple of paper flowers and a sprig of evergreen. In summer the flowers may even be real if rather shabby-genteel, but always, and where you cannot possibly help seeing it, there is a massive ash-tray which advertises some well known brand of table-water. From the walls engravings representing the royalties and politicians of a bygone day gaze benignly or severely upon the scene. Queen Victoria as a smiling young woman with pretty little ears just peeping out from demurely banded hair. Albert, the Prince Consort, in the days when he was one of the handsomest young men in Europe. The great Gladstone, hatchet-faced and gloomy. The Marquess of Salisbury in a bushy beard. There is something reposeful about the distance between these fading portraits and the really fiery passions which once raged around the men who posed for them.

Ione sat with her back to a window and laughed at Jim Severn's apologies for not having been able to find a better place for lunch.

'We ought to have gone out into the country.'

'Well, it's a very good thing we didn't, isn't it? I'm not really bigoted about the country when it's pouring with rain. Cousin Eleanor lives in a village, you know, so I've always had plenty of it, and frankly, when it comes to a wet Sunday I'd just as soon be somewhere else. Now here we can go back into the great Victorian age and be as leisurely as we like. We haven't any trains to catch, and I've got a lot of things I want to talk to you about.'

A middle-aged waitress came over to them and took their order. When she had gone he said,

'I've got a lot to talk to you about too.'

'Who is going to start?'

'Would you like to?'

She shook her head, smiling.

'Not particularly. It's the man's business to lead off.'

He leaned towards her across the table and said,

'How much does your sister really want to live in that house?'

Ione looked at him composedly.

'I don't think she wants to live in it at all. I should hate it myself, and I think it's all wrong for Allegra. She isn't strong, and the place frightens her.'

'Then why –'

'Oh, it's Geoffrey. You can't have talked to him for five minutes without seeing that he's in love with the house – besotted about it. He makes a joke of it, but that is only on the surface. He can hardly make himself stop talking about it, and I don't believe he ever stops thinking of it.'

It was curious how easily she could talk to him. He had come to Bleake to furnish Mr. Sanderson with an opinion as to the structural soundness and general condition of the Ladies' House considered as a suitable investment for Allegra's trustees, yet neither he nor she was talking about it from that angle. It was the personal and private aspect of the case which was presenting itself. Without a word of

73

explanation they had between them the two things which Ione would not have believed she could discuss with a stranger – Allegra's state, and the anxiety to which it was giving rise.

The arrival of the waitress with two plates of pink tomato soup gave both of them pause. Jim Severn thought, 'It's none of my business. Why didn't I hold my tongue?', and Ione, 'But he isn't a stranger. I've known him always – at least that's what it feels like.'

The soup was hot, and surprisingly, it wasn't out of a tin. Ione guessed at home-bottled tomatoes and thought that she would like to have the recipe. She smiled and said,

'Someone told me the food here was good. It was the daily maid from the village, Florrie Bowyer. She said the cook here was her aunt, and she had been in very good places but she liked her independence. And the other day, when she thought of having a room and going out daily just to special people, the manager asked her to marry him, so she is staying on. He lost his wife in the autumn and she is very fond of his little girl, so she is going to take him and stay.'

He was laughing.

'How on earth did you get all that?'

'Oh, Florrie likes talking.'

'Does she talk to your sister? Was it she who frightened her about the house?'

Ione nodded.

'What did she tell her about it?'

'Oh, some story about the house being called Ladies' Bane because whoever was mistress there would lose what she cared for most in the world. Allegra isn't in a state to have that sort of thing said to her.'

'All these old houses have stories about ghosts and curses. The Ladies' House hasn't got a ghost, I suppose?'

'I haven't heard of one, but I wouldn't be surprised. What Allegra wants is a nice bright modern house with lots of windows and no history.'

The waitress changed their plates and brought them each a helping of roast duck cooked to a turn. There was apple sauce, deliciously sharp, cauliflower in a creamy sauce, and

74

little potato balls cooked to a golden brown but soft inside. Jim Severn said,

'Well, your Florrie was right about one thing, the aunt is certainly a heaven-born cook. This is the sort of food which I thought had perished from the earth. Comforting to realise that it lingers here and there.' Then, without any perceptible pause or change of voice, 'You know, if you feel as you have just given me to understand about your sister living at the Ladies' House, it is all too easy. You have only to go to Sanderson – is he your trustee as well as your sister's?'

'Yes, he is.'

'Well, all you've got to do is to go to him and tell him what you've just told me. If you say the place gives you the creeps –'

She looked up quickly.

'I didn't say that.'

'You said you hated it.'

'That's not the same thing.'

'Well, does it, or doesn't it?'

She looked away, frowning.

'Well, it does – but I don't know that I should be justified – ' She bit her lip. 'You see, Geoffrey is so frightfully keen. I should feel the worst kind of double-crosser if I did it behind his back. And if I tell him I'm going to go to Mr. Sanderson to try and put him off, well, I don't see any way out of it except one of those nasty family rows which are never quite patched up. And I can't have that, because of Allegra.'

After a little he said,

'I see – ' He was thinking that she had an unusually delicate sense of honour, and then wondering if it wasn't just a little too delicate – quixotic. He couldn't make up his mind. There was, of course, another way. He said rather abruptly,

'Sanderson will surely talk to Mrs. Trent herself. I shouldn't think he could fail to discern that the house doesn't appeal to her.'

Ione said,

'I don't know. She – she is very devoted to Geoffrey, you know, and very much under his influence. She is gentle, and rather timid. If she is fond of someone she will do almost anything they want her to do. She has always been like that. If Geoffrey wants the Ladies' House, it is no use supposing for a moment that she will tell Mr. Sanderson she doesn't want to live there. It's beyond her and it's better to make up one's mind to it. I suppose you can't say anything that would put Mr. Sanderson off?'

He shook his head.

'I shall have to give an honest professional opinion. We've left the roof till Monday, but as far as the rest of the building is concerned it is remarkably sound. They knew how to build in those days. It has been continually lived in and looked after ever since, and the American's modern conveniences have been admirably contrived. My uncle drew the plans himself, and I must say he made a marvellous job of it. So unless something quite unforeseen crops up in the roof I shall have to submit a very favourable report.'

Ione drew a long breath.

'I shall just have to tell Geoffrey that I don't think the Middle Ages are good for Allegra's nerves. He won't like it, and he'll think I'm all the interfering sisters-in-law rolled into one, but it can't be helped.'

The waitress changed their plates again. She put down what looked like a piece of real English cheese and a dish of home-made biscuits. She also produced some quite admirable coffee.

It was over the cheese and the coffee that Jim Severn said suddenly,

'You'll never guess who I ran into downstairs in the coffee-room having a snack.'

'Someone I know?'

'Well' – his voice sounded amused – 'someone you have talked to.'

'With you?'

'With me.'

Something like a small cold draught drew in from the glass of the window behind her. She had not noticed it before. And Jim Severn was saying,

'You've even heard him sing. That was how I recognised

him. He was drinking a quite horrible brew of cocoa laced with whisky, which he tells me he finds very sustaining, and bursting at intervals into the *Bluebells of Scotland*.'

Ione knew why she had felt cold. She was back in that horrible night of fog, following the man whom she had just heard bargaining over the price of a life, and it was the *Bluebells of Scotland* that he had whistled and sung as he clattered with his stick along parapet and balustrade. She caught her breath sharply and said,

'Oh, *no*!' And then, 'You didn't say anything about me –' He shook his head.

'I don't know that I should have spoken to him, but he looked straight at me and waved a hand. I thought he recognised me. The gas-lamp out in the street was quite bright when he went away at three o'clock in the morning, and he could have seen me by it, but as it turned out he was just being matey and didn't know me from Adam. By the time I had tumbled to this I had already addressed him as Professor MacPhail, and he was busy swearing me to secrecy.'

'Why?'

'I haven't the slightest idea. There must have been quite a lot of whisky in that cocoa, because the tears were running down his face. He said it was a matter of his professional reputation, and got off quite a piece about the unguarded tongue, and discretion being the mother of safety. "Twa strangers in a fog, and how was it possible to suspect that I was to come across either of them again! The tongue of truth has aye been mine – except in the way of my prrofessional career. And what would hinder that truthful tongue from giving the name with which I was borrn – and not one to be ashamed of. No, no – a decent name and a decent family, the MacPhails. But" – here he buttonholed me and diffused a cloud of whisky – "*but*, for prrofessional purposes the name is Regulus Mactavish – Prrofessor Regulus Mactavish. And for the hoardings and the theatre bills The Great Prospero!"'

The imitation was very well done. Ione should have laughed, but there was no laughter in her. She felt a cold horror, and she had turned so pale that Jim Severn stretched

77

out his hand across the table and said,

'What is it – is anything wrong?'

'I don't know –'

He left his seat and came to sit beside her.

'My dear, what is it?'

She put a cold hand into his warm one.

'I'll tell you – in a minute. I'm probably being silly.'

He filled up her coffee-cup and pushed it over to her with his free hand.

'You'd better drink this whilst it's hot.'

When she had drunk the coffee she said,

'Jim, I don't want to stay here – I don't want that man to see me – I don't want him to know I'm here. I'll wait in the ladies' room while you settle up and get the car. I won't come downstairs until I see you in the hall, and if the coast is clear you can nod your head and then go straight out to the car. I don't want him to see us together.'

The next few minutes went as slowly as any Ione had known in all her life. When she came to the head of the stairs, Jim Severn was not in sight. A little man with a bald head came out of one of the side doors and tapped the large old-fashioned barometer which hung in the hall, after which he plunged down a dark passage and was seen no more. A woman in a streaming mackintosh pushed the swing-door at the entrance and came in in a very hesitating manner. She stood and dripped impartially upon the strip of red carpet and the shabby brown linoleum on either side of it, shifting her position from time to time and looking about her in a depressed and helpless manner. After some three or four minutes she appeared to lose heart altogether and wandered back through the swing-door into the rain.

There was one of those times which are probably not so long drawn out as they appear. Ione had begun to have a dazed impression that nothing was ever going to happen again, when Jim Severn came quickly in through the swing-door, looked up, nodded briefly, and turning on his heel, went out again.

With the vaguely startled feeling that she had roused suddenly from a brief uneasy sleep she began to descend the stairs. She was within two or three steps of the bottom, when a door at the end of a passage running away from the stairs to the back of the house was thrown open and a man came out. He was away out of Ione's sight and she had no inclination to turn her head, but he emerged upon a rich tide of song, and she could not have an instant's doubt as to his identity.

> 'And was'na he a roguey, a roguey, roguey,
> And was'na he a roguey,
> The Piper o' Dundee?'

It wasn't one of the songs he had sung in the fog, but she would have known the rolling voice if she had come across it in China or Peru. A quiet coldness came upon her, and without hastening her step she crossed the hall and went out through the swing-door. It fell to behind her, and the Piper of Dundee was blotted out.

Jim was drawn up just short of the entrance. She got into the seat beside him and said,

'Quick! He was behind me as I came out!'

As they slid away over the wet road, he said,

'Did he see you?'

'Not my face – and anyhow I don't suppose he ever did see that. I could only have been someone who was crossing the hall.'

He turned into a side street.

'Oh, he saw you that night. You were asleep, and the light of the street-lamp was shining in clear through the glass over the door. He had a good look at you before he went, and he said you had a bonnie face.'

She made a sound of pure exasperation. Jim Severn laughed.

'He was perfectly respectful. There really wasn't anything for you to resent – just an involuntary tribute.'

She said in a low voice,

'You don't understand. And we can't talk here. Let's get away from all these houses and things and find a country road where you can stop the car.'

They did not have to go very far. No more than two miles out of Wraydon the village of Ring has a charming green approached by broad grass verges and centering upon a pond complete with ducks. Off the road and in the lee of a hedge they could talk as privately as they chose and for as long, with the rain blurring the windscreen and the sound of trees lashing in the wind. Now that it had come to the point, Ione was wondering just what her story was worth. Seen in retrospect, the whole thing partook of the vagueness, the insubstantiality of the fog which had been its setting.

Jim Severn turned towards her and said,

'Well – what is it?'

'When I ran into you in the fog that night and asked you to say I was with you –'

He interrupted her.

'That isn't quite what you said. You wanted me to say you had bumped into me a little way back.'

'Yes – I didn't want him to know I had been following him.'

'Why?'

'I had better tell you the whole thing from the beginning. The fog had come up suddenly, and I was lost. I went on, because there was always a chance of getting somewhere. What I did get to was one of those streets where the houses stand a little way back with steps going down to an area and a stone balustrade acoss the front. It's terribly difficult to walk quite straight in a fog. I'm one of the people who bear to the right, and all at once I found myself clutching at a gate which swung away from me. As a matter of fact, I hit it pretty hard with my knee, and the next thing I knew I was falling down the area steps. I landed on some horrid wet flagstones – that is where I collected the green slime – and I was quite glad to keep still for a bit and make sure I hadn't got any broken bones. And the next thing that happened was that someone came out of the house by the front door and stood there talking to the person who was letting him out. There were steps running up from the street, and neither of them had any idea that I had just fallen down into their area.'

'How do you know that?'

'Because of what they said. The one who came out was Professor MacPhail – Regulus Mactavish – The Great Prospero – whatever he chooses to call himself. The other was just a whisper. I don't really know that it was a man. I just took it for granted, the way the Professor was talking – off-hand, you know, and not troubling about being polite. Of course I can only give you his side of the conversation, because I never got a word of what the other creature said.'

'All right, what did you get?'

'Well, the Professor began by saying what a dependable man he was, and that his word was his bond. He said there wasn't a man living who could say he had let him down, and that he was a sure friend in trouble. Then there was some whispering from the other. I think he wanted to shut the door, and the Professor had his foot in the way. Anyhow he said he was just going, and grumbled about being turned out in the fog. He said it was as black as the Earl of Hell's waistcoat, and I remembered our old Scotch nannie saying that about a very dark night. Then there was some more talk – whispering on one side, and the Professor talking about the fog. And then he said, "All right, all right – I'm going! And I haven't said I'll do it yet, but I'll give it my careful consideration and let you know." I'm not trying to do his Scotch, but I think I've got the words right. And then he went on – and I'm quite sure about this – "But mind, you'll have to think again – about the remuneration. I'll not do it for any less than two thousand. It's my neck I'll be risking, and I'll not risk it for a penny less than two thousand." And with that he came down the steps and went away up the road whistling, 'Ye'll tak the high road, and I'll tak the low road." And I followed him.'

'Why?'

'He seemed to know where he was going, and I wanted to get away from that house and the whispering creature. But I don't want him to know that I followed him, because then he would know that I could have heard what he said about risking his neck.'

'That frightened you?'

'It would have frightened you too if you had heard it, sitting in a slimy area in the middle of a fog.'

'It would certainly make it easier to put a sinister construction on the words. But you know, they might have had a perfectly innocent meaning. The Professor is in the show business. I gather he is what is called an illusionist, with a spot of hypnotism thrown in, and I dare say he is as phoney as you please. But don't you see all that about risking his neck could apply to almost any dangerous stunt?'

'Two thousand pounds? I shouldn't think that the price ran as high as that in the show business!'

'Well, what did you think at the time?'

'I thought he was being asked to get someone out of the way, and that he wasn't turning it down – it was just a matter of whether it would be worth his while or not.'

'And now?'

There was quite a long pause. Then she said very low,

'I don't know – I'm frightened –'

CHAPTER XIV

The raindrops stopped pattering upon the pond and rushing down the windscreen. The clouds were lifting. Between them there appeared first streaks, and then a broad expanse of a pale, lovely turquoise, January's gift to the English winter sky. Presently there was that clear shining after rain which makes amends for the wettest day.

They drove slowly back to Bleake, not talking very much but happy. Ione had a sense of release. She was ready to believe that it was the fog, the shaking she had just received, and her own sense of being lost, which had given a sinister tinge to the Professor's words. She was ready to believe anything so long as she didn't have to see him again, or to listen to that rolling voice. It went through her mind that he had produced the story of the unknown Chinese mandarin – if by pressing a button you would cause the death of this person, and at the same time benefit three-quarters of the human race, would you, or would you not, be justified in pressing that button? And she remembered that Jim Severn had said, there in the fog, when they were huddled together on the stairs of the empty house and she was drowsing and waking against his comfortable shoulder – he had said that he felt pretty sure the button-pusher was really only interested in one member of the human race – himself.

A warm sense of security flowed between her and the recollection. She chose her friends with a sure instinct and she always knew at once what the possibilities of that friendship were going to be. There were the people to whom you responded on the artistic, the practical, the purely personal side. There were the people with whom it was quite possible that you might fall in love, and yet at the same time there would be an inner conviction that you could not imagine spending your life with one of them. But with Jim Severn – this sense of intimacy and security. It was as if they had known each other for so long that the security was a thing tried and proved, and the intimacy a bond which could never be broken.

When they drove into the garage of the Ladies' House – converted stabling, very roomy and spacious – Ione saw that Geoffrey's car was out. He had said something about taking Allegra for a drive if it cleared, and she supposed that he had done so. Well, it was lovely now, with the clouds all drawn away to a rampart along the horizon and the whole sky of that magical rain-washed blue –

Jim Severn put a hand on her arm.

'Like to show me the gardens? Or is it too wet?'

She lifted a foot in a sensible country shoe for his inspection.

'It's not the wet, but what Geoffrey will say. He's sure to want to take you round himself.'

He laughed.

'Well, so he can. No need to tell him I've been round with you. It's rather nice with everything clear and the trees dripping. Those birches look as if they had been strung with diamonds.'

They wandered down the terraces. Looking back at the house, Ione said,

'Do you know, the garden almost persuades me. Those Americans must have loved it a lot.'

'What became of them?'

'He was killed in the war, like the last male Falconer, and she went back to the States. End of a dream.'

'Yes.'

She turned to him abruptly.

'Don't you see, the house is simply hung about with old sad stories. Allegra oughtn't to have that kind of atmosphere. There's the decaying family just petering out after five hundred years, and goodness knows how many crimes and horrors piling up all the way. If you are well, and happy, and strong-minded, you can take it all in your stride like Geoffrey does. But Allegra is neither well nor happy, and she certainly isn't strong-minded. I can just see it seeping into her and getting her down.'

He said very gravely,

'You will have to say all that to Mr. Sanderson, my dear.'

Ione took a moment before she said, 'Yes.' She felt as if she had made a momentous decision, and that once made, she was pledged to it. A weight lifted from her spirits, colour came up in her cheeks, and she turned to him with a gaiety which surprised them both.

'I've been letting myself get too intense. I do when I haven't got anyone to talk things over with. Come along and see the marvellous rock garden that the Americans made out of a disused quarry.'

She began to tell him about the trick Margot Trent had played on Geoffrey and herself the day before.

'It really was horrible. She took us in completely. And when we got to the foot of the cliff, there she was, roped to a tree near the top and laughing her head off.'

'Does she make her home permanently with your sister and brother-in-law?'

'Yes, she does. That is one of the things that worries me.

She isn't normal, and it isn't good for Allegra, but there's just nothing to be done about it. Schools won't keep her, and Geoffrey seems to be the only relation she has got in the world.'

They were approaching the quarry from rather a different angle to that which she had taken with Geoffrey on the previous day. She began to point out how beautiful it would be when the aubrietia was in flower and the bare stems of the wistaria were clothed in their feathery green and the long drooping tassels of lavender and white. She had turned back to point to a clump of wanda primroses already in bloom, when she found that he had not turned with her. He was standing on a boulder above the path and staring in the direction of the cliff. Her own view blocked by a clump of rhododendrons, she had no idea of what he was looking at. She said, 'Jim!' on a surprised note, and as he jumped down from the rock. 'What is it?'

'There's something lying at the foot of the quarry wall.'

'Something?'

'Someone!'

He began to run as Geoffrey had done. Ione followed him. She said over and over in her mind, 'It's a trick – it's a trick – it's just another trick.' But when they came out from between the bushes and up to the place where Margot lay in a sprawling heap with a bit of frayed and broken rope in her hand, the words went faint and passed into a dreadful silence. Margot had played her last trick. She lay on the stones with a broken neck and that ragged end of rope in her hand.

CHAPTER XV

Geoffrey Trent sat facing the Inspector who had come out from Wraydon, a pleasant-looking man whose fresh colouring contrasted sharply with his own haggard appearance.

'You tell me the young lady played a trick on you and Miss

Muir on Saturday at a place very near the one from which she fell on Sunday afternoon.'

'It was not exactly the same place.'

'No. We have photographs of both places of course. I'm trying to find out just how serious that trick may have been.'

'It was not serious. It was a trick.'

'But it might have been serious if the rope had broken.'

'I don't think so. The place where she was standing by that conifer – there was plenty of foothold, and there would be no strain upon the rope.'

'It was the rope you showed me?'

'Yes.'

'A good strong rope – it wouldn't have broken. But this other rope was rotten – the one she was using when she fell.'

Geoffrey's pallor became more extreme.

'After – after she played that trick – I took the rope away and locked it up in the garage. I – was – afraid – ' His voice petered out.

'Then where did the other rope come from?'

'She must have got it out of the potting-shed. There were some old ropes there. Humphreys, the gardener, says – '

'Yes, I'd like a word with him presently. He may have been one of the last people to see her alive. Now, Mr. Trent, when did you see her last?'

Geoffrey braced himself.

'She had lunch with us – as usual. Miss Muir and Mr. Severn were out, but the rest of us went into the drawing-room and had coffee there. My wife rests in the afternoon. I told her I would take her for a drive if it cleared in time. Margot and Miss Delauny went off to their sitting-room.'

'That's the governess, I take it. I haven't seen her yet. How long has she been with you?'

'Nearly three years.'

'You had tried sending the girl to school?'

Geoffrey gave a deep sigh.

'Oh, yes! But they wouldn't keep her. Good-tempered to a fault – affectionate – all that kind of thing. But she didn't fit in. There were always these trying practical jokes, and they wouldn't put up with them.'

'You had medical advice?'

'Of course. They said it was a case of arrested development.'

'It was not suggested that she ought to be under restraint?'

A slight flush tinged Geoffrey's pallor.

'Oh, no – there would have been no case for anything of that sort. She was as harmless as a child. In fact that is what she was – a child of six or seven with a particularly strong and active body ten years too old for her mind. She would have been wretched in a home.'

'You were her guardian, Mr. Trent?'

'Yes.'

The Inspector asked his next question with reluctance, but he felt bound to ask it.

'I have heard that there is some talk in the village to the effect that Miss Trent was fond of saying what a lot of money she was going to have when she came of age. Can you tell if that was true?'

Geoffrey frowned.

'Her father was a cousin of mine. He made a considerable fortune in the Middle East and left it in trust for Margot. As a matter of fact the war did a good deal of damage to his interests. Securities which were considered safe at the time are practically worthless today. In any case Margot had no idea of the value of money.'

'Who are her trustees, Mr. Trent?'

'There was another cousin who was killed in the war, and myself.'

'And who succeeds to the property now?'

Geoffrey drew another of those long melancholy sighs and said,

'Unfortunately I do. There are no other relations.'

The pause that followed was not so unduly prolonged as to be significant. With an air of turning to another subject, Inspector Grayson said,

'Well, Mr. Trent, you were telling me about the Sunday afternoon. You had coffee in the drawing-room and then separated. Will you go on from there.'

Geoffrey leaned his head upon his hand.

'I came in here and wrote a few letters. Some time before three o'clock I could see that it was going to clear. I told my wife that the air would do her good, and I went along to ask Miss Delauny whether she and Margot would like to come. She said she didn't think she would come, as she had some letters to write, and she said Margot had just gone out into the garden, but she would see if she could find her. I said I couldn't wait for her, as the afternoons were so short, and I went to get the car. Neither Margot nor Miss Delauny turned up, so I took my wife for a short round and got back at a quarter to four. My sister-in-law came out to the garage as I was putting the car away and told me that there had been an accident, and that – Margot – was dead – ' He seemed hardly able to get the last words out.

'And then, Mr. Trent?'

'I went with her and Mr. Severn to the quarry. And then I came back to the house and rang up the police.'

'How long was it since they had found her?'

'Only a few minutes, I believe.'

As this was what he had already been told by the two people concerned, Grayson had no comment to make. He said briefly,

'I should like to see the governess if I may.'

CHAPTER XVI

Miss Delauny came into the room looking pale and extinguished. In her plain black dress, without make-up, all her effects were dimmed. The absence of the bright lipstick which she used left her mouth sallow and shapeless. She looked as if she had been crying, and as if she had not troubled to remove the traces of her tears.

Inspector Grayson received a favourable impression. Margot Trent must have been a trying inmate, but these people really did seem to have been fond of her, and to be genuinely upset about her death. He began to question her on the details of her life at the Ladies' House – the amount of companionship given to Margot, and the extent of the supervision which it was considered necessary to exercise.

'Did she do regular lessons with you?'

Miss Delauny had a faint smile for that.

'I don't know that you would call them exactly lessons. One of her difficulties was that she had no power of concentration. Ordinary lessons were out of the question. Her attention had not only to be caught, but kept. I was trying to teach her a little history by allowing her to act some of the simpler dramatic scenes. She had all a child's love of acting and dressing up.' The handkerchief which had been crushed in her hand was pressed to her eyes for a moment. 'She couldn't bear sitting still or being made to read in a book. What she wanted all the time was movement, activity – something that would take up her energies. A year ago Mr. Trent got her a pony. He is a fine horseman himself, and he thought the exercise would be so good for her, but it didn't answer.'

'Didn't she care about it?'

'She adored it, Inspector! But she started playing tricks on the horses, and it simply wasn't safe. Her pony bolted with her one day, and she had quite a nasty accident. The groom found a thorn under the saddle. She said she only wanted to see how fast her pony would go!'

John Grayson had grown up on a farm. In his opinion this was as nasty and spiteful a trick as you could want. He began to think that the early death of Margot Trent was not going to inflict any particular loss upon the community. But he had his duty to do, and in pursuance of it he put the question which he had already addressed to Miss Muir and to the domestic staff.

'How was the girl treated after she had carried out one of these annoying tricks? Was Mr. Trent angry with her – was she scolded?'

A little natural colour sprang up in Miss Delauny's face. Her fine eyes brightened, and she exclaimed with emphasis, 'Oh, never! Mr. Trent was wonderful. Very few fathers would have been so kind to a child of their own. Whatever he may have felt, he never showed her that he was angry. On this last occasion, when she played that dangerous trick in the quarry, he told me he would have a serious talk with her. She came away from it in quite a softened mood and said he had been sweet. But even then – ' She broke off and looked down into her lap.

'Yes, Miss Delauny – what were you going to say?'

She lifted her eyes to his with a look of appeal.

'When anything like this happens, don't you think it is so difficult to know afterwards whether you really did have those uneasy feelings and are not just imagining that you had them?'

He looked at her keenly.

'Well, that's honest enough. But I should like to hear what this feeling was.'

She looked down again and dropped her voice.

'Well, I thought – at least I think I did – that she was – well – a little too quiet. I was afraid she might be – thinking up – something else.' She made haste to add. 'It was all just an impression – the sort of suggestion that comes to one when one's mind is disturbed.'

He considered that she was splitting hairs, and brought the question back to facts again.

'Now, Miss Delauny, I want you to tell me about Sunday afternoon. You and your charge had lunch with Mr. and Mrs. Trent?'

'Yes.'

'And then?'

'We had coffee with them in the drawing-room, after which we went to our own sitting-room.'

'That is the room I have seen – next to this one?'

'Yes.'

'What did you do there?'

'Margot was cutting pictures out of an illustrated paper. It was one of the few things she would do if it was too wet to go out.'

'Was she still in that softened mood?'

Miss Delauny shook her head.

'Oh, no – she was impatient and aggressive. It made her really angry to be kept in by the rain. I was thankful when it showed signs of clearing, and at a quarter to three I told her she could go out, only she must put on a waterproof and goloshes as everything would be streaming.'

'It did not occur to you to go with her?'

She shook her head.

'She wanted to be off by herself. She has always had the freedom of the grounds. They are large, and fortunately it never seemed to occur to her to want to go outside them.'

'So you felt no anxiety about her being out alone?'

'Oh, no – it happened every day. She has so much energy – ' She checked, caught her breath in a sob, and corrected herself. 'I ought to have said *had* – one doesn't remember these things – all at once. What I was going to say was I couldn't possibly have kept up with her. She liked to be free, and we wanted her to be happy. Then there is Mrs. Trent. You will have noticed that she is in a very sad state of health. She ought not to be too much alone, and I give as much time to her as I can.'

He nodded. It did seem all right and above board. He said,

'Well, you went on writing letters – '

'Yes. I knew Mrs. Trent would be resting. And then Mr. Trent came along and said he would be taking her for a drive, and would Margot and I like to come? I said I had letters to write, and Margot had just gone out, but I would see if I could find her. I went out on to the terrace and called, but she didn't answer, and Mr. Trent had said he couldn't wait, so I came back and went on with my letters.'

'Just a minute, Miss Delauny. How long was it after Miss Trent had gone out that Mr. Trent came to you and spoke about the drive?'

She seemed to reflect, her face turned up to his, her brows just drawn together.

'Oh, no time at all – just a few minutes – '

'And when did you hear of the accident?'

She closed her eyes for a moment.

'Mr. Severn came and told me, while Miss Muir went out to the garage to tell Mr. Trent.'

He had one more question to ask.

'How did Mrs. Trent take the news?'

Miss Delauny hesitated.

'She didn't seem to take much notice. But of course one can't really tell. It is part of her illness that she doesn't seem to notice anything very much.'

As man to man, the Inspector found himself feeling sorry for Mr. Geoffrey Trent. As if it wasn't enough to have that poor girl in the family, it seemed now that there was something odd about Mrs. Trent! He reflected, without any consciousness of being trite, that money didn't always make you happy.

He let Miss Delauny go and went out into the garden to look for old Humphreys. He found him in the potting-shed mixing compost and extremely unwilling to have his attention diverted. They were not strangers, and Grayson was perfectly well aware that he wasn't going to get any cooperation. He had married a Bleake girl who was a great-niece of old Humpy's, and there was very little he didn't know about his long association with the Falconers, his skill as a gardener, and the remarkable obstinacy of his temper. To his 'Good morning, Uncle!' Humphreys made no reply. He went on putting compost into a row of six-inch pots for some time before he said in an aggressive voice,

'Now, it's no use your coming a-bothering me, Johnny Grayson, nor a-coming the policeman over me, because I won't have it! Arh!' He sucked in his breath in a very determined manner and pressed the earth down with a broad spatulated thumb.

Grayson laughed.

'Now, Uncle, I've got my job the same as you have, and all I want is to ask if you saw or heard anything of Miss Margot Trent on Sunday afternoon. Or,' he added hastily, 'anyone else.'

He got a bright malicious stare.

'And what might you be meaning by anyone else? Flaxmans goes out Sundays regular. Lunch for the family at one, and come a quarter to three they're a-catching of the bus for Wraydon – right past my windows and a-hurrying like mad.

If that's what you mean by your anyone else, then I see'd 'em, same as I see Florrie Bowyer a-running like a rabbit to meet that young man of hers.'

Since Grayson was already aware that none of the domestic staff had been on the premises after a quarter to three on the Sunday afternoon, all this was of no particular interest. If he hoped that it argued a disposition to talk on Uncle's part he was soon to be undeceived.

Old Humpy bent to plunge his hands into the compost heap. He was a square, sturdy figure, not much above five-foot-one in height, with a face burnt as brown as a walnut and a lot of grizzled hair which like some spreading plant sent up its vigorous bushy growth in whiskers, beard, and eyebrows. It was known that he was the owner of half a dozen houses in Wraydon, and his savings were reputed to be considerable. These circumstances, together with the fact that he possessed a formidable temper, caused him to be regarded with a good deal of respect by the three hundred and fifty or so inhabitants of Bleake, to a great many of whom he was related. He had married three meek women in succession, and they had reared three respectable and obedient families. Each of them had brought him something in her stocking foot, as the saying is. He certainly wasn't going to stand any nonsense from Johnny Grayson who had married his brother Sam's grand-daughter. He stood up with his big hands full of compost and let it run through his fingers on to the old kitchen tray where the previous heap had been getting low.

'And what makes you think I'd be working on a Sunday afternoon?'

'Now, Uncle, I never said a word about working, and you know it! I suppose you could be taking a turn in the garden after the rain had stopped, and I suppose you could see Miss Margot Trent – or anyone else if they happened to be there.'

Old Humpy produced a ferocious grin.

'Arh! So I could, Johnny Grayson! Or I could be a-setting comferable by the fire with my pipe, or I could be a-walking round my own little patch a-looking at the bulbs a-coming up. Wonderful forward they are this year too.'

'And which of those things were you doing?' said Grayson good-humouredly.

'Wouldn't you like to know!' grinned old Humpy.

'Yes, I would. Come along, Uncle, don't you hinder me, and I'll quit hindering you.'

The little pots were being quickly and accurately filled. Old Mr. Humphreys bent down and came up again with more compost.

'I don't let no one hinder me,' he said, and went on filling pots.

Grayson watched him in silence. What the old boy liked was the spur of contention. Well, he just wouldn't get any more of it, and that was that. He liked the sound of his own voice, and he liked an audience for it, the old devil. He leaned against the doorpost with his hands in his pockets and waited.

Presently the pots began to be set down rather hard. The silence was broken by a loud 'Arh!'

'Pity I didn't go into the police instead of letting myself in for a job as meant hard work! Fine upstanding feller like you, and nothing to do but hang around my potting-shed of a Monday morning! Wonder you're not ashamed of yourself! Idle bones make empty stomachs – that's what my old dad 'ud ha' said! Gardener here fifty years man and boy, and head gardener near on forty of 'em! But I aim to beat him!'

Grayson gazed abstractedly through the open door of the potting-shed. He made one of those indeterminate sounds which are of all things the most enraging to anyone who has just delivered himself of a speech designed to impress. The small bright eyes which were watching from behind a bush of eyebrow took on a malicious sparkle.

'Sunday afternoon I has my pipe, and my glass by the fire, and my old woman she plays a 'ymn on the 'armonium. Arh!'

'Then you didn't see Miss Margot Trent at all.'

The stare became positively malignant.

'Don't you go a-putting words into my mouth Johnny Grayson – nor into no one else's! This isn't foreign parts where the police can carry on just how they likes! *Nor* do we want any such scandlous doings here! So don't you go a-trying of it on! I might be saying things you wouldn't like if you did! I might be saying I felt sorry for your wife! Pretty little bit of a thing she used to be afore she married you!'

The Inspector's chief aid in keeping his temper was the knowledge that nothing would delight old Humpy more than to see him lose it. He smiled and said easily,

'That's very kind of you, Uncle – I'll tell her. And now, since I'm not to put words in your mouth, perhaps you'll put them there yourself. Did you see that girl Margot Trent on Sunday afternoon, or did you not?'

Old Humpy considered. All except the last few pots were filled. He was beginning to be bored with having Johnny Grayson there. He said in a meditative voice,

'Sunday afternoon I have my pipe and my glass by the kitchen fire, and your Aunt Mary she plays a 'ymn on the 'armonium in the setting-room with the door open if so be that I've a mind to have it open – and shut if I've a mind to have it shut. Come to quarter to three the rain give over. I goes out to take a breath of air – always takes a turn, I do, when the rain gives over. I comes along this way, and I see that mischeevious girl –'

'What time would that be, Uncle?'

'Trouble with you, Johnny Grayson, is you don't listen to what you're told! Didn't I say as it had just gone the quarter? Now I don't want no interruptions *if* you please! I see that mischeevious girl coming out of my potting-shed and a-laughing to herself. Now I keeps the key in a flower-pot with a chip on it. Half full of old labels it is, and lying in the grass along of a lot more. "How d'you come by my key?" I says, and she laughs fit to burst herself and throws it at me. Spanking, that's what she did ought to have had and never got! And see what come of it! Arh!'

'Nobody corrected her?'

'Spared the rod and spoiled the child – that's what they done!'

'Uncle, was she carrying anything?'

'She'd got something humped up under her raincoat. "Something there you don't want me to see, you darned brat!" I says, and I picks up the key from where she throwed it, and it stands to reason she hadn't troubled to lock the shed. Well, I goes in, and there's nothing touched – only an old pile of ropes in the corner. She'd pulled 'em out and messed 'em about, and likely enough she'd gone off with one of 'em. Seems she must ha' done. So I coils up the ropes and puts 'em away, and I goes on with my turn.'

'You didn't go as far as the quarry?'

Old Humpy shook his head.

'That's where that mischeevious girl was heading for. I didn't want to run across her.'

'Then you didn't see her again?'

'Nor I didn't want to!'

'Did you see anyone else?'

'I heerd the governess a-calling.'

'What time would that be?'

'Church clock had just struck three.'

'You didn't see her?'

'No.'

'Nor Mr. Trent?'

'No.'

'Nor anyone else?'

Old Humpy blazed.

'I didn't see no one at all – only that mischeevious girl going off with the rope from my potting-shed! And if it 'ud been a good one I'd ha' gone after her, but since it wasn't nothing but a lot of old rubbish I let her go, and a good thing I did! A peck of trouble was what that girl was going to be wherever she was! And since it was one of her own mischeevious tricks that finished her off, I don't see no call for the police to go shoving of themselves in, nor I don't see no call for the family to take on about it! A good riddance, Johnny Grayson – that's what she was, and you won't get me from it!'

CHAPTER XVII

Inspector Grayson made his report to his Superintendent.

'Everything quite straightforward as far as I can see. The girl was abnormal and must have been a great trial, yet they really seem to have been fond of her, and to be genuinely distressed about her death. The married couple, cook and butler, and Florrie Bowyer, daily housemaid, all say she never had a scolding or a rough word from anyone – and she must have tried them high. There's nothing in it, except that Mr. Trent comes in for the property. He says there was a considerable fortune, but it isn't what it was.'

'There's precious few things that are,' said the Superintendent.

Whilst this conversation was going on – that is to say, at the agreeable hour when the curtains have been drawn and a pleasantly shaded light diffuses itself upon flowered china and the silver teapot – two ladies were approaching the same topic in Miss Falconer's cottage sitting-room. Two rooms had been thrown into one so as to have a window at either end, with a couple of black oak pillars to support the heavy beams which carried the upper storey. There was some beautiful furniture, not perhaps quite suited to a cottage, and a good deal of valuable china, but the carpet was threadbare and the curtains faded relics of former grandeur.

Miss Falconer herself was a tall angular woman with the amiable face of a horse which has been turned out to grass after years of faithful service. There was the mild, rather protuberant eye, the long front teeth, the general fading of skin and hair. In her youth, as she was presently to confide to Miss Silver, she had been known in the family as 'Ginger'. There was still no grey in the ample but rather untidy coils which slipped continually from the restraining hairpin, but the ginger had become very mild indeed. She was pressing Miss Silver to have another cup of tea – 'after your long cold journey'.

Miss Silver accepted with pleasure. She was admiring the Queen Anne teapot with its attendant milk-jug and sugar-basin, and the fine transparent porcelain of the pretty flowered cups. Miss Falconer might live in what had been a workman's cottage, her grey tweed skirt and home-made cardigan might be shabby and out of shape, but she had been accustomed to fine silver and delicate china all her life, and it would never occur to her not to use what was left of them now.

As Miss Silver put out her hand for the cup she observed brightly that the journey had not seemed long at all.

'Such agreeable people in the carriage – some well-behaved children going down on a visit to their grandmother in charge of a very pleasant nurse, and a really charming young clergyman recently returned from equatorial Africa.'

Miss Falconer gave an exclamation of pleasure.

'Do you know, I feel sure that must have been my cousin Hope Windling's youngest boy. She lives just on the other side of Wraydon, and she has been expecting him all this week. It was a terrible heartbreak to her when he decided that he had a call to go to Africa. He was most brilliant, most talented. They said he might have been anything. But we cannot arrange these things for others, can we, and at least he is alive – ' Her voice died on a sighing breath.

Miss Silver hastened to restore the conversation to a cheerful level.

'He was most interesting about the native peoples amongst whom he is working.'

After a little more talk about the Rev. Clifford Windling, together with some remarks apon Mrs. Windling's other sons – 'not quite so brilliant or so gifted, but very dear fellows', and the only daughter – 'most happily and comfortably married', Miss Silver produced her knitting and explained that the useful grey worsted stocking now depending from the needles was for her niece Mrs. Burkett's middle boy, Derek.

'With three of them, and all of school age, it is really quite beyond Ethel herself to keep them in footwear, so it is fortunate that I happen to be a quick knitter, for really a pair hardly seems to be finished before another is required.'

Miss Falconer, who had been dreading the arrival of a stranger, was by now feeling very comfortable in her company. Miss Silver knew dear Clifford, she had nephews of her own, she was interested in missionary work, she was a gentlewoman. Her mild, rather timid nature let down its defences, and she found herself speaking of the tragic accident at the Ladies' House.

'It seems so terrible that it should have taken place on a Sunday afternoon. But of course that is just what made it possible – I mean, nobody would have heard the poor girl call out or anything. You see, the butler and his wife always catch the two-fortyfive bus into Wraydon on Sundays, and Florrie Bowyer who is the daily housemaid has the afternoon and evening off. Then in the garden on a week-day there would be old Humphreys. He was with us for more than forty years, and he still brings me plants, dear old man. And two gardeners under him – the charming Americans who were our tenants before the war had four, but of course no one can keep things up in the way they used to. That would be on a week-day, but on a Sunday the two under gardeners would not be there at all, and Humphreys, who lives in the lodge, likes to smoke his pipe and listen to his wife playing hymns on the harmonium. So, you see, there wouldn't be anyone about.'

Miss Silver was knitting rapidly, her hands held low in the continental fashion.

'Where were the family?' she enquired.

'Mr. Trent had taken his wife for a drive. It was a very wet morning, but it began to clear soon after half past two. The governess was writing letters, and Miss Muir, who is Mrs. Trent's sister, had gone out to lunch with Mr. Severn who has also been staying in the house. Margot had gone off into the garden as soon as the rain stopped, and you see, there was no one about. She must have taken that crazy old bit of rope out of the potting-shed and tried to use it for climbing on the quarry face. She played a very dangerous trick there only the day before, but that was with a good bit of rope. And of course Mr. Trent took it from her.' A slight colour came into Miss Falconer's face. 'You will be wondering how it is that I know so much about it, but Florrie Bowyer who works for them is the daughter of my own kind Mrs. Bowyer who used to be our kitchenmaid twenty-five years ago and comes in every day to look after me now. I really do not know what I should do without her. I have never been clever at things like cooking and housework, and it is not so easy to learn how to do them when you are no longer young.' She leaned confidentially towards Miss Silver and added. 'I am afraid I *burn* things – oven-cloths, and toast, and my fingers – and Mrs. Bowyer says it is very much better for me not to try. So she is here a good deal, and she just tells me things as she goes along. It really seems quite natural that she should.'

Miss Silver could not have agreed more warmly. Florrie would tell her mother whatever went on at the Ladies' House and her mother would tell Miss Falconer, who seemed most ready to be confidential. She found herself presently listening to a recital of the different pranks and tricks played by poor Margot Trent upon her family or upon anyone else who was unfortunate enough to be about when she was in a mischievous mood.

'They always said she was as harmless as a child,' said Miss Falconer, shaking her head in a deprecating manner. 'But she tied an empty tin to the tail of Miss Randall's cat, and the poor thing nearly went out of its mind. And there were things like jumping out from behind a bush in the dark – really very startling indeed! Old Mrs. Spray was quite ill for a week. There was a good deal of feeling about it, and people were beginning to say it wasn't right and something ought to be done. Old Humphreys went round saying she ought to have a stick taken to her, but I believe she never had so much as a scolding. I don't know how they could be so patient with her, but they were. And now that she is gone, they seem quite broken-hearted.'

'They were fond of her? I should have thought that an

invalid like Mrs. Trent would have found that sort of thing very trying.'

'Well, I don't know about poor Mrs. Trent. She doesn't really seem to notice things a great deal. Florrie says she will sit for hours just staring into the fire or down at her own hands. I was so glad when I heard that her sister was coming to stay — it doesn't seem as if she ought to be left alone so much. Of course Mr. Trent is very good to her — he is very good to everyone. I'm sure his kindness to that poor girl, and his grief, and Miss Delauny's too — you would think Margot had been the apple of their eye. And of course the part that must distress him most is that he comes in for the money.'

Miss Silver continued to knit as she said brightly,

'The unfortunate girl had money?'

'Oh, yes. And she was very fond of telling people about it, and about what she meant to do with it when she came of age. She told Florrie Bowyer she would give her a hundred pounds for a wedding present — but of course it would have been very silly for Florrie to count on it.'

They went on talking about the Trents.

CHAPTER XVIII

Miss Silver was very glad to find that Miss Falconer had every intention of being present at the inquest on Margot Trent. Her offer to accompany her hostess being most gratefully accepted, she would have a very good opportunity of observing Geoffrey Trent and the members of his household. They would of necessity be under some considerable stress. A young girl for whom they were more than ordinarily responsible had come to a sudden and violent end whilst under their care. However blameless towards her their conduct might have been, they could hardly fail to be terribly aware

101

of their past responsibility and of the defeat which had over-whelmed it. It is at moments like these that points of character become intensified. The controlled become more controlled, the emotional slip into the easy way of tears, the person who has something to hide becomes so much aware of it as to run the risk of attracting the very attention which he is hoping to disarm.

Miss Falconer had for too many years been the principal lady in the neighbourhood to have any hesitation in making for what she considered a suitable seat. She murmured, 'Thank you – thank you,' but was really hardly aware of being made way for. At the far end of the third row on the right-hand side of the village hall she stood aside for her guest to pass her and then sat down. Nothing could have suited Miss Silver better. She had a clear view of the plat-form on which the Coroner's table had been set, and of the two or three rows on the left of the hall which were being reserved for the witnesses. There was no jury, an indication that the matter was regarded by the police as one of accident.

The hall was a small one, and had been, as Miss Falconer explained, the most kind gift of the Americans who were her tenants in the years immediately preceding the war. 'Such a boon for concerts and theatricals and dances. And of course the Women's Institute meets here too.'

When the party from the Ladies' House came in Miss Falconer was most kindly informative.

'That is Mr. Trent. Such a very goodlooking man – but terribly pale this morning. Such a shock! And then having to have an inquest! I did not think his wife would come, but I see she is here – the little one in a fur coat and a black beret. That is her sister next to her, Ione Muir. She made quite a hit in America, you know, doing monologues and sketches. I don't know whether you would call her pretty, but there is something rather striking about her, don't you think?'

Miss Silver agreed. The contrast between Mrs. Trent's little waxen face, from which all expression seemed to have withdrawn, and that of her sister was indeed noticeable. Ione Muir was pale, but it was the kind of pallor which seemed to be lighted from within. The fine eyes shone with intelligence, and, as she bent to say something to Allegra, with affection. She put a hand on her sister's and kept it there. No one who saw the gesture could fail to realise that the pressure would be warm and kind.

Geoffrey Trent sat on his wife's other side. To Miss Silver's practised eye it was obvious that he was exercising a rigorous control. Beyond Ione Muir was the governess, Miss Delauny, her head slightly bent, her hands very tightly clasped in her lap. She was the only one of the party in unrelieved black, and it gave her a curious air of being chief mourner. She wore no make-up except a very light dusting of powder which served to accentuate the pallor of her skin.

In the row behind the family, planted squarely on the outermost seat, was an old man in his working clothes, with earth on his serviceable boots and more than a suspicion of it on the big hands spread out on either knee.

'Oh, dear,' said Miss Falconer in a fluttered whisper – 'he ought not to have come like that – he really ought not! He ought to have changed. It is not respectful to the Coroner – it really isn't.' She dropped her voice still further. 'It's our old gardener, Humphreys – the one I was telling you about. I expect his wife told him he ought to change, and that would be quite enough to make him go straight in the opposite direction. She is his third wife, and they have been married for at least fifteen years, but she isn't any better at managing him than the others were – and she was a widow too, so you would have thought she would have had some practice. But I suppose the fact is he is a very obstinate old man.'

As the Coroner came in at this moment, Miss Falconer was obliged to leave the subject of old Humphreys and impart a few hurried facts with regard to Mr. Condon. They had stood up when he came in, and she had no more than murmured, 'He is a solicitor in Wraydon – very much respected,' before he took his seat and they all sat down again.

Mr. Condon was dry and brisk. After the opening of the Court with the traditional 'Oyez – Oyez – Oyez!' in its English pronunciation of 'O yes – o yes – o yes!' everything became extremely businesslike. Medical evidence. Evidence

103

of Mr. Trent. Evidence of Miss Delauny. Evidence of Edward Humphreys.

Miss Silver listened to it all with interest. She watched every smallest change in face, in voice, in manner. She heard of the tricks which Margot Trent had delighted to play. She heard Miss Delauny describe sadly but calmly the methods by which she had tried to interest her charge in other things. There was a rush of tears to her eyes when the Coroner asked her if any means of correction had been employed – scoldings – punishments. With her black gloved hands still tightly clasped before her and those wet eyes fixed on Mr. Condon's face, she said,

'Oh, never – *never!* Those things are all wrong for such cases. If you correct, you only confuse the mind. It is necessary always just to go back to the beginning again and work with kindness, patience, and love.'

The Coroner's lip tightened. He had four children at home who were growing up in a high state of discipline. He had no patience with the 'slide and let slide' school, but it wasn't his business to say so here. According to the police Superintendent there was a general concurrence of opinion that the girl had been treated a great deal too leniently. There had certainly been no severity such as might have made her think of doing away with herself.

Old Mr. Humphreys made no secret about his opinion.

'A real mischeevious brat! Always up to some of her tricks with my tools or my plants!'

He told his story of seeing her come out of the potting-shed on the Sunday afternoon with a rope humped up under her waterproof.

'And when I went in to see what devilment she'd been up to, there was all they old ropes pulled down and scattered about! . . . Sound? No, none of 'em was sound, and she didn't ought to have meddled with 'em! Just a lot of crazy old stuff – comes in handy once in a way when I wants a bit of soft packing for a graft.'

'You didn't go after her to see what she had taken?'

'I knowed well enough what she'd taken – just one of they old ropes. And it was my Sunday afternoon. She calls out a bit of cheek, and I locks up after her and goes along home.'

The Coroner remarked that there was no doubt that a most regrettable accident had occurred. The ropes had been kept in their proper place under lock and key, and the unfortunate girl had known perfectly well that she had no business to touch them. One end of the rope she took had been found fastened to a tree on the edge of the quarry. She had probably intended to descend the cliff face holding on to it, but not many feet from the top the rope had snapped and she had fallen the rest of the way. Death must have been instantaneous. She was still grasping the parted rope when her body was discovered. He found that no blame attached to anyone.

Everybody trooped out of the hall.

Miss Silver was able so to control her exit as to be just in front of the party from the Ladies' House. A turn as they came level with the door, and she was looking directly into Allegra Trent's little colourless face and blank eyes. What she saw there shocked her very much.

Her glance passed to Ione Muir, to Miss Delauny, to Geoffrey Trent. Jacqueline Delauny had a handkerchief clenched in her hand. She raised it suddenly, not to her eyes but to her lips, as if the task of controlling them had become too much for her. As she did so she looked in the direction of the door and became aware of Miss Silver's scrutiny. The lashes came down over the dark eyes. Miss Silver was left thinking about what she had seen in the instant before they fell.

CHAPTER XIX

The funeral was over. Jim Severn had gone back to London. Ione Muir was still at the Ladies' House. It seemed to her impossible that she should leave Allegra, yet to stay on was the last thing on earth that she desired. If she had disliked the place before, she had a very much better reason for disliking it now, but to her surprise neither Geoffrey nor Allegra appeared to have any such feeling. Whilst Miss Falconer was saying rather sadly to Miss Silver that of course poor Mr. Trent would not now want to go any further with his plans for buying the house, Geoffrey himself was combating this idea with a good deal of force. He was talking to his sister-in-law, or perhaps it would be more correct to say that she had been talking to him.

'Not buy the house?' He stared at her, his eyes bluer than ever. 'Because poor Margot died here? Why, scores of people have died in every old house in England, and nobody suggests that the families shouldn't go on living there. If you were to look them up, I expect the most appalling things happened in this very place, and nobody thinks about them now.' He looked at her frankly. 'Do you know, you surprise me. I should never have given you credit for being morbid about that sort of thing. Why, my dear girl, what would you propose doing after a death in the house? I've heard of people who kept the room just as it was – wouldn't use it, wouldn't even have it cleaned. And how soon after that do you suppose it is before someone begins to say the place is haunted? I'm not going to have anything like that started about poor little Margot, and I not only hope, I *insist*, that you shouldn't put any such ideas into Allegra's head.

As it turned out, Allegra had no morbid views.

'I don't know why you should think I would mind staying

on here – because of Margot. After all, nobody can really mind about her very much – can they? She was a terribly inconvenient person to have in the house, and of course the older she got the worse it was going to be. I was always afraid she was going to jump out on me from behind a door. She did once, and that was the only time Geoffrey ever really scolded her. He said if she did it again she would have to be sent away to a very strict Home.'

'When was this?'

'Oh, about two years ago,' said Allegra vaguely.

'And she didn't do it again?'

'No – but I was always afraid she might.'

Ione went in search of Geoffrey, and found him in his study. She went and stood by the fire and said,

'You were right about Allegra. I don't think she likes the Ladies' House, but she doesn't dislike it any more because of what happened to Margot.'

He sent her a challenging look.

'So you've been talking to her about it?'

Her deep voice had a note of impatience.

'Naturally. I had to find out what she felt. Well, I have found out. She is just where she was before the accident happened, except that – she's better.'

He nodded.

'I've found where she keeps her stuff. There are some hiding-places in this old house, you know. I daren't cut it off all at once, but I'm managing so that the amount is being diminished gradually. The tablets she's taking now are not what she thinks they are. I'm in touch with Whichcote about it, and he has been very helpful. I'm glad you notice the difference.'

She stooped forward over the fire as if to warm her hands, and said as easily as she could,

'I suppose Miss Delauny won't be staying on here now?'

She was not looking at him, but she was aware of his being startled.

'Jacqueline! Why? Has she said anything to you? She doesn't want to leave, does she?'

Ione stood up and turned round. He was looking at her with a troubled and distressed expression.

'Well, Geoffrey, she was Margot's governess, and her job has come to an end.'

He said very warmly indeed,

'I can't agree about that, you know. Allegra needs her just as much as Margot did, and she will have more time to give to her now. Don't you see, it's exactly what we need – someone to give Allegra the constant care and companionship she ought to have, and to make sure that she doesn't get hold of any more of that wretched stuff.'

Ione was reminded, and disagreeably reminded, of something she could not immediately place. And then she did place it. Geoffrey was speaking of Jacqueline Delauny and the benefits her companionship would confer upon Allegra in the same tone and with very much the same enthusiasm as he had brought to his panegyrics on the Ladies' House. The impression was the more startling because ever since Margot's death he had been silent and very evidently under the influence of shock. There had been no trace of his former good humour and easily stirred enthusiasms until now, when Jacqueline Delauny called them up. Ione refused the implication. Geoffrey was like that – easily cast down, and as easily roused by some fresh project. He was pleased at Allegra's improvement, and regarded Miss Delauny as an adjunct to a more complete recovery. She said,

'I certainly don't think Allegra ought to be alone. All that sitting about is bad for her. She needs to do things. I was thinking we might go into Wraydon this morning and do a little shopping.'

His face clouded.

'Well, I don't know – I have a good deal of business to get through this morning – I couldn't drive you – '

Ione laughed.

'That is just what I mean, Geoffrey. Allegra needs to do things for herself, not to have them done for her all the time. There isn't the slightest necessity for you to drive her. We shall take the bus from the church, and the whole thing will do her a lot of good. You want to get rid of the cottonwool wrappings, you know. She wasn't brought up like that any more than I was. And by the way, if she's pleased and interested, we shall probably have lunch at the George.'

She carried the day, but there was a certain undercurrent of disapproval, and in the end, to her disappointment, he announced that he would put his letters on one side and take them to Wraydon in the car.

'You can come back in the bus if you want to, and I think that will be enough of an experiment for today.'

When she and Allegra came down to get into the car Ione was surprised and not at all pleased to find that Jacqueline Delauny intended to accompany them. She had planned a little cosy shopping of trifles with Allegra – the kind of thing which may be used to recall expeditions which have been shared in the past. She definitely did not want a third person and a stranger, to give Allegra a chance of slipping into one of her abstracted moods. The face which was so expressive upon the stage must have showed at least some trace of this feeling, for Miss Delauny made haste to say,

'I won't be in your way, Miss Muir. I have just the one place to go to, and Mr. Trent very kindly offered me the lift.'

She got off at the station, and Ione and Allegra where Cross Street turns into the High Street. It was a pleasant day with a hint of February softness in the air. There were actually a few snowdrops and a yellow crocus or two in the little sheltered gardens in Cross Street where half a dozen old cottages have managed to linger on. Due for demolition before the war, the housing shortage has for the moment deferred their doom. They have no amenities, but they are easy on the eye, and the snowdrops were coming out bravely. Allegra actually noticed them, and stood for a moment to look.

The High Street is like a great many other High Streets. There are the large shops which have swallowed their neighbours, and the little ones not yet quite squeezed to death. The elegances are advertised by the plate-glass window where a single hat like some exotic flower is displayed against a length of shimmering brocade. The exiguous purse is attracted by the scarlet and gold front of a famous emporium.

There is the usual conglomeration of prams on the pavement, bicycles propped at the kerb, and motor-buses pursuing their rather dashing way along the crowded street.

The principal shop in the High Street is Kenlow's. From small beginnings it has expanded into one of those glittering glass-fronted affairs with a department for almost everything you can think of. Everything for the bride, everything for the baby, everything for the schoolboy, the schoolgirl, the home – it does not matter what your need may be, Kenlow's can always, or nearly always, supply it.

Ione was thinking of a small flat in London. The idea was to interest Allegra in materials for curtains. Mentally reflecting that she could always give the stuff away if she felt that she couldn't bear it, she was preparing for a certain amount of self-immolation. A good deal to her surprise, she found that this would not be necessary. Kenlow's really had lovely materials, and at not unreasonable prices. Allegra began to sit up and take notice. She pulled off a glove to finger the stuffs, asked to have them held up to the light, and was so much the old Allegra that Ione's heart was warmed.

'And you know, darling,' Allegra was saying, 'I wouldn't decide anything in a hurry if I were you. Are you sure of the flat?'

'Yes. It is Louisa Blunt's. She can't afford to stay on, but she isn't in a hurry to get out, so I don't have to make up my mind till I want to.'

Allegra was quite animated.

'Then I'll tell you what you must do! Go up to town and measure everything properly. They will give you patterns of these lovely stuffs, and you can look at them on the spot, which is always a great help, and then come back and give your order.' She turned to the salesman. 'You would let us have the patterns, wouldn't you?'

Kenlow's was delighted to do anything that would please the customer.

It was surprising how much time had already passed. It was a quarter to one, and the idea of lunch at the George was pleasant.

As they emerged upon the pavement, Allegra said,

'I'm rather surprised that Jacqueline wanted to come with us.'

'Why?'

'Well, she's in a fuss you know – about those things of Margot's that have gone missing.' Her tone was the usual dreamy one. It gave the impression that she really cared nothing at all for what she said.

'Ally, I haven't the slightest idea what you are talking about.'

Allegra looked at her vaguely.

'Oh – didn't I tell you? That tiresome girl used to keep some kind of a diary – just now and then, you know, when the fancy took her. I saw a bit of it once, and it might have been written by a child of eight – frightful spelling mistakes and all that. She was writing in it that very afternoon before she went out and fell over the quarry, and Jackie is worried because she doesn't know what she may have put in it.'

Ione said a little contemptuously,

'Why, what could she have put?'

Allegra could not have looked less interested. Her voice was indifference itself.

'Oh, I don't know. She was very angry with Geoffrey because he took away her rope – she might have put down something frightful about him.' She gave Ione one of those odd sideways looks. 'Or about me.'

'What could she possibly say about you, Ally?'

Allegra said angrily,

'She found something I had put away to keep it safe. She was a dreadful child. You don't know how glad I am that she is dead.'

'I wouldn't say that to anyone else, Ally.'

Allegra flushed.

'I'm not – I'm saying it to you! And I don't want to go on talking about it anyhow. And I wouldn't have said anything about it now if I hadn't wondered why Jackie didn't stay at home and go on having a good look for those torn-out pages. You see, she has got an idea that Margot may have hidden them in your room. She was awfully fond of

111

going in there, you know, and of course it would be much easier to have a good look for them if you were out of the way.'

It was things like this that brought it home to Ione how far from normal Allegra still was. She was surprised at her own anger – not against poor Ally, but at just the bare idea of Jacqueline Delauny searching her room. And for what? An abnormal girl's scribblings. She said quickly,

'You say these were just some torn-out pages at the end. But what about the rest of the diary? Has Geoffrey got it?'

Allegra shook her head.

'Oh, no, Jacqueline and Geoffrey burned it,' she said in a perfectly matter-of-fact kind of way.

They walked on down the sloping pavement in silence.

There is a four-cross-way at the bottom of the High Street which is the centre of all that is busiest and noisiest in Wraydon. A frightful clock-tower rears itself upon an island in the middle. It is supported by symbolic statues. Like most efforts of this kind, the less that is said about them the better. Fortunately, very few people ever notice them. They are too much taken up with getting safely across to the island, and from there to the opposite side of the four-cross-way.

Allegra held Ione tightly by the arm.

'It's the worst crossing in the world – I really do think so. I can't ever remember which way the traffic goes when the lights change.'

Ione laughed.

'Don't bother! There's getting to be quite a crowd. Nobody is going to run us down if we all keep together.'

There really were more people on the island than it was intended to hold. Ione and Allegra, in the front rank, were not only squashed together but in some danger of being pushed off the kerb. But the lights were due to change at any moment, and they would get across. Thinking it over afterwards, Ione was to puzzle over just what the people behind could have seen. They would see that she and Allegra were being pressed together in the crowd, but would they be able to see that it was Allegra who was holding on to her, and not she to Allegra? That was the point which

112

was to keep on coming back. She did not think that the people behind would have noticed Allegra's clutch on her arm. She was so much smaller, and her hold was so low down. She did not think it would be seen. She did not think — but she was never to be sure.

What happened was violently, bewilderingly sudden. The lights were due to change at any moment and a large double-decker bus came hurrying by. Just before it was level with them Ione felt the impact of a blow. It took her glancingly on the side to which Allegra clung, and it loosened her grip. Whilst Ione braced herself to avoid being dislodged from the kerb Allegra was sent staggering forward right in the path of the bus.

CHAPTER XX

Two women screamed, there was a man's warning shout, the ranks of the crowd divided, and before Ione could recover her balance a tweed-covered arm shot out and a stick with a large open crook linked itself about Allegra's outflung arm. It jerked her back. She took a stumbling step or two and went down. The lights changed, people crowded round. Ione sat on the edge of the kerb with Allegra's head in her lap. The tweed-covered arm and the crooked stick had disappeared. Amongst the murmur of voices one reached her with a note of calm and kind authority.

'Miss Muir, I have managed to procure a taxi. Miss Falconer informs me that the George is a good and quiet hotel. If we could take your sister there we could ascertain whether a doctor should be sent for, but I believe she has only fainted from the shock.'

With feelings of deep gratitude Ione looked up and saw that she was being addressed by the little governessy person whom she knew to be Miss Falconer's paying guest.

With the assistance of the taxi driver and another man Allegra was lifted into the car. As they drove away, Ione felt no surprise at finding that Miss Silver was still with them. The name had come back to her, though she had not been able to recall it in the first shock. But she remembered it now, and Miss Falconer making the introduction in the village shop – 'Miss Silver who is so kind as to come and stay with me at this bleak time of the year. It is nice to have a guest who is not afraid of the winter.'

It came to Ione to wonder whether Miss Silver would be afraid of anything. With everybody else gasping, crowding, and exclaiming, she had not only presented an appearance of perfect calm but she had conjured up a taxi. With her fingers at Allegra's wrist, she now gave a slight cough as if to command attention and said,

'Her pulse is quite steady. I am sure there is no cause for alarm.'

As she spoke, Allegra opened her eyes, gave a faint cry, and attempted to sit up.

'Oh, what has happened?'

Ione said,

'Nothing. We were pushed off the kerb, and you had a fall.'

'I can't remember. Am I – hurt?'

'I don't think so. Do you feel as if you were?'

She did sit up this time, turning her head and moving her arms and legs. In the end she said in an almost disappointed tone.

'No, I don't seem to be, do I?' She looked down at her hands. 'Oh, I've split my glove!'

By the time they arrived at the George she only needed Ione's arm to steady her, and was presently able to come into the dining-room for lunch.

Warmly pressed to stay, Miss Silver did so. There were things she wished to say, and she hoped that she might have an opportunity of saying them. It came when the excellent lunch had been disposed of and they had withdrawn into a comfortable small sitting-room with the assurance from the manageress that no one would disturb them there. She even produced a rug to cover Allegra if she cared to rest upon the sofa. Ione tucked her up, and by the time the others had finished coffee she was deeply asleep.

Ione moved a little nearer to Miss Silver and dropped her voice.

'What happened? Were you behind us? What did you see?'

Miss Silver shook her head regretfully.

'Very little, I am afraid. There was a very big man in front of me wearing one of those old-fashioned Inverness capes. It was he, of course, who saved your sister's life. No one could have reached her in time, but he caught her arm with the crook of his stick.'

Ione drew in her breath.

'I didn't see him,' she said – 'only his arm – and the stick. He must have gone away.'

Miss Silver said in a non-committal voice,

'He may not have wanted to be thanked.'

Ione said very earnestly indeed,

'Did you see him? Could you describe him?'

Miss Silver's gaze dwelt on her with interest.

'He was a big man, and of course the cape made him look bigger. I did not at that time see his face. But there are two small points to which I may perhaps draw your attention –'

Ione broke in upon what promised to be a leisurely sentence.

'Yes – what were they? Oh, please forgive me, but you don't know how important it is!'

Miss Silver smiled at her kindly. Youth is always in a hurry.

'He had quite a broad Scottish accent,' she said.

'You heard him speak?'

'To a child who asked him the time. He replied, "Look up at the clock tower, laddie." '

Ione felt as if she had been waiting for a door to open. Now, of all things in the world, she wanted it to stay shut. And it wouldn't – not for her or for anyone else. She said in a lagging voice,

'You said there were two things – what was the other?'

'I was behind him as we crossed the street to the island. He was humming to himself.'

'Did you know the tune?'

'Oh, yes, it was one of the better known of the Scottish airs. I knew it at once. It was *The Bluebells of Scotland.*'

The door was open with a vengeance. What lay beyond it was terrifying and incomprehensible. Every instinct spoke of danger, and connected that danger with the Professor. She knew him to be in Wraydon. She knew him to be the great Prospero whose presence was advertised on every hoarding, and she could have no doubt that it was he who had crossed the road humming *The Bluebells of Scotland* and had stood on the island behind her and Allegra. When she had heard him bargaining over a life in the fog, whose life was it? Was it Allegra's life? But he had saved Allegra. It was the crook of his stick which had snatched her back from the impending death. Had he pushed her, and then had his moment of remorse? There are mysterious promptings under which we snatch back the not quite spoken word, recall the not quite accomplished act. Had Allegra been saved because of such a prompting? But that would mean that it was Allegra's life she had heard bargained about in the fog. The clear, hard voice of commonsense said, 'Nonsense!' And something else said, 'Margot died.' She was what is called an encumbrance. Perhaps Allegra was an encumbrance too.

She was aware of Miss Silver's scrutiny. It was deep and searching. She felt as if a light was being turned upon her thoughts. It was a kind and beneficent light, but very keen. The curious thing was that she did not resent it. She said,

'Miss Silver, I think I had better tell you that I know why you are here.'

Miss Silver retained her kindly expression.

'Yes, my dear?'

'Josepha Bowden wrote and told me. She is an erratic, interfering person, and I was – angry.'

'Very naturally so, Miss Muir.'

'And then I met you. I could see that you were not at all the sort of person I expected. Josepha had really no right to butt in on a delicate family matter, but she is, and always has been, devoted to Allegra, and if you love anyone, it is hard to stand by and not know how it is with them. I don't want you to think that Allegra's family has been neglectful. The cousin who brought us up has had an illness, and I could not leave her. I had been out in the States, and returned to find her between life and death. Then, when she was better, every plan to see my sister fell through. There was always a perfectly reasonable excuse, but – we didn't meet. I was getting desperate, when this visit of mine was proposed, and this time it actually came off. Apparently Josepha was getting desperate too, and when she is desperate she really can be very alarming. I am always expecting her to get mixed up in a libel action, or a slander case or something, because she doesn't care what she says.'

Miss Silver agreed in her own way.

'She is perhaps inclined to vehemence. When she first spoke to me I was doubtful about taking the case, but on reflection it seemed to me that I could do no possible harm by coming down here for a week. If I found that Miss Bowden's fears were groundless, that Mrs. Trent was living happily with her husband, and that no undue pressure was being put upon her in the matter of the Ladies' House, then Miss Bowden's fears would be relieved, and I felt she would consider that I had earned my fee. If, on the other hand, there was anything wrong, it would be as well that someone who had Mrs. Trent's interests at heart should know of it.'

Ione was looking at her earnestly.

'And what conclusion did you come to?'

'I became aware that your sister was taking drugs.'

The colour rushed into Ione's face.

'I know! But she is better, Miss Silver, she is really better. Someone must have persuaded her to take the stuff in the rush before the wedding. Geoffrey discovered it on their honeymoon. He has told me all about it. He took her to a French doctor, and he thought she was cured, but it has cropped up again. Today he told me that he had found out where she kept her supply, and that he and Doctor Which-cote were weaning her from it with diminishing doses. She very, very much better than when I arrived – I couldn't think what had happened to her then. Of course it explains why she wouldn't meet me and everything.'

Miss Silver said, 'Yes.' Then she folded her hands in her lap and looked very directly at Ione.

'Miss Muir, are you in your own mind quite satisfied about the death of Margot Trent?'

CHAPTER XXI

There was a sense of tingling shock. The colour which had risen so brightly as she spoke of Allegra now faded out. She said in an uncertain voice,

'What do you mean?'

Miss Silver coughed.

'It could doubtless have been an accident. The girl was careless, and not possessed of any high order of reasoning. She has been described to me by a number of people, and I have been left with the impression that, so far as mental development went, she was an irresponsible child of seven or eight years old. Does this agree with your own judgment?'

'Yes – I think so. But many children of seven or eight would have a great deal more sense. I don't think she had any.'

'That being the case, what do you suppose would have been her reaction if someone had suggested to her that she should take one of those old ropes and practise some kind of climbing trick upon the quarry face?'

'Miss Silver!'

'Would it have appealed to her?'

'Of course it would. She would have jumped at it. Anyone who knew her would know that. But no one – no one would do such a thing! It is horrible to suggest it!'

Miss Silver agreed mildly.

'But I believe that it may have happened. I will tell you something which I had not meant to repeat. As you say, the suggestion is horrible. But Margot Trent is dead, and if it had not been for a most curious and unexpected interposition Mrs. Trent might have met with the same fate. It is not possible at the moment to relate these two matters more closely than that, but after what happened this morning I feel that I ought not to keep any information back from you.'

'Yes – ' said Ione.

There was a sound in her voice which moved Miss Silver's heart. She gave Miss Muir the smile with which she had been wont in the schoolroom to encourage a hesitant pupil. It had never yet failed of its effect, and it did not do so now. There was a sense of support, and a promise that difficulties would be overcome. She continued to look kindly in Ione's direction as she said,

'Old Humphreys, the gardener at the Ladies' House, came down to see Miss Falconer last night. I was at the other end of the room, and I am sure now that he did not realise I was there, but of course that did not occur to me at the time. He had been forcing some hyacinths for her, and they were just coming into bloom – three lovely bowls with four bulbs in each. Miss Falconer was doing her best to be vexed and telling him he ought not to use Mr. Trent's bulbs and the heat of his greenhouse to force things on for her, and Humphreys was being very downright about it. Of course everyone knows how devoted he is to Miss Falconer, but he really was quite rude.'

'He probably remembers her when she was a little girl.'

Miss Silver smiled, but retained a faint shade of disapproval in her voice.

'Oh, yes, he has been forty years in the place, and so was his father before him. He quite flared up and said, "You don't need to think nothing about it, ma'am! What's a few bulbses to Mr. Trent? And I put it to him straight when he come – Miss Falconer she'll have her bulbses brought along same as she's always had them. And he says, "That'll be all right, Humphreys." '

119

'Yes, I'm sure,' said Ione.

'Miss Falconer said she would thank him, and Humphreys said a very curious thing. You must remember that I was on the other side of the room in one of those deep armchairs, and I realise now that he could have had no idea that I was there. He said, "Mr. Trent don't want to be thanked, ma'am, and least said soonest mended. I kept my mouth shut at that there inquest. Never did hold with lawyers asking a lot of questions, and none of their business." '

'What did he mean?'

'I was very much startled, and so, I am sure, was Miss Falconer. She said at once what did he mean, and that if he had not told all he knew at the inquest, it was very wrong of him. He just stood there shaking his head and saying his tongue was his own and he didn't hold with lawyers. Then he said there were some that were better out of the way, and Miss Falconer became very much distressed. I could see she was afraid the old man might have done something to the girl himself. I think Humphreys saw that too, because all of a sudden he changed his tone. "Now don't you take on, ma'am," he said, "for there's no call. I told Crowner that mischeevious girl let fly a piece of cheek at me. Well, he never asked me what it was, did he? It weren't for me to tell him if he didn't ask, so I kept a still tongue. But I'm telling you, ma'am, because I don't want you to think no such thing as I can see you're a-thinking. I up and says to that girl, 'There's one of my ropes you've got under that coat of yours, for I can see the end a-dangling.' And she makes a face at me and calls out, 'Geoffrey says I can have it,' and off with her, laughing fit to bust herself".'

Ione drew in her breath sharply.

'Miss Silver, he couldn't!'

Miss Silver coughed.

'We do not know that he did. She had been caught taking something out of the gardener's shed. Would it not be quite natural for her to say that she had authority from Mr. Trent?'

'I don't know. It would have been very awkward for Geoffrey if it had come out at the inquest.'

Miss Silver agreed.

'It would not have looked well. Miss Falconer was a good deal upset. She said yes, yes, she thought Humphreys had been quite right to hold his tongue. It was just the kind of thing a naughty girl might say, and most likely not true in the least, and she hoped he wouldn't repeat it to anyone, because it would be very painful for Mr. Trent. And Humphreys said, "That's just what I thought, ma'am," and he went away.'

There was a long odd silence. Then Ione said,

'Why did you tell me this?'

'I think you know why, Miss Muir.'

'Yes, I know why. But you – I don't know why you should have thought it necessary. You see, there is something I haven't told you.'

'Are you going to tell me?'

'Yes, I must.'

Miss Silver listened attentively to her story of being lost in the fog, and the conversation she had heard after her fall down the steps of an unknown house.

'I could only hear one side of the conversation, because the person on the inner side of the door never got beyond a whisper. But the other one spoke quite loud. He said he was a very dependable person and he had never failed anyone. He said his word was his bond. He had a strong Scottish accent and he rolled his r's. And he had his foot in the door. He said he would take it out when he was ready, and not before. The person on the inside was in a hurry to get rid of him, and no wonder, but he just stood there and talked. He wasn't drunk, but he had had as much whisky as was good for him, and this is what I heard him say. "If you think it's reasonable to turn a man out in a fog like this you can just consider who'll do your dirty work for you if I'm run over. And I haven't said I'll do it yet, but I'll give it my careful consideration and let you know. But you'll have to think again about the remuneration. I'll not do it for any less than two thousand, and it's my opinion I'd be a fool to do it for that. It's my neck I'll be risking, and I'll not risk it for a penny less than two thousand pounds.' And he went off up the road whistling *The Bluebells of Scotland.*'

Miss Silver's expression was one of alert attention.

'What did you do?'

'I followed him. I was quite lost, and he seemed to know where he was going.'

She told about the meeting with Jim Severn, and how the three of them went into the empty house of which he had the key and sat on the stairs waiting for the fog to lift.

'I am afraid I went to sleep with my head on Jim's shoulder, but I did wake up once when the Scot was saying his name was Professor Robert McPhail, and another time – at least I think it was another time – when he was arguing about the old problem of the mandarin in China. You know – suppose you could benefit threequarters of the human race by pressing a button and destroying this mandarin. Jim Severn was saying that the button-pusher would be wondering what he was going to get out of it himself, he wouldn't be worrying about the rest of the human race. They were still arguing about it when I went to sleep again. And when I really did wake up the fog had gone, and so had the Professor. But on that Sunday when Margot was killed Jim and I were lunching here, and Jim ran into him in the coffee-room. He said Robert McPhail was just his private name, but he was here professionally as Professor Regulus Mactavish or The Great Prospero.'

Miss Silver said,

'You interest me extremely. Miss Falconer and I came in to the matinee yesterday afternoon. He is an illusionist, and his act is a very clever one. I recognised him immediately when we were crossing the road to the island.'

Ione leaned forward.

'Miss Silver – did he push Allegra – could he have pushed her?'

Miss Silver shook her head.

'I cannot tell you whether he pushed her. He certainly could have done so. That roomy Inverness cape would hide the movement of an arm. But if he pushed your sister, why should he have saved her? Do you really believe that it was she whom he intended to push? Did you feel nothing yourself?'

Miss Silver in her black cloth jacket and her second-best hat, one of those durable felts which survive the buffetings of many winters – her whole safe, kind governessy appearance, receded. They were a long way off, like something seen through a diminishing glass. The worn yellowish fur tippet discarded because of the warmth of the room and hanging over an arm of Miss Silver's chair, the strong black woollen gloves neatly rolled up in Miss Silver's lap, the shabby handbag which had seen so much useful service – these were all present in miniature at the end of a constantly lengthening vista. Everything shook and was unstable.

Miss Silver's small, firm hand came out and took her own.

'Just put your head down, my dear. You will be all right in a moment.'

Ione did as she was told. Everything was coming back into its place. She said,

'I'm all right now. It was just – a shock. You asked me if I did not feel anything myself. And of course I did. I felt a kind of glancing blow down my left side. We were being pressed from behind, and I was afraid we might be forced off the island on to the roadway, so I took a step to the right and got hold of the foot of one of those statues. If I hadn't –'

Miss Silver said gravely,

'That blow would have struck you between the shoulders.'

The silence settled. It was a long time before Ione could bring herself to say,

'He meant to push *me*?'

'If you had not moved, it was you who would have been pushed.'

'I see –'

'Miss Muir, will you tell me something?'

'What is it?'

'Miss Bowden informed me that both you and your sister have money.'

'Yes.'

'Then in the event of your death –'

'The money would go to Allegra.'

'And in the event of Mrs. Trent's death?'

'Her share would come to me.'

'Then Mr. Trent would have no possible motive for desiring his wife's death.'

'Of course not – Miss Silver!'

Miss Silver said equably,

'There would be no motive for Mrs. Trent's death. There was a motive for the death of that poor girl Margot. She had a good deal of money, had she not, and it passes to Mr. Trent. In your own case there would also be a motive. You have a considerable fortune, and it would pass to your sister.'

Ione's pallor was quite unbroken. Her eyes had a wide, dark stare. She said only just above her breath,

'No – no – it's too horrible –'

CHAPTER XXII

Geoffrey Trent was writing letters in his study. He frowned over them and drove his pen hard. A letter to his cousin's solicitor about probate. A letter to Margot's old nurse, a silly, fond old woman to whom she was still the healthy bouncing baby of so many years ago. A letter to Iris Morley who had practically written to congratulate him. He had had a passing affair with her, and his gorge rose at it. One of those women who look as if butter wouldn't melt in their mouths and go about distilling poison. He would have liked to tell her what he thought of her now, but it wasn't safe to rouse that deadly tongue. As he signed his name he became aware of Flaxman at his elbow with the coffee-tray.

'And if you have a moment to spare, sir –'

When anyone said that, it generally meant something fairly unpleasant – a domestic quarrel, or an intention of giving notice. His heart misgave him. Mrs. Flaxman was a very good cook, and Flaxman a very efficient butler. Their wages were high, but everything ran on oiled wheels. He braced himself to hear that Mrs. Flaxman was feeling unsettled – 'after the young lady's death, sir' – and was relieved to find the conversation opening in quite a different though equally time-honoured manner.

'I was wondering, sir, if you would consider the question of a rise for Mrs. Flaxman and myself.'

He had set down the tray and come round to the far side of the table, where he stood in a respectful attitude, his slim figure very neat in the grey linen house-coat, his rather sharp features darkened and thrown into relief by the light from the window behind him.

Geoffrey said, 'Well – ' in a tone which he contrived to make as doubtful as possible. They had been with him for the best part of two years, and they had been more than satisfactory. He supposed he would have to give them their rise, or they would be wanting to go elsewhere, but he had no intention of making things too easy, so he put all the doubt he could into his voice,

'Well, I don't know, Flaxman – '

Flaxman went over to the fire and began to make it up.

'After two years we thought you would consider it. The young lady's death has been a good bit of a shock to Mrs. Flaxman. Not that either of us is wishful to leave, having your interests at heart the way we have.'

'That is very nice of you,' said Geoffrey in a half absent tone.

'Not at all, sir. Just the motto we've always gone on – the employer's interests first.'

Geoffrey came back with a start. Was there, or was there not, a meaning note in Flaxman's voice? He thought there was, and found himself saying sharply,

'What on earth do you mean, man?'

Flaxman turned round from the fire, dusting his hands. He kept his eyes down.

'The employer's interests come first,' he said. 'If it hadn't been for me making that my motto, there were things I could have stood up and said at the inquest.'

125

'What things? Speak up, man!'

'Well, sir, I'm saying to you what I'm not thinking of saying to anyone else. You're a gentleman, and you'll know how to treat us right. The Sunday afternoon Miss Margot had that fall – ' He paused, not hesitating, but as if to give time for this preliminary to sink in.

Geoffrey Trent, very nearly facing the light from the window, was, and perhaps felt himself to be, at a disadvantage. He drove his chair back and turned it so that he now sat sideways to the table. He leaned an elbow upon it and screened that side of his face with his hand. The movements were natural enough, the position he now assumed an easier one.

Flaxman stood where he was upon the hearth. When Geoffrey said, 'Well?' he continued in his previous respectful strain.

'On the Sunday when Miss Margot had that fall, sir, you will perhaps remember that the morning had been very wet.'

Geoffrey Trent had certainly not forgotten. He said, 'Yes.'

'Mrs. Flaxman and myself, we were catching our bus – two-forty-five from the church. Mrs. Flaxman, she don't like to be hurried, and we were there by the half hour. And right about then the rain began to clear off, and there she was, with her thick mackintosh over her coat and the sun coming out as hot as you please. Mrs. Flaxman, she says to me she can't drag those two heavy coats all around Wraydon and I'd have time to nip up to the house and bring her down her light fawn coat instead. She feels the heat, sir, being so stout. Well, I says, "I don't want to miss the bus," and we were having what you might call a bit of an argument about it, when Ted Boulter comes by on his bicycle, and he says the bus has had a hold-up at West Eldon and he's got a message to say it'd be all of three o'clock before they got to Bleake. Well, that meant I had plenty of time, so I took Mrs. Flaxman's things up to the house and got her the coat she wanted. Very troublesome things ladies' clothes, if I may say so. I was coming out by the back way, when Miss Margot come running past me. She was laughing to herself, and I

126

thought she was up to something. She called out, "I thought you'd gone, Fred. Don't tell anyone you saw me!" Well, I looked at my watch, and it wanted a minute or two of the quarter, so I'd a quarter of an hour in hand, and I thought I'd see what she was up to. She was off in the direction of Mr. Humphreys's potting-shed. Well, I thought he would be wild if she got up to any of her mischief there. She must have known where to find the key, because she was inside when I come along. The church clock went the quarter, and she come out laughing and holding something up inside her rain-coat. She didn't see me, and I didn't want to start anything that was going to make me late. I was just thinking it wouldn't be anything that mattered, when Mr. Humphreys come along. He was in a fine taking, but no matter what he said it only made her laugh. I was just going, when he says, "That's one of my ropes you've got there, and you've no business with it!" and she makes a face and calls back, "Well then Geoffrey said I could have it!' And I didn't wait to hear any more because of not running any risk with the bus.'

Geoffrey Trent looked past Flaxman at the fire. He had the same ghastly pallor which had shocked everybody on the day of Margot's death. When the normal colouring is unusually strong and bright, its absence is bound to produce a somewhat startling effect. Flaxman, however, appeared quite undisturbed. If Mr. Trent wanted time to think of something to say he could have it – there was no hurry. In the end he would see reason. After all, their interests were identical.

Geoffrey said in a controlled voice,

'Miss Margot had no authority from me – that goes with-out saying. I should not have dreamed of allowing her to touch those ropes. If she said what you say you heard, it would be just a trick to get her own way. And if she said it, why didn't Humphreys say so? He was examined on his interview with her, but he never said a word about her having claimed my authority for taking the rope.'

His colour was coming back. He took his elbow off the table, straightened up, and fixed his eyes on Flaxman's face. He observed there an indefinable trace of complacency.

Flaxman's tongue was glib to answer.

'The employer's interests come first, sir. Mr. Humphreys has a long tradition of service in connection with the Ladies' House. I am sure you can rely upon him not to repeat what was said.'

The touch of complacency had deepened. Geoffrey Trent said,

'Are you blackmailing me, Flaxman?'

An archbishop could not have looked more shocked.

'Mr. Trent! How can you say such a thing!'

Geoffrey's eyebrows rose.

'As easily as you yourself.'

'Mr. Trent, I never expected! I bring to your notice a circumstance of which I consider you should be apprised – '

Geoffrey laughed harshly.

'For God's sake, man, stop talking like a grammar book! I never gave that poor girl any authority to take one of those crazy ropes. I did give her a good talking to about the trick she played on Miss Muir and myself the day before, and I hoped I had made an impression. It seems I didn't. She was like a weathercock, poor child. I certainly never told her she could take one of those ropes. They were rotten.'

'A story of that kind can be very damaging, sir.' Flaxman's tone was without any expression. 'So far as I am concerned, you can of course rely on my discretion.'

'The employer's interests!' Geoffrey could not keep the sneer out of his voice.

An expression of pain appeared upon Flaxman's face.

'Yes, sir – the employer's interests. But I am sure it is not necessary for me to point out that these things are, if I may use the expression, reciprocal. Loyalty on the one side is stimulated and encouraged by generosity and trust upon the other. In fact, sir, if you take me, the benefits are mutual.'

Geoffrey Trent threw back his head with an angry laugh.

'Oh, I take you, Flaxman, I take you! You needn't worry about that – you have made yourself perfectly clear! It is just a question now of how much you expect me to pay you for holding your tongue!'

'Mr. Trent, I must beg of you to be more moderate in

your language. I have declared myself to be a loyal servant who is devoted to your interests. There would, I think, be nothing inappropriate in the suggestion of a rise in salary.'

'And what do you mean by a rise?'

In a manner that was at once firm and respectful Flaxman said,

'Double for Mrs. Flaxman, and the same for myself, with a bonus to be agreed upon between us.'

He went out of the room and shut the door.

CHAPTER XXIII

For the moment all that Geoffrey Trent could feel was relief. Flaxman was gone. He had not to take any immediate decision. He was being blackmailed – skilfully, delicately, and respectfully blackmailed. There were severe penalties for blackmail, but if he were to ring up the police at this moment and accuse Flaxman, it would only be one man's word against another. He had no doubt at all that Flaxman would keep his head and produce the perfect explanation. He and Mrs. Flaxman had been at least two years with Mr. Trent. They hoped that they had given satisfaction, and they considered that they were due for a rise. As for the matter of Miss Margot saying that about the rope, he would not have dreamed of bringing it up if Mr. Trent had not done so.

It would have been brought up. If he sent for the police he would have brought it up himself, and once it had been spoken aloud it could never be taken back. 'Miss Margot, she said, "Geoffrey says I can have it".' Hearsay words, but just what Margot might have said, making a mischievous face and throwing the words at Humphreys as he stormed at her. Chance, idle words – just something to throw at Humphreys – but once they were repeated they would never be forgotten. The whispers would follow him everywhere. 'That poor girl, his ward, she went climbing with a crazy rope and was killed. They say she told the gardener she had Trent's leave to take it. She had quite a lot of money, and he came in for it.' Nothing that would hold water in a court of law perhaps, but enough to damn him socially from one end of his world to the other. That sort of thing stuck. He began to know inside his own mind that he couldn't face it.

Flaxman went out to the kitchen. He was whistling, and he looked pleased. Mrs. Flaxman wondered what had pleased him. She was mixing a cake without hurry. Cooking done in a hurry was cooking spoiled in her opinion. She could have taken a job as a chef, but it wouldn't have suited her – not all that rush and bustle. She liked to have her mind easy, and all her ingredients of the best. She looked up from her smooth, creamy mixture and said,

'What's got into you? I don't know when I heard you whistle.'

He said good-humouredly,

'Inquisitive, aren't you, old dear?'

She went on stirring.

'Meaning I'd better not ask?'

'That's your meaning, not mine.' He picked up a sultana from the table and nibbled it.

She began to put in the fruit. When she had the consistency to her liking she turned the mixture into a buttered cake-tin and slid it into the oven. Then she came back to her place at the table, wiping her hands upon her apron.

'I hope you're not up to nothing, Fred.'

He put his hand in his pocket, jingled some money that was there, and said,

'Why should I be?' Then, sharply, 'Where's that girl Florrie?'

She stared at him.

'It's her half day – you know that as well as I do. She's been gone this quarter of an hour.'

There were two more doors to the kitchen. He opened them both and came back laughing.

'Nothing like making sure. And now, Mary, you just listen to me! I'm not up to anything, and you'll be careful you don't as much as think that I am! We've been two years with Mr. Trent, and I've asked him for a rise, and that's all there is to it – you can just remember that!'

She was a very large woman. Everything about her lacked colour – her hair, her skin, her eyes, the short thick lashes which had been sandy when she was young. She looked steadily at her husband for a while before she said,

'You're up to something, and I don't like it.'

'Now, Mary, I ask you – have I been a good husband to you, or haven't I?'

Remembering a number of times when she hadn't thought so, but not being wishful to bring them up, Mrs. Flaxman made brief reply.

'In reason.'

'Well, there you are! What more do you want? I never ran off and left you, did I?'

'Men don't run off and leave a woman that can cook the way I can. They are fools, but they're not such fools as that. Leastways I never heard of one that was.' She dropped her voice to an almost indistinguishable mutter, but he thought what she said was, 'More's the pity.'

'What's that?' he said sharply.

'Oh, nothing, Fred.'

'Do you think I didn't hear? Want me to clear out, do you?'

She shook her head.

'I wouldn't go as far as that. All I've got to say is, if you're up to anything, you can leave me out of it. Crooked ways and crooked plans, they come to crooked ends, and I'm not getting mixed up in any of it, Fred Flaxman!'

He laughed.

'Now you're trying to get me angry with you. But not today, my girl, not today. You see, you've done me a good turn without knowing it, so I don't mind letting you have the run of your tongue.'

'I've done you a good turn?' The words came out slowly, as if she could hardly believe in them.

'Yes, you. And it only goes to show you never can tell. Many's the time I've put it across you over that stupid

131

jealousy of yours – couldn't see me speaking to a good-looking woman without thinking all sorts of things you didn't ought to!'

'I don't know what you're talking about.'

'I'm talking about you being jealous, my dear, and the day Miss Margot had that accident and we had to wait for the bus on account of its being held up at West Eldon. You wasn't going to let me have the chance of talking to Nellie Humphreys for that twenty minutes – was you? So you had to say your coat was too thick and you wouldn't be wanting your raincoat now the weather was clearing, and had to ask me in front of all those people to go off up to the house and bring you something light. Well, I couldn't say no, could I – not with everyone listening. But I was going to take it out of you afterwards. Didn't you ever wonder why I didn't? You must have known you'd got it coming to you – doing a thing like that to me! But as it happened, you done me a good turn, and you needn't ask how, because I'm not telling.'

She sat there at the kitchen table, rubbing a finger up and down on it. Her face had a brooding look.

'That Nellie Humphreys is no better than she ought to be.'

'She's a handsome woman, my dear, which is more than anyone could ever have said of you.'

Mrs. Flaxman flared suddenly.

'Then why didn't she marry and get a man of her own? Forty if she's a day! And Miss Humphreys here, and Miss Humphreys there! She did ought to have had a wedding-ring on her finger these twenty years, bringing up a family respectable like other people! But no, she stays on with her father and keeps herself free to turn anyone's head that's fool enough to let her! A bad lot – that's what your Nellie Humphreys is, and I wouldn't mind telling her so if I got the chance!'

He walked over to her and slapped her across the face. It was a hard stinging blow and it left her dizzy. She blinked up at him as he stood over her.

'That's all for now!' he said. 'Because you've done me a good turn – see? But you keep your tongue off Nellie Humphreys!'

He went out of the kitchen whistling.

Mrs. Flaxman put up her floury hands and covered her face.

CHAPTER XXIV

Allegra woke quite refreshed and not at all the worse for her adventure. She was, in fact, brighter than Ione had yet seen her. They returned home by bus, which she declared to be more amusing than having a car. But when they had said goodbye to Miss Silver and were walking up the drive to the Ladies' House she said after rather a long silence,

'I don't know whether to tell Geoffrey or not.'

Ione had a startled sensation. She said, 'Why?' and found her voice a little more urgent than she had meant it to be.

'Oh, well – I don't know – he might fuss and say that I wasn't to be trusted to go out alone – and that would be a bore, wouldn't it?' She had a quick sidelong look for her sister.

Ione didn't like it. Was she still bent on getting hold of the drug which had been destroying her? She pushed the thought away vehemently. As for telling Geoffrey about that near-accident, she intended that he should know. Allegra could tell him or not just as she liked, but he was going to hear all about it from Ione Muir. There were horrible things stirring on the fringes of her mind. She meant to bring them to the test of Geoffrey's reactions. There might be no reactions at all except the natural ones of shock and relief. If there were anything more, she thought she would not miss it. Everything in her was so tense, so much on guard, so keyed to the point of discernment, that she felt it would be impossible for her to miss even the slightest indication of what she feared.

Allegra went up to her room. Ione after a moment's hesitation turned in the direction of the study. If she was going to talk to Geoffrey she had better do it at once.

To reach the study she had to pass the sitting-room which had been shared by Margot and Miss Delauny. The door stood open, and as she went by she was arrested by a sound from within. She could not have said quite what sound it was – an exclamation of a cry but muffled as if it came from a distance. She stepped into the room and looked about her. There was nobody there. The afternoon was a bright one, and in spite of the dark panelling there was still plenty of light. But there was certainly no one in the room. She was just about to leave it, when the second sound reached her. This time it did not resemble a cry so much as a deep and angry vibration. It seemed to come from the direction of the fireplace. A wide oak panel covered the chimney-breast, flanked on either side by much smaller ones.

As Ione stood looking in the direction from which the sound had seemed to come she saw that a panel immediately to the right of the chimney-breast had started and stood an inch away from the wall. Before she did anything else she went to the door and shut it. Then she returned to the panel. It measured about eighteen inches by two feet, and it stood about five feet from the floor. It looked to be what she thought it probably was, the door of a cupboard. Pulled on, it opened like a door, and as soon as it was open the sound of voices on the other side of the wall became not only unmistakable but insistent. The wall, like all the walls of the Ladies' House, was thick enough, but this odd cupboard, if it was a cupboard, had made use of a stone shaft which ran between the rooms. Ione had seen similar openings in the chancel of more than one old church. They were called Lepers' Squints, and existed to enable the leper to view the Elevation of the Host without mingling with the other worshippers. For what purpose this shaft had been made she could form no idea, but there it was, closed at this end by a stout oak panel, and at the other by something which must have been a great deal thinner, since the sound of the voices was hardly impeded at all.

Staring into a dark space which appeared to be empty

except for a couple of exercise-books and one or two loose sheets of paper, Ione heard Geoffrey Trent say in an agitated voice,

'No! No, Jacqueline!'

Miss Delauny's response was one for which Ione was really unprepared. Had it been other than it was, she would, or at least she hoped that she would, have closed the panel and come away, but when she heard Jacqueline Delauny reply to Geoffrey's 'No!' with a warm and heartfelt 'Oh, Geoffrey, my darling!' it was beyond her. The ugly things which she had been telling herself could not possibly be true all came a step nearer. It might be Allegra's life that was in question, it might be her own. She leaned into the shaft and listened for what Geoffrey would say. He said, '*No,*' again in the tone of a man who has a woman crying in his arms and doesn't know what to do about it. Jacqueline was certainly crying, or as near as makes no difference. She sobbed his name, and there was the sound of more than one kiss.

Il y a toujours l'un qui baise et l'autre qui tend la joue. Ione didn't think that it was Geoffrey who was doing the kissing. She thought it was the weeping Jacqueline, and she considered that she had probably got her arms round Geoffrey's neck. It was at any rate Geoffrey who said with a commendable approach to firmness,

'Jacqueline, you mustn't – you really mustn't! Suppose anyone were to come in. Allegra and Ione may be back at any moment.'

'We should hear the taxi.' Miss Delauny's tone was crisp, but she sounded as if she had released Geoffrey. His voice was farther off as he said,

'It won't do, Jackie, and you know it. You can't stay on if you are going to make these emotional scenes. You must see for yourself how dangerous they are. It only needs a whisper, a single whisper about the relations between us, and I should be sunk. If Ione thought there was anything, she would only have to go to that solicitor of hers and I should never see a penny of Allegra's money. I want it for the house, and if you don't know how much I want the house, you don't know very much about me after all.'

She seemed to have come nearer to him again. Her voice was low but perfectly distinct.

'How much do you want it, Geoffrey?'

'As much as anyone can want anything.'

She said, 'As much as you want me?' and then broke into a ripple of sobbing laughter. 'Oh, you need not answer that, my dear! There is always something that men want more than they want any woman. And since the men that are not like that are not worth loving at all, I shall just have to put up with it. But if you were free, Geoffrey – if you were free – would I at least come second to this house which you adore?'

'What is the good of saying that kind of thing?'

'I say it because I want to know the answer. If you were free, would you marry me, Geoffrey? Or would you put me off as you did before?'

'Jacqueline – for God's sake!'

She laughed.

'I did you one or two good turns in the old days, but you didn't marry me. Allegra had money, and I was getting to be an old story. But you were very much in love with me once, and you could be again. Try – and see! And I can help you. I can give you your heart's desire – not me or any other woman, but the Ladies' House. You won't get it without me. I won't tell you why, but you won't. You may do your damndest, but you won't! You've done quite a lot already, haven't you? Do you ever dream about Margot and that crazy rope you told her she could take? I didn't think you would go as far as that, you know.'

'Jackie, you're mad!'

'Oh no, my dear. And I'm not a fool either. You told her she could take the rope, and that is that. You will have to shut Flaxman's mouth, but nobody will ever hear about it from me. Unless you were to do something stupid like trying to send me away. I couldn't bear that, you know. Oh, Geoffrey, I couldn't!'

She had thrown herself into his arms again. Their voices murmured. There were kisses. For the moment at any rate Geoffrey was responding to these warm currents of emotion.

Ione stepped back from the panel and shut it. One part of

her wanted to slam it hard, the other guided her fingers to a careful noiseless closing. She stood back in the middle of the room and drew a very long breath.

So this was what had been going on behind Jacqueline Delauny's air of superiority – an old affair with Geoffrey, or perhaps not quite so old. It had sometimes been a matter of surprise to Ione that so obviously poised and competent a person should content herself with such a trying job. She thought she must have been a fool not to guess before now that Geoffrey Trent was the gilding on the pill. Standing there, she began to try to sort out what she had overheard. There was the affair with Geoffrey. If it was to be resumed, it would give Allegra grounds for leaving him. Would Allegra leave him? Even if she knew that he was unfaithful? Ione doubted it. There was the indifference following upon the drug which she had used. There was improvement in this direction, even great improvement, but she was still far from normal in her reactions. And what evidence was there? Nothing that you could take to a solicitor. Jacqueline Delauny had been flinging herself into Geoffrey's arms, and for the greater part of the interview he had been doing his best to stop her.

Ione frowned. She couldn't upset Allegra, and there wasn't anything that you could really call evidence against Geoffrey. He was too goodlooking, and too fond of trying to please. Jacqueline had fallen for him in a big way and carried him off his feet, as she was probably doing at the moment. The horrible thing which was now beginning to emerge from all this welter of emotion was the fact that, in love with him and alone with him, Jacqueline had not hesitated to assume that Geoffrey Trent had connived at Margot's death. 'Do you ever dream about Margot and that crazy rope you told her she could take? I didn't think you would go as far as that, you know.' Geoffrey had certainly exclaimed in a tone of horror. He had said she must be mad. To which she replied that she wasn't a fool, and that he had told Margot she could take the rope. Too horrible to be true? Even Jacqueline had said, 'I didn't think you would go as far as that.' Suppose he had gone as far. Suppose he was ready to go farther still.

Suppose there was nothing he wouldn't do to get the Ladies' House – his heart's desire. She thought, 'If I had gone under that bus this afternoon, all my money would have come to Allegra.' If she had not moved just those few inches to the right, the blow which had struck Allegra would have landed fair and square between her own shoulders.

Geoffrey? Impossible! Why? Because he wouldn't? Or because he couldn't? What did she know about the mind of a man who had set his heart on something to such an extent that he would allow nothing and no one to stand between him and his desire? That it could not have been his hand which delivered the blow went for just nothing at all. She knew very well whose hand it was which had done that, and she remembered that she had heard the Great Prospero making terms for the risk of his neck. 'Two thousand pounds, and I'll not do it for less.' The voice that whispered and gave him his orders had not left her with a single word to remember. It remained what it had been from the beginning a whisper in a fog. It had no sex, no character, but it was briefing a man to take a life. It came to her now that the life was her own.

CHAPTER XXV

Ione did not know how long she stood there. The time might have been long, or it might have been short. It went by her. She came back from the distance to which her mind had retreated and began to think what she was going to do next.

There were two things.

She could walk into the study here and now and confront Geoffrey and the Delauny woman.

She could go quietly away and tell Allegra what she had overheard.

She couldn't tell Allegra. The minute she thought of herself doing so it became a flat impossibility. Neither she nor anyone else could say what effect that kind of shock might have upon the balance of a wavering mind. She knew with a most positive certainty that nothing would induce her to risk it.

If she were to walk into the study it would force the situation with a vengeance. Did she want to force it? She thought she did. She thought whatever else happened, Jacqueline Delauny must go.

All at once her mind felt clear. It was foreign to her nature to allow a decision to remain in the balance. One way or the other the scales must be tipped, and once this happened, she would never look back. She came out into the passage, to see that the door on the left was opening. She was able to retreat some little way and be walking back again by the time that Jacqueline Delauny emerged, eyes shining, cheeks glowing, and with some slight disorder of the usually perfect setting of her hair. At the sight of Ione she did not exactly check, but there was a change – an attempt at the usual composed manner – which did not quite come off.

'Why – Miss Muir! Is Mrs. Trent back too? I thought we should have heard your taxi –'

'We came by bus.'

'Oh – I hope Mrs. Trent is not too tired –'

'No, she seems quite fresh. My brother-in-law is in the study, is he not? I want to speak to him.' ('And if she likes to go next door and listen she can, and much good may it do her!')

With this thought flaring in her mind, Ione went into the study and shut the door behind her.

Geoffrey was standing by the hearth gazing moodily down at the sunken fire. He looked up with a hint of impatience which changed to rather a half-hearted smile.

'I didn't hear you come.'

'No – we took the bus.'

'Allegra all right?'

'Oh, quite.'

Her tone roused his attention. He threw her an anxious glance.

'Ione – is anything the matter?'

'A good deal, I think.'

'What do you mean?'

'I am going to tell you.'

She gave him the incident on the island at Wraydon in as few words as possible.

'There was a violent push – it came from behind us. Allegra couldn't keep her hold on my arm – she went tottering out into the road. Nothing could have stopped her falling under one of those motor-buses if a man in the crowd hadn't caught her arm with the crook of his stick and jerked her back.'

Nobody could have looked more horrified.

'*Ione* – you don't mean it! How horrible! Is she hurt? You shouldn't have left her! I must go to her at once!' He came across the room almost as if he could not see his way.

Ione went back against the door and stood there. She said briskly,

'She isn't hurt, and she isn't suffering from shock. I took her to the George, where we had lunch, and afterwards she went to sleep on a very comfortable sofa.'

'Who could possibly have pushed her?' said Geoffrey Trent in a bewildered voice.

'I wonder. Anyhow I do not think the push was meant for Allegra. I think it was meant for me. I had just moved about six inches to the right so that I could take hold of the foot of one of those awful statues – there were too many people on the island, and I was afraid we might be crowded off it. If I hadn't moved just then, that push would have taken me right in the middle of the back.'

'But who – but why? You can't mean you think – there was anything deliberate!'

Ione said,

'I am not really thinking about it at present, Geoffrey. There are other things –'

'What do you mean!' Tone and expression held a mixture of alarm and surprise.

She dropped her voice.

'Did you know that there was a shaft in the wall between

this room and the one next door?'

'A *shaft*?'

She walked towards the fireplace.

'This end of it would be covered by one of those lattice-work panels . . . Yes, I should say it would be this one. That would account for the voices being so plain. The other end has a solid oak door. It must have been left ajar by mistake, and just now as I was passing I heard someone calling out. There wasn't anyone in the room, but the panel was open, and I could hear Miss Delauny addressing you as "Geoffrey, my darling".'

He turned abruptly and walked to the window. The failing light was thick and cold. In the study it was already dusk. Ione went over to the door and switched on the overhead light. As if it startled him, he said,

'You listened?'

'I did. I hope you don't expect me to apologise?'

'I don't expect – ' He flung round suddenly. 'Ione, for God's sake let me explain!'

'I heard everything she said to you, and everything you said to her. I don't know that there is anything very much left to explain.'

'But there is!'

'Then I will listen.'

He began to walk up and down in the room.

'If you heard what she said you must have realised that she was in a very emotional state.'

'Oh, yes, I realised that.'

'She wasn't herself at all – you must have seen that. In the ordinary way she is one of the most sensible and controlled people I know.'

'Do you want me to say that she was being sensible and controlled just now?'

'No – of course not. She had completely lost her head. You have got to remember that Margot's death was the most frightful shock to her. She had known her since she was a child. She was, as a matter of fact, my cousin's secretary, which is how I first came across her. When my cousin died and the business went down in the war, she was at a loose

141

end, and when she offered to take charge of Margot I was more than grateful. The old nurse was retiring, and I didn't know what to do – '

He came to a standstill. Ione wondered whether he thought he had really explained anything.

Seeing that she continued to wait in an expectant manner, he flushed and went on.

'We were thrown a great deal together. I suppose we got fond of each other. It didn't last very long. I had to go out to the Middle East on business, and when I came back I think we both took it for granted that the affair was over. I ought never to have begun it. For one thing, Margot might have noticed.' His colour deepened considerably. 'I couldn't take the risk of that. You know, in some ways she was very quick. She seemed to have a sort of instinct – ' There was another pause.

Ione said, 'Yes?'

'Well, then I met Allegra.'

'Yes?'

'I suppose you heard what Jacqueline said about the money?'

'I heard everything.'

And it wasn't going to be easy to explain some of it away. It wasn't being easy. His hands were clenched as he said,

'Ione, I swear it wasn't just the money – it wasn't, really! You know how she was before all this drug business started – little and appealing and – sweet. It got me. But it's true that I couldn't afford to marry her if there hadn't been some money. When I went out to the Middle East I found my cousin's affairs in the most frightful mess. Well, I had put quite a lot of money into them. It was a question of what could be saved from the wreck. I couldn't have asked any girl to marry me who wasn't financially secure. That is how it was.'

Ione looked him straight in the face.

'You married Allegra, and brought your mistress to live under the same roof.'

He threw up his head.

'You have no right to say that! She didn't come here as

142

my mistress – such a thought never entered either of our heads! She came here as Margot's governess, and to help me with Allegra!'

What fools men were! 'It never entered either of our heads!' Did he really believe that! He looked and sounded as if he did. Could he have lived in the house with Jacqueline Delauny for two years and not been aware that she had a devouring passion for him? It had rung in every tone of her voice in the scene which Ione had overheard. But that wasn't all. Looking back, she knew that she had rather taken it for granted that the Delauny had what school-girls call a crush on Geoffrey. She had supposed such things would be apt to happen when a man was as 'sinfully good-looking as Geoffrey Trent' – Fenella's expression came back to her. She had been a little amused, a little contemptuous, but somehow it had never occurred to her to think that the feeling might be reciprocal.

He was watching her now to see if she was going to believe him. Those very blue eyes of his were like those of a dog who isn't at all sure whether he is going to get the bone on which his hopes are fixed. Had he put it across, or hadn't he? Ione wasn't sure herself – not under that pleading gaze. She said,

'Well, that's your case, Geoffrey. I don't know whether I believe it or not. It could be true, or it could be' – she made a slight pause – 'very well put together. I would much rather believe that it was true.'

He said in a despondent tone,

'It's true – but I can't make you believe it.'

'Well, anyhow it leaves a good deal unexplained. When Jacqueline Delauny asked you whether you would marry her if you were free – just what did she mean? You see, there are two ways in which you might be free to make a second marriage – Allegra might die, or she might divorce you. Which of those two things was Jacqueline suggesting?'

He broke in, voice and manner very much disturbed.

'Ione – you've got it all wrong! Don't you see Jacqueline was just upset? She's a very controlled person as a rule – you must have noticed that. But this business about Margot

143

has really thrown her right off her balance. She was fond of her, and of course it was a constant occupation. Now she is all at a loose end. What you overheard gives a very unfair picture of what she is really like. It was an emotional outburst, and when she gave way to it she believed that we were quite alone. After all, I'm fond of her, you know – and I suppose she is of me. We have known each other for a long time, and she just let herself go.'

Ione agreed.

'Oh, yes, she let herself go. But I still want to know how she thought you were going to be free. Had you ever discussed a divorce?'

'No – no – of course not!'

'Then the alternative would be Allegra's death. If she had been pushed under that bus this morning, you would have been free, Geoffrey.'

He stared at her with an effect of stupidity. Ione repeated her words.

'If she had gone under that bus she would have been killed, and you would have been free.'

He still went on staring at her. When words came they were hoarse and choked.

'You can't – possibly – mean what you're saying – '

'You would have been free.'

He went down suddenly on his knees by the table and hid his face against his outflung arms. His shoulders heaved with sobs. He kept saying Allegra's name and choking on it. It was the most complete and sudden breakdown Ione had ever witnessed. She hoped with some fervour that Jacqueline Delauny was not listening. If she were to be added to the scene, she did not feel that she could continue to cope with it.

There was, however, no dramatic entry. Geoffrey's sobs became quieter. He lifted a ravaged face, got to his feet, and sank into the armchair by the fire. There had been no tears. That ravaged face bore no sign of them, but it was horribly drawn. There was no doubt that he had received an overwhelming shock. She did not mean to speak first, and she had to wait for some time before he said in a low stumbling voice,

'You – mustn't – say things like that. I love Allegra. When you spoke of her going under that bus it was just as if you were telling me that it had happened.'

Two voices spoke in Ione. One said, 'He was shocked through and through. He really loves her.' And the other, 'If Allegra had been killed today, her money wouldn't have gone to Geoffrey – it would have come to me.'

She came over to the fire and stood there looking down at him.

'What did Jacqueline mean when she said you had let Margot take that crazy rope?'

His face twitched. He said in a tone of utter weariness,

'It just shows you how off her balance she was.'

'She said it twice, and she laughed when you denied it.'

'Am I to deny it to you? The thing nobody seems to understand is that I loved Margot. She was a child, and I'm – fond of children. I want them. Some day, I hope, Allegra – ' He broke off, lifting his head. 'You see, that is how it was – she was just a child that I was fond of. Sometimes she was a naughty child, but you don't stop loving children because they are naughty. That was one of the reasons I've been fond of Jacqueline – she loved Margot too. You don't know how patient she was. You heard her today at her worst, but she has lived with us for two years, and I have seen her at her best.'

Yes, Jacqueline Delauny had been endlessly patient. It did not need anyone to tell Ione that. She had seen it for herself. Everything that Geoffrey said about her was true. And Geoffrey had made out a good case for himself. A man with a drug addict and an abnormal girl on his hands would not lightly part with devoted efficiency in the shape of a Jacqueline Delauny. All the same, she would have to go. Amongst all the uncertainties which filled her mind Ione took firm hold of this necessity. She said,

'She will have to go, Geoffrey.'

'For a single breakdown after years of self-control?'

'It went a little farther than a breakdown, I think. There was a definite proposal that Allegra should be got rid of, and that you should marry her.'

'She didn't know what she was saying.'

'My dear Geoffrey, she knew perfectly well. And I don't think – you know, I really don't think that it was the first time she had tried to get an answer to that question. And right on the top of that she was asking you why you had let Margot have the rope that killed her. Doesn't it strike you that anyone who is capable of throwing that sort of bomb is a good deal too dangerous to be under the same roof as Allegra?'

'She didn't know what she was saying. If you were listening, you must have realised that she was beside herself. I have told you just how it all happened. I can't make you believe me. We had better stop talking about it now, because I want to go to Allegra.'

CHAPTER XXVI

Miss Silver took a journey to town next day. She explained to Miss Falconer that she might be obliged to stay the night, but she would let her know in good time.

Arrived at the terminus, she entered a telephone-box. After some little delay she was connected with the extension for which she had asked. To a familiar voice saying, 'Hullo?' she replied, 'Miss Silver speaking.'

The voice, which was that of Detective Inspector Frank Abbott, immediately took on a tinge of warm affection.

'My dear ma'am – what can I do for you?'

Miss Silver coughed.

'I have been down in the country, but I have come up for the day. I am speaking from a call-box. I wondered if it would be possible for you to see me for half an hour.'

He permitted himself to laugh.

'Someone been getting himself murdered amidst bucolic scenes?'

Miss Silver's tone rebuked him.

'I hope to *prevent* a murder. I think perhaps the Yard may be able to give me some information.'

'Well, anything we can do. Come right along!'

It was a tribute to the importance of her errand that she took a taxi. When she entered his office Frank Abbott gave her as warm a welcome as if she had been a favourite aunt. There were, in fact, very few people who had seen his glance soften and heard his voice change as they did for his Miss Silver. No two people could have provided a more complete contrast – the tall fair young man with the beautifully cut suit, his hair slicked back above a bony nose and ice-blue eyes, and the ex-governess with her flavour of the family photograph-album of some forty years ago. She was wearing the good black cloth coat which had served her for many years and her best hat, not new but freshly trimmed with a ruche of magenta velvet ribbon and two rather irrelevant bows. The hat, of course, was black. All her hats were black, like the stout laced shoes upon her feet, the worn handbag, and the shabby kid gloves.

She smiled at Frank with great affection as she seated herself, and observed,

'I was sure that you would help me if you could. What I should like to know is whether the Yard has any information about a Mr. Geoffrey Trent.'

'In any particular connection?'

Miss Silver coughed in a deprecating manner.

'I did just wonder if there was any link with drugs and drug-running. I will be quite frank with you and tell you that I have no knowledge or evidence of any such link. I have no knowledge of any illegal activity on Mr. Trent's part. He is just one of a group of people around whom some odd things have been happening. There has been a death attributed to accident. There has been a very narrow escape from a second accident which would almost certainly have proved fatal. One of the members of the group has been taking an illicit drug. And there are connections with the Near East.'

Frank whistled.

'It might add up to something,' he admitted. 'Wait a minute and I'll call up Howland – drugs are his pigeon. What's the fellow's name? Geoffrey Trent? Geoffrey with a G, or a J? . . . All right, I'll just get him on to it.'

'One moment, Frank. You might at the same time enquire whether anything is known of a Miss Jacqueline Delauny.'

He cocked an eyebrow.

'Sounds as if it might be an alias – or even one of a series.'

A slight frown rebuked him.

'I know nothing at all to Miss Delauny's discredit. I merely mention her because she is one of the group of which I was speaking. I believe she did at one time occupy a secretarial position.'

'Which is not in itself a crime. All right, if they don't know anything about her she leaves the court without a stain upon her character.'

He turned to the telephone, had a short friendly conversation of which Miss Silver could only hear his side, and finally hung up, to turn back to her with a smile.

'He says he'll get on to it right away. He's an astonishing fellow – industrious past belief – in fact King Beaver number one. And now perhaps you'll tell me all about these people.'

He listened attentively whilst she told him what she knew – things she had observed herself, and things which she had heard from Josepha Bowden, from Miss Falconer, from old Humphreys, and from Ione Muir.

Knowing the meticulous accuracy with which she could repeat a conversation, Frank did not doubt that he was hearing word for word what these people had told her. But what a confused, unintelligible business it all was. Or was it? Geoffrey Trent coming in for his cousin's business in trust, together with his cousin's abnormal child. The girl saying she had a big fortune, and Geoffrey Trent saying that the war had more or less smashed it, and that there wasn't much left. It might be a case of fraudulent conversion, and a day of reckoning ahead when the girl's money would have to be accounted for. Motive enough there for a contrived accident, especially if she was a bit of a problem anyhow.

Well, suppose that was one thread clear of the tangle.

What about the others? The fog story – Ione Muir hearing somebody bargaining over whether he would risk his neck for two thousand pounds. It might have meant anything. It might have meant murder. Miss Muir insisted that she followed the bargaining gentleman, who was diffusing a Scottish accent and an aroma of whisky, and that having run into a rising architect of the name of Severn, the three of them spent the best part of the night together in an empty house waiting for the fog to lift. The Scottish gentleman's remarks during that time might, or might not, shed some light upon his previous conversation in the fog. He produced the old chestnut about the Chinese mandarin whose death was somehow to prove immensely beneficial to the human race – if by pressing a button you would kill this person, would you press it? As a sequel to the conversation about risking one's neck for two thousand pounds, there was certainly something suggestive about this artless tale. There followed Miss Muir's identification of the narrator as a Variety artist known as Professor Regulus Mactavish or The Great Prospero, and the very narrow escape experienced by Mrs. Trent and herself when the Professor was standing in the crowd behind them on a street island in Wraydon.

He turned, frowning, to Miss Silver.

'He could have pushed them?'

She shook her head.

'I cannot say. I was standing behind him, and I had no view. I believe that he could have done so.'

'You say Mrs. Trent went staggering out into the road right in the track of the bus, and that he then reached out with the crook of his stick and snatched her back. You did see that?'

'Everyone saw that. He is very tall, or he would not have been able to save Mrs. Trent. What he did was to reach across over the shoulders of the people in front of him and catch her arm with the crook of his stick.'

Frank got up and walked over to the hearth. Standing there looking down at Miss Silver, he said,

'But it doesn't make sense. Why should he push her one minute, and snatch her back the next?'

'I do not think that he ever intended to push Mrs. Trent. She was holding her sister's arm. Miss Muir had just moved some inches to the right. The blow therefore fell more or less between them, causing Mrs. Trent to lose her hold and totter out into the road.'

'You mean that the push was intended for Miss Muir?'

'I do.'

'Why?'

'Mrs. Trent and Miss Muir are considerable heiresses. If Mrs. Trent had suffered a fatal accident, her share of the inheritance would have passed to her sister. If it had been Miss Muir who was killed, her portion – her very considerable portion – would have passed to Mrs. Trent, who could then have made a will leaving both shares to her husband. I think you can see now why I find myself in some anxiety about the position of Miss Ione Muir.'

Frank nodded.

'Might be something – might be nothing. Might be one of those mare's nests the Chief is so fond of casting up at us. There is, of course, no evidence.'

Miss Silver said with gravity.

'I would not wish to wait until the evidence of another crime was forced upon us.'

The telephone bell rang. Frank strolled across to his writing-table and picked up the receiver. There ensued a long and mostly inaudible conversation during which the telephone gurgled and Frank occasionally said things like, 'Oh, there was, was there? . . . Well, well – ' and finally, 'Good work!' and, 'Thanks very much, old chap.' He hung up, came back to stand in front of the fire, and said briefly,

'That was Howland.'

'Yes?'

'Well, there is a certain amount of information, but I don't know what you will think about it. Here it is. The Trent cousin ran a very lucrative business in the Near East. He called himself a general exporter. I suspect he had a good many of the local people eating out of his hand, but the police of one or two other countries were beginning to sit up and take notice. All this, by the way, was before the war.

There never was what you might call actual concrete evidence, but there was a very strong suspicion. Trent died some time in the early forties. Some idea that he had been trying to run with the hare and hunt with the hounds. He was found shot, with a revolver in his hand. He may have done it himself, or someone may have done it for him – double-crossing is not a particularly healthy game. After the war was over Geoffrey Trent came out to clear up the mess. Quite a job! But there were, of course, the remnants of a legitimate business. He got it on its legs again, put in a manager, and left things running. Since then nothing has happened to revive the former suspicions. The business now appears to be a perfectly ordinary one – nothing like so extensive or so lucrative as it used to be, but no longer of any interest to the police.'

Miss Silver said, 'Dear me!'

Frank laughed.

'It doesn't get you any farther with your supicions, does it? Except for just one thing. You do get the drug motif cropping up – not in Geoffrey Trent himself, but in his predecessor. Of course a cynic might say that the business owes its present blameless reputation to the fact that Geoffrey Trent is being cleverer than his cousin, and has so far been able to avoid being found out. But then you and I, my dear ma'am, are not cynics.'

Miss Silver took no notice of this. She said in a meditative tone,

'Is that all, Frank?'

'Oh, yes. Except about Miss Delauny. Nothing on record about anyone of that name, but as I said, it has a very strong smell of the alias. You say she was a secretary?'

'Miss Falconer gave me that impression. She said she was a great help to Mr. Geoffrey Trent with his business correspondence.'

'Besides looking after the abnormal girl? Well, well! She must be a tiger for work! And what is Geoffrey Trent like – how does he strike you?'

Miss Silver was not immediately ready with an answer. This was in itself something of a portent. In the end she said,

'You will probably laugh if I say that his extreme good looks make that a very difficult question to answer. With some people this would predispose them in his favour. With others it would have an exactly opposite effect. I know quite a number of women who would distrust so good-looking a man at sight. I myself greatly prefer the type whose features have been shaped by character and by the stress of events rather than that which appears to have been cast in a perfect mould. But I should, of course, use every precaution against allowing myself to be prejudiced against a man because he is unusually handsome.'

Frank considered that his Miss Silver was excelling herself. He could not resist saying,

'Let me be grateful that I have been spared the fatal handicap.'

He received a slight frown of reproof.

'The matter is a very serious one. Miss Falconer appears to be much attached to Mr. Trent. She describes him as the soul of consideration and kindness, and she has greatly admired his goodness to his unfortunate ward and to his invalid wife.'

'Then what is troubling you?'

'The old Venetian saw, Frank – *cui bono* – who profits? Geoffrey Trent is hard up. He has one of those strange passions for the fourteenth-century house which he rents from Miss Falconer. He wants to buy it, but he cannot produce the money himself, and so far Mrs. Trent's trustees have refused to allow any of her capital to be used.'

'And pray, how do you know all this?'

'From Miss Falconer, and from Miss Muir.'

'One at the seller's, and one at the buyer's end! Should be reliable. Well, go on.'

'The ward's death gives Mr. Trent whatever was left of her fortune. If Miss Muir had been killed yesterday, as she very well might have been, everything she possessed would have passed to her sister, who could then have done what she liked with it. I cannot refrain from asking myself how long, in these circumstances, Mrs. Trent might have been expected to survive. She is known to be a drug addict. There is a reputable local doctor in attendance, and a husband to whose solicitude everyone can testify. How easy to arrange for an overdose! Drug addicts are known to be incredibly cunning. She obtains a supply and, impelled by her craving, she takes a fatal quantity. Geoffrey Trent would be free, and a very rich man. He could buy the Ladies' House and have it for a possession.'

Frank said,

'Well, you are making out a case – you always do. That could be the plan of it, but – no evidence, just a lot of threads that seem to lead in the same direction. In fact, "much suspected, nothing proved".' He paused, then went on abruptly. 'You said just now that Trent had "one of those strange passions" for this house he wants to buy. What exactly did you mean by that?'

'Just what I said, Frank. It obsesses him – he has a craving to possess it. Miss Muir tells me there are times when he can hardly think or speak of anything else. Miss Falconer confided to me that if she could bring herself to sell, it would be to someone who thinks the world of the place, as Mr. Trent does. "Sometimes, do you know," she said, "I feel as if he cares about it too much. In the old days people might have said that it had bewitched him. But then, of course, they were very superstitious in those times, and we ought not to take any notice of their fancies." '

'And what did she mean by that?'

Miss Silver folded her hands in her lap, looked him straight in the face, and said,

'You see, my dear Frank, she believes that there is a curse upon the place.'

'My dear ma'am!'

'That is why she hesitates to sell, though the money would be very welcome indeed.'

'A good thing the Chief isn't here! There would have been a major explosion! Of course the bother with him is that deep down inside he has the remnants of a lurking belief in curses, witches, ghosts, bogles, and things that go bump in the night. Now what about this curse? Does Trent believe in it? It might have a bearing if he did. Anyhow, what is it?'

'It is extremely old. It goes back, in fact, to the fifteenth century. The young Falconer who was Lord of the Manor went over to France and came back with a French wife instead of the heiress his mother had planned for him to marry. She was portionless, and she spoke hardly any English. She was a stranger, and she had strange ways. She would go out and gather herbs by moonlight, and she made potions. It began to be whispered that young Falconer had had a spell cast upon him. In the end there was a formal accusation of witchcraft, brought by his mother. The girl stabbed herself and left a dying curse. Since she had lost the thing that was dearest to herself in all the world, every mistress of the manor should likewise lose the thing upon which she had set her heart.'

He was looking at her with his quizzical smile.

'And how did it work out?'

Miss Silver coughed demurely.

'Miss Falconer is a little vague about that. There were some deaths of children. Young Falconer married the heiress whom his mother had chosen for him, and their eldest son was killed in the tiltyard at the age of seventeen. This would naturally be put down to the French girl's curse.'

'In fact once you've got a curse like that in the family, everything would go down to it. People had fourteen or fifteen children and didn't expect to rear more than half of them, but every time a Falconer child died it would be the curse. But to come down to more modern times. Any further evidence?'

Miss Silver said dryly,

'Miss Falconer's great-grandfather lost a fortune on the turf, and her grandmother, who had been left a famous parure of emeralds, was robbed of them whilst staying on the Riviera.'

'Not really!'

Her tone changed.

'I am afraid Miss Falconer does believe in the curse, Frank. She was herself in some sort mistress of the Ladies'

154

House when her nephew was killed in the war. He was the last male Falconer, and she had certainly set her whole heart upon him, poor thing. It is difficult to argue with anyone when such feelings as these are involved.'

He said,

'Yes.' And then, 'Difficult to see how all this might affect Trent. Difficult to see anything in this case of yours – if you can call it a case. It began in a fog, and it seems to me to have stuck there. All I can do is to give you a bit of advice which you can pass on to Miss Ione Muir. If there is anything in the yarn, she ought to clear out of Bleake as quickly as she can. If there is anything in the story at all, Mrs. Trent is safe so long as Miss Muir is safe. Nobody is going to attempt Mrs. Trent's life if her money is going to her sister. Her danger only begins if and when something happens to Miss Muir. So Miss Muir must get out and stay out, and look after herself as well as she can.'

Miss Silver shook her head.

'I am very much afraid that she will not go.'

CHAPTER XXVII

Fred Flaxman was talking big in the local. He had been in foreign parts, not just as so many of them had, under the tedium and discipline of army life, but in a kind of glorious splashing freedom.

'When I was valet to the Honourable John de Bent – ' he would begin, and before you knew where you were you were in the midst of most thrilling adventures – lovely women, dark secrets, nightclubs more astonishing than could be imagined, murder, mystery, and what have you.

'Cross my heart, chaps, he said good night to us with no more than fifty yards to go – up one street and round the corner – and no one never saw him again!'

Or it might be, 'Nobody hadn't seen her come in. No noise, no sound of the door – nothing. And there she was, staring at us out of those big eyes and holding her cloak tight up under her chin. Till all of a sudden she drops down dead with a great stab wound in her side, and no one to say how she come by it?'

'This was a side of Flaxman's character which would have greatly surprised his present employer. On the whole, it went down well in the Falcon. Some of the men laughed at him behind his back, but they found him good company and were willing to be entertained. It was only Tom Humphreys who kept his shoulder turned and stared moodily down at his beer while the tales went on. He was old Humphreys's second son and the father of the handsome Nellie.

There had certainly been stories about Nellie in the past. She had a roving eye, and no disposition to keep anyone's house but her father's. She had always been perfectly frank about it. 'Marry, and you have half a dozen kids under your feet before you can turn round! It's no thank you for me! Look at poor Milly – up nights with that baby teething and looking fit to drop, and another one on the way! You'd never think she used to be better looking than me – now would you? Well, she was, and see where it's landed her! I'm not walking into anything like that, thank you!' Tom Humphreys was said to be afraid of her. At any rate he knew when he was well off. His house was spotless and his food well cooked. He worked at some big nursery gardens at Wraydon, and he could be relied on to drink his couple of pints most nights and make them last till closing-time.

It wasn't much after nine o'clock when Flaxman looked at his watch, finished his beer, and said he must be off. He went out with a laughing 'Good night, all!' and the darkness swallowed him up. He had not been gone for more than ten minutes, when Tom Humphreys muttered something to which nobody could put words and went lurching out after him. There was a loose joke or two, and then no more about it.

But Fred Flaxman didn't come home that night. Mrs. Flaxman sat waiting, seething with jealous anger, until round about three in the morning the anger died in her and she was cold. He wouldn't stay out all night, not with Nellie Humphreys – he darsn't! Everyone knew Tom Humphreys went home as soon as the pubs were shut. Ten o'clock. Even if he'd stayed in Wraydon and gone to the Rose or the Gardeners' Arms he'd be home by the half hour or the quarter to. And Nellie wouldn't dare keep a man in her room if her father was home. Or would she? *Would* she? She fell into uncertainty again. Her code was a very simple one of black and white. There were good women and bad women. Good women were good, and bad women were bad. The bad woman was the enemy from the beginning. She would take a man from his duty, she would take him from his wife and children, she would spend his money. There was nothing bad she would not do. She was badness itself. She had to be fought. But the good woman had no weapon. If she spoke her mind, the man only ran the more eagerly to the woman who spoke him fair. She began to be sure that Nellie had kept Fred there in the dark cottage, with her father asleep and deceived under the selfsame roof.

At four o'clock she left the back door unlocked and went heavily upstairs to bed, where she fell into a dreary sleep, and waked with a start to the sound of the alarm clock. It was half past six, and Fred Flaxman had not come home.

CHAPTER XXVIII

Come nine o'clock there was a ring of the front door bell. When Florrie went to answer it she found a tall policeman there. She knew more about him than he did about her. His name was Ben Sales, and he was new at Wraydon. All the girls had seen him on point duty, and they thought he was lovely. She wondered what he had come for. If it was tickets for the police dance, perhaps Mr. Trent would give them all

157

one like he did last year. She put on her best smile as she took him to the study, and tripped away to tell Geoffrey that there was a policeman to see him.

Geoffrey had not yet sat down to his breakfast. He was warming himself at the dining-room fire. He said in a tone of annoyance,

'What an hour to come bothering one! What on earth can he want?'

Out of the abundance of the heart the mouth speaketh. Florrie looked at him with eyes like saucers.

'Please, sir, I thought it might be about the police dance.'

Geoffrey went out frowning. When he had shut the study door on himself and the good-looking young man who towered between him and the light, any opening he had intended was quashed by the enquiry.

'You have a butler of the name of Frederick Flaxman?'

'Certainly.'

'Are you aware that he did not return to your house last night?'

Geoffrey's 'No!' was sharp. 'What on earth –'

Constable Sales said,

'I'm afraid you must be prepared for a shock, sir. The man was found dead this morning on the piece of waste ground at the end of Marsham Lane.'

'Dead! You don't say so! He never complained of any illness!'

'He didn't die of any illness, sir. He had received a charge of shot about the head and shoulders, but it would not have proved fatal. The cause of death was a stab wound.'

When Mrs. Flaxman was told she did not cry. She just sat in a kind of heavy daze and thought of all the times that Fred had run after women. And now it was a woman who had brought him to his death – because there was nobody doubted but that Tom Humphreys had let his temper get the better of him and done murder on the man that was making his daughter the talk of the place.

Tom was arrested at the nurseries where he worked. Mrs. Larkin who had the next cottage could testify to hearing high words the night before. The time would be round about half past nine. The voices were so loud she come out on to the front door step to listen. There was Tom Humphreys carrying on something shocking, Nellie crying, and Mr. Flaxman standing off out in the road trying to smooth it all down, saying things like, "No harm done," and "Couldn't anyone drop in for a friendly chat?" And Mr. Humphreys says, "Not in a single woman's bedroom he can't! And not in my house he don't!" '

Mrs. Larkin was more than willing to repeat her statement to all and sundry.

'And with that he goes in, and comes out again with his gun, and, "You be off," he says, "or you'll get a peppering! And if I ever catch you here again, you'll get something worse!" Mr. Flaxman he calls out something, and he turns to go. I couldn't hear rightly what he said, but it must have aggravated Mr. Humphreys, for he let fly with his gun. Nellie she lets out a screech, and Mr. Humphreys takes her by the shoulder and pushes her into the house. Then he goes in himself and locks the door. Mr. Flaxman he stands there shaking himself and swearing. But when I called out to him was he all right, and was there anything I could do, he said I could mind my own business. Real nasty of him, I thought it was, so I went in and shut my door and went to bed.'

It may be imagined how Bleake seethed.

Old Humphreys came up to Miss Falconer's on the evening of the second day. He had changed his boots and put on his Sunday suit. Standing in the middle of Miss Falconer's faded Persian carpet, he shifted an aged cap from one hand to the other and said,

'I was wishful to speak to you, ma'am.'

Miss Silver had been brought up with the manners of a gentlewoman. There was really nothing for it but to rise to her feet and gather up her knitting. But to her immense relief the sacrifice was not required. Old Humphreys jerked his head in her direction and said,

'The lady can stay if she's a mind to – I've no objections. Arrh! 'Tis the evildoers that needs to say their says and do their deeds in secret. Those that lives respectable and speaks the truth, they haven't got nothing that wants hiding.'

'Sit down, Humphreys,' said Miss Falconer in her benevolent voice.

'Thank you, ma'am, but I'm more at my ease standing. They've arrested my boy Tom, and what I've come here to say is he never done it.'

Miss Silver lifted a bright, intelligent glance to his face. That he was affected by it is certain, since he tended more and more to address himself to the stranger lady rather than to his own Miss Falconer. When at times he seemed to become aware of this he would once more direct himself to the accustomed quarter, only to experience the same gradual falling away.

'Tom never done it,' he said firmly. 'He's got a temper same as every man that calls hisself a man did ought to have. I've got a temper myself. If a chap was interfering with a daughter of mine, I might give him a walloping, or I might loose off a charge of small shot at him same as what Tom did. But I wouldn't go a-murdering of him with a knife. Think I'd be such a fool as to hang for a chap like that? Arrh! Well, Tom isn't a fool neither, nor he isn't the sort to go sticking knives in people. I've got things against him. He don't keep his daughter in order, for one thing. I'd like to see any gal of mine that darst act the way that gal of Tom's does. Took a stick to 'em, I did, when they was young. Arrh! That was what that there Nellie needed and didn't never get!'

Miss Falconer said, 'Oh – ' and then stopped. The idea of a young woman being beaten by her father was really very shocking, but on the other hand this hardly seemed the moment –

It was Miss Silver who said,

'Your son went into his house and shut the door, and Mrs. Larkin saw Flaxman go away. Your son did not follow him?'

'No, ma'am, he didn't. He was giving that Nellie what she'd been asking for, a right good hiding – and pity she didn't get it sooner.'

Miss Silver considered. Could Tom Humphreys have beaten his daughter and still had time to follow up a badly peppered man? Whoever had stabbed him, Flaxman had got no more than a hundred yards from the Humphreys's cottage. The waste piece of ground where his body had been found was on the other side of the road and about that distance nearer the village. Flaxman could have been in considerable pain. He could have stumbled off the road without much idea of what he was doing. If Tom Humphreys had come up with him there, a knife in his hand and murder in his heart, the crime might have been an easy one. She said,

'Flaxman received a fatal wound. If it was not your son who stabbed him, who was it?'

Old Humphreys said, 'Arrh – ' in a meditative manner. Then, lowering his voice to a churchyard whisper.

'There's those that knows too much. There's those that don't know when to keep a still tongue in their head. And there's those that think theirselves too clever by half.'

Miss Silver coughed.

'You are alluding to Flaxman?'

He gave his head an affirmative jerk.

'My son Tom, he got his grudge against Flaxman all right, and put a charge of shot into him on account of it. Scandalous goings on with his daughter and bringing of us all to shame. But maybe there was others that got things against him too – and weightier matters than a light wench.'

'What do you mean, Mr. Humphreys?'

He was turned wholly towards Miss Silver now. Miss Falconer looked on in astonishment. She heard him say,

'Before I answers that question, ma'am, there's one as I'd like to put to you, and here 'tis. Be you, or be you not the Miss Silver as was staying in Greenings in the autumn and found out who done the murders there?'

If Miss Silver received any shock of surprise, it did not appear. She said soberly,

'I was in Greenings in the autumn.'

He nodded, as if with satisfaction.

'Arrh! That's my sister as keeps the shop there – youngest of the family – Mrs. Alexander. Come visiting us at Christmas, and a wonderful lot to say about they murders and how clever you found them out – said the police thought the world and all of you too. So when it come to my lad Tom being took I thought maybe I'd come up and talk it over like.'

'Then you had better sit down, Mr. Humphreys. It will be easier for us both.'

To Miss Falconer's continued astonishment he accepted this ruling, fetched himself a solid Chippendale chair, and sat down. Then, with a hand firmly planted on either knee, he addressed himself to Miss Silver.

'I said there was others might have their grudges let alone my Tom, and I can tell you one of 'em straight away, and that's Mr. Geoffrey Trent.'

Miss Falconer threw up her hands.

'Oh, *Humphreys!*'

'Sorry, ma'am, but there 'tis. That Flaxman, he knew too much. When that there Miss Margot come after my rope, he needn't think I didn't see him a-watching atween the bushes, for I did. Arrh! There he was, and must ha' heard every word that was said. And one of the things he must ha' heard was me saying she'd no business to take my rope, and that audacious brat a-calling back, "Well then, Geoffrey said I could!" No two ways but what he heard that, and off between the bushes like a weasel. Well now, maybe you're wondering what I'm a-driving at. I didn't say nothing to nobody – it wasn't any of my business. But there's some might make it their business – and the kind of business that might put a pretty penny in their pocket.'

'You mean, or you have some reason to believe, that Flaxman was attempting to blackmail Mr. Trent?'

'Arrh! Mr. Trent wouldn't ha' liked for to have that piece about the rope repeated. That there brat saying as he told her she could take one of they old crazy things! 'Twould ha' caused a powerful lot of talk to my way of thinking – him coming in for the money and all!'

'Undoubtedly. But have you any reason to suppose that Flaxman did indeed make an attempt at blackmail?'

He gave her a vigorous nod.

'That's what I'm a-coming to. When I heard as how Tom had been took I went round to see that Nellie and find out the rights of it. I knew she'd had a good lambasting from her father, and I thought maybe she'd be singing a bit small. Well, there she was, and all the pride gone out of her. Tom had beaten her proper. She couldn't hardly move without a-calling out. "Well, my gal," I says, "you've brought your pigs to a fine market," and she bursts out a-crying and says as how everyone is against her. "Well," I says, "blood's thicker than water, and you're my granddaughter and Tom's my son. There's a time for hard words, and there's a time for telling the truth, and if you don't want your father to hang, that's what you'll be telling me now." And when she'd quieted down a bit that's what she done – and a heap of it not what I'd like to repeat to you ladies. Proper bad lot she'd been, and a pity Tom didn't take the stick to her afore.

> "A woman, a whelp, and a walnut tree,
> The more you beat 'em the better they be."[1]

That's a proper good old saying.'

Miss Silver coughed. She could not possibly approve such sentiments, but like Miss Falconer she could not feel that this was the moment to say so.

'Did she say anything which would lead you to suppose that she knew of an attempt on the part of Flaxman to blackmail Mr. Trent?'

Humphreys lifted one of his big square hands and let it fall again upon his knee.

'That she did, ma'am! Said as how Flaxman told her he'd as good as come into a gold mine. And when she arst him what he meant by that, he up and laughed and said it was just a little bit of something he knew, and maybe there was some that would pay good money for him to keep a still tongue about it.'

Miss Silver had become very grave indeed.

'To blackmail a criminal is an extremely dangerous thing. When that criminal is quite possibly a murderer, the attempt may very well prove fatal. A person who has killed once will not feel the same reluctance to kill again. If he has killed twice without incurring suspicion, his conscience will have become indurated and he will be in a dangerous state of self-confidence.'

'Too clever by half – that's what he'll be thinking he is – thinking he's diddled everyone, and putting the blame on my poor Tom! Tom's pruning-knife, that's what they say as that Flaxman was stabbed with. But there's other pruning-knives aside of Tom's, and here's what I found in my potting-shed.' He pulled a newspaper parcel out of his pocket and spread it open across his knees. The light shone down on a knife with a sharp, bright edge. ' 'Tis my knife certain sure, but I keeps it on the shelf, and 'twasn't there. 'Twas shoved in with a lot of old muck where I'd never keep nothing as has got an edge on it same as this. What 'tracted my 'tention to it was the way there was a fly a-buzzing round the thing. These warm days we've had there's been one or two of 'em about, but 'twasn't natural the way that fly kept a-buzzing round this here knife. So I takes a look, and there's a brown smear right up by the handle, and what with the fly and the colour of it, it come to me as it was blood.' He pointed with a horny finger. 'There ma'am, you can see for yourself! The blade it was clean enough – looked to me as if it had been pushed into the earth to clean it. But right up by the handle there's the stain. So I thinks about they finger-prints as the police is so set on, and I wraps it up in a bit of paper and I brings it along. And maybe you'll tell me what I'm to do with it, ma'am.'

He sat there with the newspaper across his knees and the bright edge of the knife under the light.

Without any hesitation at all Miss Silver said,

'You must take it to the police, Mr. Humphreys.'

CHAPTER XXIX

It was next morning that Ione Muir betook herself down the drive and along the village street to Miss Falconer's cottage. After three sleepless nights she had come to a point from which she felt that she could not go on. Geoffrey and Jacqueline Delauny, who had certainly been his mistress once whatever she was now! And Geoffrey so frank about the whole thing – or should the word be plausible? An old affair which ought never to have been, but all quite over and done with now. Anything she had overheard the fruit of a temporary hysterical breakdown! So why not let the dead past bury its dead? She didn't know whether she believed him or not. She didn't even know whether she ought to try to believe him. The matters involved were soo weighty. She had no scales to weigh them in. The balance could tip too violently, too dangerously, for her handling.

On the one side, and in the light of that whispered conversation in the fog, that near escape from death in Wraydon, could it be safe for Allegra to go on living in the house with the woman who had demanded so passionately of Geoffrey Trent, 'If you were free, would you marry me? . . . You were in love with me once, and you could be again. Try – and see! . . . I can give you your heart's desire – not me nor any other woman, but the Ladies' House! You won't get it without me . . . You may do your damndest but you won't!' A bait and a threat, and a woman who thought her own heart's desire might be within her grasp. 'If you were free –' And in what way was he to be free? Ione had the same thought as Frank Abbott – how easy to say that a morphia addict had somehow contrived to get hold of an overdose. Matter heavy enough to weigh a scale down into the depths!

And on the other side herself as the home-wrecker, dragging up a dead and gone affair out of Geoffrey's past to thrust between him and Allegra and shatter their marriage. Whichever way you looked at it, the tipping of the scale could so easily be fraught with disaster. As she pressed the electric bell which supplemented Miss Falconer's old-fashioned knockers she was, in fact, in that state of mind which had brought Miss Silver so many of her clients. She no longer felt that she could go on alone.

It was Miss Silver herself who opened the door. Miss Falconer had gone out to visit a blind woman, and her very efficient daily was busy in the kitchen. Ione was taken into the pleasant living-room and ensconced in a comfortable chair. Since it was no use beating about the bush, she came directly to the point, and a very interesting point Miss Silver found it. She listened with profound attention to a description of the shaft in the wall between the study and the sitting-room next door.

'I suppose I really should not have listened, but I am afraid I would do it again. You see, Jacqueline Delauny was speaking, and the very first words I heard her say were "Oh, Geoffrey, my darling!"'

In the course of her professional career Miss Silver had frequently been obliged to draw a distinction between the code of a gentlewoman and the duty owed by a detective to her client. Repugnant as it might be to her feelings to listen to a private conversation, she had quite often felt obliged to do so, and where it was a question of a life to be saved, an innocent person cleared, or a criminal brought to justice, she had had no compunction in the matter. She therefore diffused a very comforting atmosphere of approval as she said,

'Pray proceed, Miss Muir.'

Ione proceeded.

When she had heard everything Miss Silver looked very grave indeed.

'Certainly Miss Delauny should go,' she said. 'It is not at all suitable that she should be there.'

Ione had to suppress a laugh. Suitability and Jacqueline Delauny were by now such poles apart!

166

'Geoffrey won't send her away. He says it isn't fair. The whole thing has been over and done with for years, and if she had this outburst, it was because she was so overdone and upset about Margot.' She changed colour and hurried a little over her next sentence. 'He just digs his toes in and says how wonderful she was with Margot, and how good she is with Allegra. And how difficult it would be to replace her. Of course that is just what he would say if there was something between them. But at the same time, isn't it just what a decent man would say if he was speaking the truth and didn't think it fair to send Jacqueline away for an old affair which was just as much his fault as hers? You know, the time I came nearest to believing him was when he stuck it out that he was fond of her. He kept saying she had been so wonderful with Margot, and he really did sound as if he meant it.' She propped her chin in her hand and gazed at Miss Silver out of those big eyes of hers. 'But of course that is what the really first-class liar does – he sounds as if he was telling the truth.'

Miss Silver had a new grey stocking on her needles. Johnny's three pairs had been completed, and this was the first of Derek's. She was knitting in her usual smooth and rapid manner, her hands low in her lap, and her attention apparently entirely given to Ione.

'Miss Muir, I do not think that you have told me everything.'

'What do you mean, Miss Silver?'

She received the smile with which Miss Silver had been wont to encourage the backward pupil.

'It is something about that poor girl Margot Trent, is it not?'

Ione said, 'Oh –'

'There were parts of your narrative where it was obvious to me that something had been omitted. Later you showed signs of discomfort when, in a quite unembarrassing connection, you were obliged to mention the girl's name. If the subject of Margot Trent's death was mentioned in the conversation which you heard between Mr. Trent and Miss

Delauny, it might be of great importance. Will you not tell me whether it did so occur?'

Ione was pale. All along it had seemed to her that she must keep this one thing back. Whatever Geoffrey had done, he was Allegra's husband. What touched him would touch her. But now, with Miss Silver's level gaze upon her, it came to her that she couldn't hold anything back. If Geoffrey was guilty of Margot's death, then might he not have been guilty, through his agent, of the Wraydon attempt, and might he not even now be planning something against herself, or even against Allegra? She said in a distressed voice,

'You mustn't make too much of it. It's all just heresay, and Jacqueline was behaving as if she were off her balance.'

'It was something Miss Delauny said?'

'Yes. It was just after what she said about his never getting the Ladies' House, not if he did his damndest. And then she said, "You've done quite a lot already, haven't you? Do you ever dream about Margot and that crazy rope you told her she could take? I didn't think you would go as far as that, you know." '

Miss Silver's needles clicked. Derek's grey stocking revolved.

'And what did Mr. Trent say?'

'He said she was mad. And she said oh, no, she wasn't – "You told her she could take the rope, and that is that!" And then she went on – ' Ione's voice faltered and broke off.

'Yes – you had better tell me.'

'Jacqueline Delauny said, "You will have to shut Flaxman's mouth, but nobody will ever hear anything about it from me! Unless you were to do something stupid like try to send me away!" '

It was as she repeated the words that it came to Ione how impossible they made things look for Geoffrey Trent. She should have shut her mouth on them and kept it shut. But if they meant something as bad as all that, to what might she then be exposing herself – Allegra? With that shuddering thought she passed the point at which the mind can be brought to bear clearly and definitely upon its object. She heard Miss Silver say in her kindest voice,

'Believe me, my dear, the truth is always best.'

Ione drew in her breath sharply.

'You really think so?'

'I am quite sure of it. Let us take your own case. As you spoke to me you became afraid of the words you were repeating. They placed vividly before you the possibility that your brother-in-law had contrived the death of his unfortunate ward, and that being blackmailed by Flaxman, he had intervened to silence him. This upset you so much that you began to regret what you had just told me.'

She saw through you just as if you were made of glass. It was no good trying to keep anything back —

Miss Silver went on speaking.

'If it is true that Mr. Trent has committed these two crimes, you are yourself in considerable danger. He knows that you have overheard his conversation with Miss Delauny. He is therefore aware that you heard her accuse him of being a party to Margot's death. He would also know that you had heard the allusion to Flaxman and the necessity of stopping his mouth. He already has a financial interest in your death. Would it not be strongly reinforced by all this? You must remember that with each successful killing the murderer becomes more inflated with his own self-importance and more certain of his own ability to flout the law. In the end he thinks himself infallible, and so perhaps makes a false step. But in the meanwhile how much suffering may be caused, how much irreparable damage may be done!'

'Miss Silver —'

'One moment, Miss Muir. I do not say that Mr. Trent is guilty of these or of any other crimes. If he were, the bringing of the truth to light would still be the best course, for him as well as for others, since the longer a sinner remains undetected the more terrible will be the reckoning. But assuming that he is not guilty. Circumstances may look very black against an innocent man, you know, and if he is innocent, it is only the truth that can prove him so.' She quoted from an older poet than her usual favourite Lord Tennyson:

"Trust thou in Him and let thy ghost thee lead,
And Truth shall thee deliver, it is no drede."

169

Ione said, 'Yes.' Her deep, beautiful voice was firm again. Miss Silver looked at her kindly.

'There are certain facts which must be the foundation of all our reasoning. Margot Trent is dead, and Flaxman's mouth has been closed. We have to ask ourselves very seriously who benefits by these two events.'

CHAPTER XXX

The Chief Constable of the county looked testily at Superintendent Cole and Inspector Grayson. He rapped with his fingers upon the edge of the writing-table and demanded,

'What do you suppose anyone can do with a story like that?'

He was a small man with a lively blue eye and what had been a tendency to red in the hair now going grey. All his movements were quick, and so was his temper.

The Superintendent on the contrary was a large, affable man with a fatherly manner, slow to take offence and always ready to pour oil upon the official waters should they require it. He and Inspector Grayson – smart, intelligent, and for the moment respectfully silent – were on the other side of the table.

The Superintendent said in his comfortable voice,

'Well, sir – '

Colonel Marsden snapped at him.

'What's there well about it? Perhaps you can tell me that! First you put up a damned good case, and then you come along and try and knock it down again! And what have you got to knock it down with? A lot of gossip and hearsay – word-spinning!'

'Well, sir – '

Colonel Mardsen thumped the table.

'I tell you it isn't well! It's a damned mess! Now there was a perfectly good reason against that fellow Humphreys – don't know what you want with a better one! He finds Flaxman in his daughter's room getting on for ten o'clock at night, orders him off the premises, fires a charge of shot at him, and beats his daughter. Whole affair witnessed and testified to by next door neighbour. Corpse of Flaxman subsequently found on waste piece of ground not a hundred yards away. Been stabbed. Pruning-knife corresponding to stab wound in Humphrey's possession. Beautiful case without a hole in it. And then you come along and say Tom Humphreys didn't do it because his father says so!'

'Well, sir' – the Superintendent's tone was placid – 'I don't know that I went so far as all that, but that knife old Mr. Humphreys brought in – well, it looks like he's got something there. The stains up by the hilt are blood – I've brought the report along for you to see –and the blood belongs to the same group as Flaxman's, which is one of the kind you don't so often come across.'

Colonel Marsden gave the impression that he was emitting sparks.

'My good Cole, don't you ever think – just for a change? You might even read a detective story or two – it might broaden your mind!' He leaned forward, tapping on the table. 'It didn't occur to you, I suppose, that old Humphreys might have changed knives with his son?'

'No, sir. And begging your pardon, it doesn't occur to me now. I make so bold as to say that old Mr. Humphreys is a man that is very highly respected in Bleake. A very honest, respectable, hard-working family, and nothing against any of them till it comes to poor Tom's daughter. Old Mr. Humphreys wouldn't do a thing like accusing an innocent man – and that man his employer. He's got a temper, and he's dry and surly, but his bark's a deal worse than his bite, and you won't find anyone to believe he would do a mean trick like changing those knives.'

Colonel Marsden threw himself back in his chair.

'So Mr. Geoffrey Trent told his ward she could take a crazy rope and go hang: *"Geoffrey said I could have it."* Old Humphreys says that's what she said to him, and he says that Flaxman heard her say it. Well, perhaps he did, and perhaps he didn't. Again we have only got old Humphreys' word for that!'

'I believe there is something Miss Muir could say, but she is holding back. Mr. Trent is her brother-in-law, after all.'

'Too many relations mixed up in this affair for my liking! Too many loose ends everywhere, and too many fingers in the pie – gardeners – sisters-in-law – old maid visitors! And as if there wasn't enough and to spare without anyone else taking a hand, the Yard has been on to me this morning!'

Grayson, silent, attentive, watchful, was able to remark that the temperature of the interview had cooled perceptibly. Old Cole was no longer enemy number one, but a possible reinforcement. He was being confided in rather than attacked. It was in a tone of sympathy that the Superintendent exclaimed,

'The Yard, sir!'

Colonel Marsden jerked open a drawer, rummaged in it, and flung a crumpled sheet across the table.

'There you are! Read it for yourself! Dope! Accidents and murders aren't complicated enough, it seems! That girl who fell off the quarry, her father ran a business in the Near East. Suspected of trafficking in drugs – nothing proved. Interval for the war. Fellow commits suicide and Geoffrey Trent goes out to clear up the mess. Nothing against him until just now. Seems they've had advices from the Mediterranean area that there are some quite lively deals going on. More loose threads, but one of them connects with Geoffrey Trent and his business, and they want to send a man down – name of Howland. Well, of course no objection to that. We don't pretend to handle international dope traffic – well, do we?'

The Superintendent said, 'No, sir.' His tone was a little on the dry side. He had served for fifteen years under the Chief Constable, and he was wondering what it was that he had got up his sleeve. He was to know in a minute.

Leaning back in his chair, and in a manner which could hardly have been more casual, Colonel Marsden said,

'Seems to be some idea that Mrs. Trent has been taking the stuff. Heard anything about that?' His eye travelled from Cole to the Inspector.

'Well, yes, sir.' Grayson was brisk. 'There's been a bit of talk in Bleake about her being strange. I don't know that it went further than that.'

Colonel Mardsen grunted.

'Nice household, I must say! And that girl who fell over the quarry – odd in the head, wasn't she? And her money all came to Trent. Ever think there might have been more in that case than met the eye, Cole?'

'No evidence, sir.'

'And now Humphreys comes along with a yarn that she told him that Trent had given her leave to take that rope. Rotten, wasn't it?'

Grayson said,

'Yes, sir – I handled it. It wouldn't have held a dog's weight, let alone that poor girl's. You could break it almost anywhere with a good pull.'

The Chief Constable said in his testiest voice,

'The Yard seem to have got hold of that too! They got on to me this morning, and they said some information had been brought to them. Well, the whole thing ties up together, doesn't it? If they've got all this stuff they'd better use it and be done with it! Seems there's a suggestion that Mrs. Trent or her sister may be exposed to some risk. Can't quite see it myself! But of course I haven't got their information! I don't want to be told afterwards that something has happened, and that we ought to have known it was going to happen and have prevented it!'

'No, sir.'

The Chief Constable banged his knee.

'How do you mean "No, sir"? I tell you I'm not going to take any responsibility in the matter! They can send down anyone they like, and they won't be able to say we made difficulties about it! If the whole thing turns out to be a mare's nest, well then, that's their look-out! We can just sit back and say we said so all along!'

Grayson's face allowed none of his angry thoughts to

173

show. What old Marsden meant was that he had called in the Yard, and that if anyone was going to get a pat on the back over the case, it wasn't going to be John Grayson.

The Superintendent was saying,

'You mean that you have asked them to send someone down besides Howland?'

Colonel Marsden nodded.

'Well, they suggest Abbott – Inspector Abbott. Seems some of this information was brought to him, and they think he might as well come down and see if he can dig up anything more. Don't know if you've ever run across him. Very competent fellow. Used to know a cousin of his – extraordinarily pretty woman, but no brains. Not that I'm partial to your clever women – too dashed earnest about it, if you know what I mean. But there's a limit the other way!'

Superintendent Cole said with slightly strained good humour,

'Am I to take it that these chaps from the Yard will be coming down immediately?'

CHAPTER XXXI

Inspector Howland was a slight middle-aged man with a retiring manner. There were, in fact, times when it became so hesitant that the person to whom he was talking might feel a kindly impulse to help him out. He saw Geoffrey Trent, and asked him a number of questions relating to his business in the Near East. Geoffrey, at first annoyed, passed to a state of rather contemptuous tolerance. If a check-up on these things was required for Customs purposes, he could not imagine why a more competent and businesslike person had not been sent down. In any case, as he told the embarrassed Howland, there were a number of the questions which he could not possibly answer without access to the books of the Company, in which he held an interest.

'That would be as trustee for your late ward, Miss Margot Trent?'

The question was put in so small and shy a voice that no offence could be taken.

'Certainly.'

'These interests have now passed to you?'

'Yes, I am sorry to say they have.'

'Sorry, Mr. Trent?' Howland peered through the thick lenses behind which his short-sighted eyes blinked at the world.

'I was very fond of my ward.'

'Ah, it was a sad accident. But to return to this Company. You hold a majority of the shares?'

'About fifty-five per cent – besides some which I hold in my own name. May I enquire why I am being asked all these questions? So far as I am aware everything is in order. If there is an idea that there has been some breach of the Customs regulations –'

'I have no connection with His Majesty's Customs, Mr. Trent. If you jumped to that conclusion, it is not my fault.'

Geoffrey frowned.

The questions went on, still in that diffident tone, but becoming more and more difficult to answer.

'Do you know a man called Muller?'

'Well, yes.'

'He was the assistant manager of your general trading company?'

Geoffrey raised his eyebrows.

'Was?'

Howland blinked.

'I am afraid he has been arrested.'

'What for?'

'Trafficking in illicit drugs.'

Geoffrey Trent clapped a hand to his head and exclaimed, 'Oh, my God!'

Another person interviewed by Inspector Howland was Florrie Bowyer.

'You work by the day at the Ladies' House?'

Florrie felt pleased and important.

175

'Oh, yes, sir – I'm housemaid.'

'Like working there?'

'Oh, yes – Mr. Trent is ever so kind.'

'And what about Mrs. Trent?'

She wouldn't have answered just anyone who asked her that, but this poor little man did seem so shy you kind of felt you'd got to help him out. She dropped her voice and said,

'She's been ill – sometimes she's ever so strange. You won't say I said so.'

'What makes her strange?'

They were in her mother's front room, but she looked over her shoulder as if someone were listening for what she was going to say.

'It's the medicine she takes – white stuff in a powder. Mr. Trent he asked me had I ever seen any such, doing her room and putting her things away. And when I said yes, he said to show him, and he took the whole lot and put it on the fire – said it was making her ill and she mustn't have any more of it.'

'And did she seem to get better after that?'

'Oh, yes, she did. Dr. Whichcote came up to see her once a week. He thought she was better too, because I was in the hall once when Mr. Trent was letting him out, and he said something like "definite progress", and, "we'll just go on with the diminishing doses".' She looked up suddenly with a flush on her face. 'I wouldn't say nothing about it, not to anyone, only you can't be in a place without knowing when there's talk, and if it's anything against Mr. Trent, well, I thought I'd better tell what I see with my own eyes, and heard too, because there never was a gentleman that took more thought for his wife. Never an unkind word, and she used to be ever so queer sometimes – enough to put any gentleman out. But Mr. Trent never!'

Howland looked through his thick lenses at the little pleading face. Earnest child with every appearance of being truthful. He said.

'You were quite right to tell me what you know.'

Florrie felt a good deal uplifted.

There was another interview, and a longer one, with

Jacqueline Delauny. She made an effective entry in her black dress, and avoided the chair which he had set for her facing the light.

'Thank you, I should prefer to stand, and as I am feeling cold I should like to warm myself a little.'

She took up a graceful bending position with a hand on the mantelpiece and a foot raised upon the kerb of the hearth. She was thus only half facing him and could look away or down into the fire as she wished. He began to think that she was clever, and then to wonder whether it would not have been cleverer not to take so obvious a precaution. But then she probably put him down as a fool – people very often did.

She stood there waiting for him to begin, her dark eyebrows a little raised. When he let her wait, she bit her lip and said,

'I'm afraid I don't quite understand. May I ask why you wanted to see me?'

'Certainly. I am an officer from Scotland Yard. A question has arisen out of the affairs of the late Mr. Edgar Trent. I believe you were his secretary.'

She really did look genuinely surprised.

'That seems like a very old story. And I am afraid I must correct you. I wasn't really Mr. Edgar Trent's secretary. I did some translation work for him, and he would occasionally ask me to help him with a foreign letter.'

'Our information is that you lived in his house and acted as his confidential secretary.'

She shook her head.

'Oh, no – nothing like that. I went to live in his house because he asked me to take charge of his daughter. He was a widower, and the child, who was then about eight or nine, had been left to run quite wild.'

'That was the girl Margot Trent who met with a fatal accident here?'

The tears rushed to her eyes.

'Yes, it was Margot. She had been terribly neglected, and she was not quite normal. I can assure you that looking after her left me with very little spare time on my hands.'

'But you were in Edgar Trent's confidence?'

'With regard to his daughter, I may say that I was. I could not have stayed with so difficult a child if I had not had the full support and confidence of my employer.'

'Miss Delauny, I was not talking about your employer's daughter, I was talking about his business. Were you not equally in his confidence about that?'

'But of course not! I knew nothing about his business except what everybody knew. He was a rich man who had done very well at it, but just what he did – ' She shrugged her shoulders. 'I'm afraid business has always seemed very dull to me. I really wasn't interested in it.'

Howland looked at her hard.

'Are you going to say you didn't know he was running dope?'

Her hand dropped from the shelf, her foot from the kerb. She stood up straight and angry.

'That is a most insulting question!'

'I am afraid it is one that you will have to answer.'

'Naturally. I should insist upon answering it. Of course I have no knowledge of the sort you imply.'

'You knew that your employer committed suicide?'

'I was no longer in Alexandria by then. Naturally I heard of his death. He sent Margot home in '39 just before the war broke out, and I accompanied her.'

'You remained in charge of her?'

'Not entirely. Margot was for a time with her old nurse, a very suitable person. I used to visit her constantly and report to her father. After his death Mr. Geoffrey Trent invited me to take charge again. Nurse was getting old and felt that she could not go on. When Mr. Trent married two years ago we joined him here.'

A perfectly natural, simple, straightforward story, and no evidence to break it down. There is a long sliding scale between the nursery governess who looks after your difficult child and occasionally writes a foreign letter for you and the confidential secretary with every detail of your business at her fingers' ends. Their advices had not mentioned the child. If she was really there, and Jacqueline Delauny in charge of her, it was going to be very difficult to get her where they wanted her, at the incriminating end of that scale. He went away with a feeling that he hadn't got very far.

CHAPTER XXXII

Howland had gone and they were all at lunch, when Allegra turned one of her rather vague looks upon her husband and said,

'Did I tell you that Miss Falconer and her friend are coming to tea?'

Geoffrey started. His fresh colour was less in evidence than usual, and his thoughts appeared to have been wandering.

'What did you say?'

'I just wondered if I had told you that Miss Falconer and her friend are coming to tea.' Allegra rather dropped than raised her voice.

'No. I don't think you did. I didn't think we were having anyone just now.'

'I thought it would be nice for Ione. Miss Falconer knows so much about the house.'

'And she has had two years to tell us what she knows!' said Geoffrey Trent.

It was the first time that Ione had seen him put out about a domestic matter. Allegra's face puckered up as if she were going to cry, and all in a moment he was his old smiling self again.

'Darling, that was horrid of me. But I've got a lot of letters to write, and I shall just have to run away as soon as tea is over. After all, you and Jackie and Ione ought to be enough to entertain two old ladies. By the way, what is the friend's name? I keep forgetting it.'

It was Jacqueline Delauny who said,

'It is Miss Silver – Miss Maud Silver – and she is like all

179

the old maids in the world rolled into one.' She had a short
dry laugh for this.

Geoffrey said,

'*Really*, Ally!'

He used what was Ione's own special name. No reason
why he shouldn't of course, and there had to be a first time
for everything, but she didn't like it.

Allegra smiled vaguely and repeated,

'I thought it would be nice for Ione. But Jackie must
stay too, because I don't always want to talk – I get so tired.'

The two ladies arrived punctually at half-past four, Miss
Silver wearing her best hat with the magenta trimming, and
the plum-coloured cashmere dress which had been new in
the autumn. Since she invariably bought the stuff and had
it made up by an elderly dressmaker in Chiswick, the pattern
of these garments changed very little. A bog-oak brooch in
the form of a rose with an Irish pearl at the heart fastened
the folds in front. Miss Falconer never varied now from her
shabby black, and wore, as always, a wide-brimmed felt of
a mushroom shape and a limp discouraged scarf about her
neck. But the pearls which showed occasionally were real
and had been her mother's. Where so much else had gone,
she held on to them, and would continue to do so until con-
fronted by some final emergency.

Geoffrey Trent made himself perfectly charming during
tea, and then vanished with the time-honoured excuse of
letters to write. Whilst Allegra lapsed into one of her
abstracted moods and Ione led Miss Falconer on to talk
about the family history Miss Silver found herself practically
tête-à-tête with Jacqueline Delauny. Her hands occupied
with her knitting, she explained that the stocking on her
needles was for her niece Ethel Burkett's second boy Derek.

'There are three of them, Miss Delauny, and all at school
now, so they get through their stockings very quickly indeed.
I have finished three pairs for the eldest boy, Johnny, and as
soon as these are done I shall be knitting a set for Roger who
is the youngest.

'Indeed?'

Miss Silver beamed upon her.

180

'And then I shall be able to think about a pretty knitted frock for little Josephine.'

It was not until the conversational possibilities of the Burkett family had been thoroughly explored that Miss Silver sighed and observed that she was afraid she talked too much about them.

'But when you are as fond of children as I am – I was for some time engaged in the scholastic profession –'

Miss Delauny's lip twisted.

'It is very hard work.'

'Ah, yes, but so rewarding. I am sure you must have felt that too.'

A sudden failure of the blood beneath the skin made Miss Delauny's lip rouge stand out with a rather ghastly emphasis. The effect was for a moment only. Then Jacqueline said with a kind of bitter composure,

'I am afraid I did not find it so.'

Miss Silver was all compunction.

'My dear Miss Delauny! I had no intention of making any reference – do, pray, believe me!'

'It doesn't matter. Mr. Trent and I are, perhaps, too sensitive on the subject. You see, we were both very fond of Margot. But nobody seems able to believe that. They write and talk as if it was all very painful but it must of course be a great relief to us.'

Miss Silver observed that far too few people had been endowed with tact.

'Even if they thought such a thing, it is really the height of bad taste to say so.'

'Mr. Trent feels it very much.'

In spite of her remark about tact Miss Silver did not seem able to get away from the subject of Margot Trent. She asked a number of small and quite harmless questions about her tastes, her temperament, and the difficulties which attend the education of an abnormal child, the whole copiously illustrated by anecdotes from her own experience and from that of friends also engaged in the scholastic profession. If Miss Delauny had any idea of breaking away and joining the other group, it was made quite impossible for her to do so.

Ione and Miss Falconer were away in one of the half dozen centuries which had elapsed since Robert the Falconer received his grant of land and built himself a house upon it.

Allegra took no part in either conversation. She sat in the sofa corner and did not pay any attention to what was going on until right at the end, when she broke in suddenly with an irrelevant,

'Ione has had such a charming flat lent to her. Her friend Louisa Blunt. She is going abroad or something, and wants to get it off her hands. Where is she going, Io?'

Thus directly addressed, Ione returned from the middle ages.

'I don't think she is going anywhere, except just for a short holiday in Paris. And she isn't lending me the flat. It is too much for her, and I am taking it over.'

'So much nicer,' said Allegra. She spoke to the company at large. 'You see, she can have her own furniture and things. We were looking at materials for curtains at Kenlow's the other day.'

Miss Falconer nodded approval.

'They have very good materials at Kenlow's, only everything is so expensive –' She ended with a sigh.

Ione said gently,

'Yes, they are. But my friend will leave her things there for as long as I want them, so I need not get everything at once.'

There was a little more talk. About the position of the flat – 'So convenient for shopping. And your sister can come up and stay with you – it will do her good.'

Allegra said brightly, 'Oh, yes,' and then appeared to lose interest again. She leaned back in the sofa corner and closed her eyes. It became obvious that the tea-party might be considered to be over.

The front door was no sooner closed behind the visitors than Jacqueline Delauny swept tempestuously into the study. She shut the door with what was almost a bang and said,

'Of all things in the world I detest a prying old maid!'

Geoffrey Trent looked up with half a smile.

'My dear Jackie – how fierce!'

She flung round at him from the hearth.

'It is all very well for you – you ran away!'

It was an effort to maintain the smile. She had become a great deal too prone to make scenes. It seemed painfully probable that she was going to make one now. He found himself for the first time not altogether unsympathetic towards Ione's demand that Jacqueline should go. You could not count on what an hysterical woman might say. What the situation demanded was the appearance of a perfectly normal household – saddened, it is true, by a recent death but at peace within itself.

'My dear Jackie, be reasonable!'

She threw up her head.

'Do you suppose that I feel reasonable?'

He did not suppose anything of the sort.

Her voice choked as she hurried on.

'For one whole hour that damned prying old cat has been grilling me! First she bored me with her relations till I could have screamed, and then she got on to Margot – Margot, oh, my God!'

There was no question of a smile between them now. He dropped his voice.

'What did she say?'

'Oh, it didn't amount to anything. It was just one niggling question after another. Did she read – did she write? A friend of hers had been very successful with a similar case. The girl could write a passable letter, *and had even made some attempts at keeping a diary!* Of course I could see at once that someone had been talking – Allegra, or Florrie. And there was this inquisitive old devil all set to find out whether Margot kept a diary!'

'What did you say?'

She flung out a hand.

'What was there to say? I said she scribbled a lot of nonsense, and as often as not destroyed it. But do you think I could get that woman off the subject? She just went on, and on, and on!'

'Well, she has gone now. Sit down and have a cigarette.'

She shook her head impatiently.

'You think you can shrug everything off and smooth it

183

down, don't you! I tell you I don't know what Margot may have put in those missing pages! She was in her very slyest mood that afternoon and brim full of spite! She kept looking sideways at me and laughing to herself!'

'She was writing in her diary then?'

'I told you she was! But I didn't know she had torn the pages out! I'd never have let her go out of the room with them if I'd known!'

He said uneasily.

'Well, after all, Jackie, the most of what she wrote was only a child's scribblings. I don't see you need be in such a state.'

'Don't you? I tell you she was just as full of spite as she could be! Are you prepared for those pages to turn up, and find out that she had written, "Geoffrey says I can take one of those old ropes from the shed and so I shall"? I can just see her sitting there, putting down things like that and hiding them for someone to find!'

There was a silence. He was staring down at his blotting-pad. In the end he said,

'Don't you know where she used to hide things?'

'Those pages are not in any of the usual places. Do you suppose I haven't looked? I believe they are somewhere in Ione's room.'

'Why?'

'She had been fairly haunting it. It was her last new craze, and I believe she stumbled on some hiding-place. The trouble is I never really have a chance of getting down to looking there. I thought I would get one the day Ione and Allegra went into Wraydon. I came back as quickly as I could, and there was Florrie turning out the room!'

He bent a frank look upon her.

'But why don't you tell Ione and ask her to help you?'

She broke into unsteady laughter.

'You damned, damned fool! Can't you get it into your head that what Margot wrote on those missing pages may very well put a rope round your neck? Not the rope you told her she could have, but one that can be trusted to do its

184

job!' She came up close to him and went down on her knees by his chair, catching him by the wrist and arm. 'Geoffrey – Geoffrey – can't you see the danger you are in? They are raking up all that old business of Edgar's again, and if they get only half a chance they'll try and pin Margot's death on you! They haven't got anything on me, but they could be made to believe that they have quite a lot on you! You don't seem to realise it, and you've got to! There's nothing I wouldn't do for you – *nothing!* But I can't help you if you won't help yourself!'

He disentangled himself from her clinging hands and got up. What an unbridled lust for emotion women had! But not Allegra. She came into his mind, passing through it as she might have passed through a room, small, and pale, and cool. He went round to the farther side of the table and stood there.

'Get up, Jackie!' he said. 'Get up and take a pull on yourself! You're seeing everything through a magnifying-glass, and at least threequarters of what you see is in your own imagination. You and I are going to quarrel if you keep trumping up this damned story about my having told Margot she could take that rope. It is utterly and wickedly untrue, and I absolutely forbid you to bring it up again!'

She got to her feet, stumbling on the edge of her skirt, catching at the table for support. When she was up, she leaned on it shaking, her eyes ablaze in an ashy face.

'You don't dream about her?' The words only just reached him.

He said, 'No.'

'You don't feel as if you might meet her on one of those damned staircases – closed in, the two of you?'

'Certainly not.'

She leaned a little nearer. The slightest breath – the least sound of words –

'She doesn't come in the night and – show you – the rope?'

He drew back a step.

'My dear Jackie, I'm not an hysterical woman. You are, and I suggest that you should go up to your room and use

185

enough cold water to steady your nerves.'

He went over to the door, opened it, and went out, leaving her standing there by the study table.

CHAPTER XXXIII

At half past eight that evening Frank Abbott betook himself to see Miss Silver. The two elderly ladies would have partaken of a light meal, and the sacred ritual of washing up would have been accomplished.

Miss Falconer, who opened the door to him, was a good deal fluttered. There had been a time when young men came in and out of the house laughing and talking with Robin, but it was all so long ago, and not this house. There was nothing to bring young people here any more – not since Robin went away to the war and never came back. Just for a moment the sight of Frank's tall, light figure and the tone of his voice brought everything up. Time did take away the worst of the pain, but you could never tell when it would come upon you suddenly like this.

She showed him into the little dining-room, switched on the electric fire, and went away to find Miss Silver. He was wondering what he had done to frighten her, when Miss Maud Silver came in, knitting-bag on arm. She was wearing last year's summer dress – art silk of a shade rather too reminiscent of boiled greens – this garment being reinforced by the now aged black velvet coatee without which she never went down into the country. Even in the height of summer she knew only too well how draughty the English cottage, the English vicarage, and above all the English country mansion could be. But with her coatee, so cosy, so comfortable, she felt secure.

When she had seated herself and extracted Derek's last stocking from her knitting-bag she smiled and said,

186

'Well, Frank?'

A leaf of the dining-table had been let down, and they sat one on either side of the hearth in Windsor chairs. Miss Falconer never lost her secret regrets for the Chippendale set which she had been obliged to sacrifice, but Frank, who had an eye for such things, allowed it to rest appreciatively upon the Windsors and thought how perfectly they suited the room. He laughed and said,

'And why should it be you who say "Well?" in that tone to me?'

She smiled demurely.

'You would not have come to see me if you had not had anything to say.'

He had a protest for that.

'I might have wanted to hear what you had got to say. Or I might, who knows, have had an urge to come and sit at your feet. As the late revered Tennyson has put it:

> "An infant crying in the night,
> An infant crying for the light,
> And with no language but a cry".'

'My dear Frank, you really do talk very great nonsense.'

'*Dulce est desipere in loco!*'

Miss Silver coughed.

'I am not familiar with Latin. It was not considered a necessary part of a girl's education when I was in the school-room.'

He cocked an impudent eyebrow.

'Something you don't know! My dear ma'am, let me make the most of it – it will probably never occur again! I was merely remarking that it is sweet to play the fool sometimes.'

She regarded him with indulgence.

'If you have anything to tell me, do you not think you had better begin?'

'Unless you would like to shoot first.'

She considered this.

'There is one point upon which you should be informed.

Miss Muir has not, I believe, communicated it to Inspector Grayson.'

'But she told you.'

'And I have given no pledge of secrecy. It concerns a conversation which she overheard between Mr. Trent and Miss Delauny. I think that I had better repeat it to you.'

He listened to the careful, accurate repetition of what Ione had heard through the shaft in the wall. As soon as she had finished he said,

'She can't keep that back, you know. She'll have to come across with it.'

'Yes, I have told her so. She is in a painful position.'

He said in his most cynical tone,

'Murder does make it painful for the relations, doesn't it?'

She could have nothing but reproof for this. It was expressed by a brief silence, after which she observed with some restraint,

'And now I believe that you will have something to tell me.'

He laughed, and then was as serious as she could wish.

'Well, I suppose you would like to know what Howland's impressions are. He's the dope expert, and we came down together bright and early this morning. He's gone back to town to make his report whilst I linger on the scene.'

'And what does Mr. Howland think?'

He laughed again.

'Inspector – same as me. But so very, very much more like a plain John Citizen. I should like to have been a fly on the wall whilst he was talking to Trent and Miss Delauny. He manages to give the impression that he is almost too shy to ask any questions at all, and yet out they come one after the other. I believe he really is shy, you know, but he has managed to polish up his natural diffidence until it has become a very effective technique.'

Miss Silver's needles clicked.

'I should be interested to know what he thought of Mr. Trent and Miss Delauny.'

'Well, they both put up very good stories. Trent admitted frankly that he had been horrified by some of the things which had cropped up when he went out after the war to settle up his cousin Edgar's affairs. Chap committed suicide in '42, and there was a pretty bad mess to clear up. Trent said he hadn't the slightest idea of there being anything wrong since then. Couldn't understand it, and couldn't be expected to go into business details without having access to the books. Professed himself ready to fly out to Alexandria and go into everything with the police.'

'And is he going to do that?'

'Not if I can help it, but I don't know whether I can. You see, if there's anything in this idea that he may be tied up with a couple of murders, Alex would be a great deal too convenient for him. Back doors and back stairs *ad lib*, and if his trading company has been up to any funny business, there will be plenty of keys to open those back doors. The question is, how much is there in this idea that there was some hanky-panky about his ward's death, and that he may have stuck a knife into his butler for knowing too much about it. Grayson was telling me about what they had got, and frankly it doesn't amount to much, does it? Grayson is a very nice chap and as honest as they come. But then he has married into the Humphreys family, and you can't expect him to want Tom Humphreys to hang – to put it no stronger than that. So however hard he tries to be impartial, he can scarcely help at least hoping that there's something in old Humphreys' story.'

Miss Silver coughed in a gently meditative manner.

'Do you want me to tell you what I think?'

He was quite serious now.

'Yes, I do.'

'Very well then, I will do so. Where evidence is slight and possibly biased, I have always felt that the best results may be obtained by going behind the evidence to what springs directly from the disposition, character, and temperament of the people concerned. In this case we have a young woman of loose morals engaged in an affair with Mr. Trent's butler who is a married man. They are surprised by her father, and after a violent scene Tom Humphreys fires a charge of shot at Flaxman, who is by this time too far off to be dangerously affected. He staggers away. Tom Humphreys pushes his daughter into the house and goes in and beats her. Up to this point the whole scene has been witnessed by the next door neighbour, Mrs. Larkin. According to her account she calls after Flaxman to ask if he is all right, and he tells her to mind her own business. After which she would have us believe that she went into her cottage and took no further interest in the proceedings, though she has already stated that she knew Tom Humphreys was beating his daughter. Bearing in mind that she is an extremely voluble and inquisitive woman, does that strike you as credible?'

'Frankly, no. What do you think she really did?'

The busy needles clicked.

'I think she would go into her house. Tom Humphreys was in a violent state, and he had a stick in his hand. He might have adopted a threatening attitude towards an eavesdropper. But she could go into her house and look out of an upstairs window. There is hardly a woman on earth who would not have done so. She would be listening for Nellie's screams and watching to see whether Flaxman was going away. The night was overcast, but there was a moon behind the clouds. I am told that Mrs. Larkin prides herself on her good eyesight. I think she could have commanded quite a considerable field of vision from her upper window.'

He whistled.

'You mean that she would have seen Tom Humphreys if he had left the house?'

'I believe that she must have done so. If she did not see him leave the house, it was because, having beaten his daughter, he went to bed.'

'My dear ma'am, he could have waited until he was sure that a prying neighbour had given it up, and that he would be able to slip out unobserved.'

Miss Silver shook her head.

'You are not really thinking,' she said in grave reproof. 'When you have peppered a man with shot you do not expect him to hang about waiting for you to come out and stab him. And you are getting away from what we agreed to consider – the characters of the people concerned. Tom Humphreys has the reputation of being a man surly in manner but not given to violence in action. On this occasion he received very grave provocation, with a consequent lack of control which led him to fire a charge of shot at Flaxman and beat his daughter. That is to say, in the first immediate heat of anger he turns to a shotgun. The firing of the gun was not followed up. His anger turned towards Nellie, and he beat her with a stick. By this time his first violence would have expended itself. If it had not done so, he would, I feel sure, have gone out stick in hand to make sure that Flaxman had cleared off. I find it impossible to believe that at that period of the proceedings he took a pruning-knife and went out to stab a man who he could not really have supposed would still be there. And if he had done so, Mrs. Larkin would have seen him.'

Frank said,

'You're making out a case, but I don't know what a jury would say to it. And if Mrs. Larkin was really looking out of her window and didn't see Tom Humphreys come out again, why doesn't she say so and clear him?'

Miss Silver pulled on her ball of wool.

'Mrs. Larkin has been a widow for ten years. Miss Falconer tells me that she has made several very determined attempts to marry Tom Humphreys. She has had high words with Nellie, and not very long ago there was quite a violent quarrel with Tom himself. Since she talked about it all over the village, it is common knowledge that he told her to keep out of his affairs and leave him alone.'

'In fact, "No fury like a woman scorned". You know, the immortal Sherlock was perfectly right when he pointed out that the English countryside fairly seethes with material for crime. I seem to remember that Dr. Watson couldn't believe him! But I can!'

Miss Silver looked some slight reproof, and opined that human nature was very much the same wherever you found it, but that of course in the country people did know more about their next door neighbours.

Frank got up and stood in front of the fire.

'Well, Tom Humphreys couldn't have done it, because Mrs. Larkin didn't see him leave the cottage, and she won't say so because he spurned her. As a matter of fact, the daughter is going to swear that her father didn't go out again – but she would probably do that anyhow. Now where do we go from there?'

'We look for someone coming from the village,' said Miss Silver soberly. 'Tom Humphreys is indoors beating Nellie, Mrs. Larkin has gone upstairs to look out of her window. Someone comes down the road from the village and meets Flaxman at or near that waste piece of ground. Let us consider Flaxman for a moment. He has been bragging to Nellie that he knows something which is going to be a gold mine to him. It is a sign of his weakness that he needs someone to whom he can figure as a bold, determined fellow. A really determined man would have held his tongue. Flaxman is weak. He feels the need of someone to bolster him up. Then observe him in the scene at the cottage. He has been found out, and his conscience has made a coward of him. He makes no attempt to stand up to Tom Humphreys or to protect Nellie. He just slinks off with his charge of shot, and there, by the waste piece of land, someone meets him. He is probably feeling extremely sorry for himself. If the person is known to him, he will be glad of an arm and of help upon his way. There would be every opportunity of administering that fatal stab.'

Frank looked at her in an enigmatic manner.

'And who do you suppose that someone to have been?'

Miss Silver coughed.

'There are four possibilities, one of them a very shadowy one, but we may as well examine it with the others. Of the four people who might have stabbed Flaxman, three would have come from within the Ladies' House, and one from the gardener's cottage.'

'Old Humphreys?'

'It was to him that I was alluding when I spoke of a shadowy possibility. I do not, in fact, entertain it at all seriously, but he might have heard someone who was returning from the Falcon remark upon the fact that his son Tom had left unusually early. He might have heard some coarse speculation as to whether he had done so in order to catch

Flaxman with his daughter. Miss Falconer informs me that the affair has been the subject of village gossip for some time past. Mr. Humphreys could have decided to go and see what was happening. He could have put his pruning-knife in his pocket and yielded to a sudden temptation to use it.'

One of Frank's very fair eyebrows lifted quizzically.

'We began by talking about character, didn't we? Having regard to old Humphreys's character, you think that likely?'

Miss Silver smiled.

'I think it extremely unlikely. In fact, now that the bare possibility has been mooted, I believe that we may rule it out of court. In view of his known character, I find myself unable to believe that he would stand by and allow his son to be arrested for a crime which he had committed himself. He would, I feel sure, have gone straight to the police.'

Frank nodded.

'I think you are right there. And now let us have your three real suspects – the ones from the Ladies' House. I will leave you to name them.'

She said gravely,

'I do not think that we can entirely rule out Flaxman's wife. Stabbing is not really an English crime. When it does occur, it is more often the work of a woman than of a man. It is the frightened woman who picks up a knife to defend herself, where a man would use his fists. It is the suspicious, angry, jealous woman who strikes with a knife at the man who has betrayed her, or at the rival who has taken him away.'

'Yes, you are right there.'

'Miss Falconer tells me it is common talk in the village that Flaxman's behaviour has caused his wife a great deal of distress. I do not think that we can rule out the possibility that she may have waited for him outside the Falcon and followed him to Tom Humphreys's cottage. On the other hand she is, I think, much less likely to have gone to the potting-shed for a weapon than either of the other two suspects. When you consider the variety of knives with which a kitchen is equipped, I would certainly never expect a cook to go past them in the choice of a weapon.'

He burst out laughing.

'She leaves the court without a stain on one of her kitchen knives! And now perhaps we may get down to Trent and the alluring secretary.'

An involuntary look of surprise touched Miss Silver's small, neat features. Men were incalculable. You just had to allow for it. Even Frank –

'You found her alluring?'

He laughed.

'I do not allow myself to be allured when I am on duty.'

Quite, quite incalculable! That pallid, haggard creature with the uneasy something that would not let her rest! She said quite soberly,

'She does not seem like that to me.'

'You saw her plain and pale, didn't you? But you may take it from me that there are banked-up fires.'

Miss Silver put down her knitting for a moment and looked at him.

'And they are for Geoffrey Trent.'

'Now, do you say that because of what Ione Muir told you, or because it just came across and hit you in the eye?'

Her 'Really, my dear Frank!' reproved the expression, but she continued placidly enough.

'Miss Muir had told me of the conversation she overheard between them, a conversation which made it quite clear that there had been an intimate relationship. Mr. Trent assured her that the whole thing was over and done with before his marriage, and the substance of what Miss Muir overheard does bear that out. But when I had tea at the Ladies' House I became aware that as far as Miss Delauny's emotions were concerned they had by no means been relegated to the past. She was aware of Mr. Trent in the kind of way in which a woman is only aware of someone for whom she has a very deep feeling.'

He nodded.

'And Trent?'

'I could not discern that there was any response.'

He looked down on her from his place on the hearth. The rather mouse-coloured hair, no more visibly touched with grey than when he knew her first, was piled up in a fringe above the small face with its smooth, pale skin. He had never known a single hair to be out of place either in the fringe or in the neat coils at the back. There was the control of a net, but the still more potent one of a very exact and orderly mind. The brooch which fastened that hideous spinach-coloured dress was never by the smallest fraction out of line. The bog-oak rose had been temporarily supplanted by an ornament in the ample Victorian style. It contained the hair of her deceased parents enclosed in a wide border of plaited gold. The real affection of his glance was touched, and perhaps heightened, by a humorous appreciation. She was his esteemed preceptress. She was unique! He said,

'Well, ma'am – and which of them did it?'

CHAPTER XXXIV

Mrs. Larkin was singing in a loud cracked voice:

> 'If I was on a desert island,
> I'd – love – you.'

The tune was a catchy one. Under her erratic guidance it wandered from key to key, but retained a strident quality. She was engaged in hanging out a few kitchen cloths and dusters. Even with a clothes-peg in her mouth the horrid sounds continued.

Inspector Abbott, lifting the latch of the garden gate, surveyed the scene. It was not his first visit, but he now looked upon a good many details with fresh interest. Mrs. Larkin had gone in, and could be heard proclaiming shrilly:

> 'Up in an aeroplane
> I'd – love – you.'

He therefore had ample opportunity of looking about him.

The two cottages were no more than twenty yards apart. Each had a small square garden in front, a narrow strip at the side, and a good long piece at the back. Tom Humphreys's garden was a model of neatness – a row of crocuses on either side of the front door, signs of springing life in the tidy beds, and at the back a glimpse of spinach, broccoli, and winter greens. Mrs. Larkin's front patch could not really be called a garden any more. It was ten years since there had been a man to dig it over. The back was a wilderness, and the creepers on the house a neglected tangle. His eye went from them to the ordered roses, the blooming yellow jasmine next door. His lip lifted as he wondered whether it was not so much a husband as a gardener Mrs. Larkin had wished to acquire.

He went up the untidy path and knocked on the door. She opened it, her sleeves still rolled up, her hair blowing in wisps. It had not occurred to him yesterday, but this morning, with her small sharp eyes fixed upon him, he was reminded of a ferret. He said,

'Good morning, Mrs. Larkin. I wonder if I might have a word with you.'

'You were here yesterday with that Grayson.'

He smiled.

'You made a very interesting statement, you know, and you can't expect me not to be interested.'

He could have sworn that the tip of her nose twitched. She said with conscious virtue,

'It wasn't no more than the truth.'

'I'm sure it wasn't. But when it comes to putting down what is the truth there aren't so many people who can do it clearly. Now that is what struck me about your statement – it was so clear.'

She preened herself.

'I've always been one for telling the truth. "Tell the truth and shame the devil," was what my father used to say, and I'm sure he would have taken a stick to any of us that didn't. "Spare the rod and spoil the child," that was his motto. And not like some that I could name, with the lies

all piling up until there's a scandal and the police called in!'
She tossed her head in the direction of the Humphreys's
cottage.

Inspector Abbott said, 'How well you put it!' And then,
'Do you know, it would help me very much if you would run
through that scene in the garden again – just where you
were, and Tom Humphreys, and his daughter, and Flaxman.'

Mrs. Larkin was willing enough. It appeared that she
herself had been right up to the boundary fence. There was
a green hedge on the far side of it, but she had fetched the
kitchen stool and was able to look over the top.

'And Tom Humphreys, he never come no further than
that there gravel path going up to the door. He stands there
and he curses, and then he rushes in, and comes out with his
gun and lets fly at that Flaxman that was just the other side
of the road. He screeches, and Nellie screeches. And Tom
takes her by the shoulder and pushes her into the house, and,
"If you never took a thrashing in your life you'll take one
now!" he says. And bangs the door.'

'I see. You put it all very clearly. And what happened
then?'

Mrs. Larkin's face was puckered up with malicious enjoyment. She was very lined and brown, and she had the kind
of small sharp eyes which see everything. The fact that they
had no lashes gave them the appearance of windows without
blind or curtain. She said with zest,

'There was that Flaxman cursing away on the other side of
the road, so I called out and arst him is he all right, and he
uses language I wouldn't demean myself by repeating and
says I can mind my own business. So I went in and shut my
door.'

'And then?'

She tossed her head.

'There wasn't any "and then". I hope I know when I'm
not wanted. I went in and I locked up careful.'

Some time during the last minute or two she had found
herself leaving the garden for the house. It had happened
in the most unobtrusive way, with the tall plain-clothes police
officer suiting his step to hers and listening to her for all the

world as if she was the Queen of England. You couldn't have told him from one of the high-up gentry either, except that none of them had ever paid her so much attention. When he opened the sitting-room door and stood aside for her to pass, she was a good deal gratified.

The room was for high days and holidays only. It housed a photographic enlargement of herself and Jim Larkin on their wedding day, and the red plush suite which they had bought with their savings. It was with a glow of satisfaction that she sat down now on the extreme edge of the 'lady's easy chair', and watched Frank take his seat in the 'gent's ditto'. Quite at home he looked in it too. She had been parlourmaid to Lady Emily Crosby before she married, and butler-trained. Those small sharp eyes took in the cut of Inspector Abbott's suit and the quality of the shoes on his long, elegant feet. She knew something about gentlemen's clothes. The glow of satisfaction deepened.

He leaned forward with a smile and said,

'Now, Mrs. Larkin, let us take it from when you came in and locked up. What did you do after that?'

The wispy hair flew up as she tossed her head.

'I minded my own business same as that Flaxman told me!'

'Well, I don't know that we need bother about what he said. I think you put in your statement that he went off cursing.'

'You never heard such language!'

He made a mental note that she could hear it all right, and pursued the point.

'And whilst he was doing that and you were locking up, Tom Humphreys was beating his daughter?'

'And if anyone arst for it!' said Mrs. Larkin with a virtuous sniff.

Frank said,

'Quite. And how long did he go on beating her?'

The sharp eyes stared at him.

'That's not for me to say. I was in my own house minding of my own business.'

'Then you can't really say whether Tom was beating her or not?'

She gave a sniff that was almost a snort.

'Not say? I've got ears in my head, haven't I? Why, I could hear Tom Humphreys a-laying of it on, and her letting out a scream with every whack!'

'You would be upstairs in your bedroom?'

She closed down again.

'It's my own business where I was.'

He laughed agreeably.

'Mrs. Larkin, you are much too intelligent a woman not to have been taking an interest in what was going on next door. Don't tell me you were not looking out of one of the upstair windows using your ears and your eyes to the very best of their capacity. And that would be pretty good, wouldn't it? I shouldn't say there was much you would miss.'

The sniff this time was a modest one.

'I've been known for it from a child.'

'That doesn't surprise me at all. I could see at once that you have unusual powers of observation and the gift of putting what you have observed into words. A combination of the two is not at all common.'

Thus credited with uncommon gifts, it was up to Mrs. Larkin to display them. She said in a yielding voice,

'Well, and if I *was* in my bedroom – I suppose there's nothing out of place about that?'

'No, of course not. Now how long did that beating go on?'

Mrs. Larkin considered.

'All of five minutes,' she said.

'Five minutes from when you came indoors, or five minutes from the time you got upstairs and opened your window?'

She gave him that hard stare.

'Who says I opened my window?'

'But of course you did. It would have been very stupid of you if you hadn't. You wanted to hear what was going on, didn't you?'

She slid away from that.

'I didn't know but what murder would be done.'

'Exactly. Now just which way does this window of yours look? Do you mind letting me see?'

Oh, no, she didn't mind. Why should she? If her garden

was untidy, her house was always neat. The bedroom was tidy enough, with a clean cotton spread on the bed.

There was a casement window looking to the front. By setting it wide and leaning out Frank could see the Humphreys's cottage and its approaches, whilst more or less straight ahead lay the road to the village and the piece of waste ground where Flaxman's body had been found. Mrs. Larkin had certainly had a front seat for anything that might have been going on.

He returned to the charge.

'Well, Mrs. Larkin, how long did that beating go on after you got to the window?'

She gave him the same answer as before.

'About five minutes.'

'You could hear the sound of the blows?'

'Anyone could have heard them.'

'And Nellie screaming?'

'Every time the stick come down,' said Mrs. Larkin enjoyably.

'And when Tom stopped beating her?'

'Upstairs to her room, and bawling all the way.'

'And Tom Humphreys?'

'How do I know? I reckon he'd get himself a drink. Beating's thirsty work, and getting in the sort of temper he was in was worse.'

'Then he didn't come out of the house again.'

She gave him a look of sharp resentment.

'That's putting words in my mouth! I tell you I don't know nothing about what Tom Humphreys did!'

He nodded.

'My dear Mrs. Larkin, I wouldn't try and put words in your mouth for anything in the world. You are much too clear and careful a witness. As I told you before, you have an uncommon gift of observation, and what I want from you is just what you saw and heard. Come now, you were at your open window – what about it?'

She had drawn back, but she was not insensible to the fact that she was being treated with appreciation. If Inspector Abbott on his side could salve his conscience with the reflection that he had flattered her with nothing but the truth, Mrs. Larkin for her part accepted what he had said with the same conviction. She was a keen and accurate observer, with the kind of memory which can reproduce a narrative without varying a single detail. It is the kind of memory which is commoner in the country than in the town, and which used to be commoner still.

Appreciation was therefore only her right. But it had to struggle with a grudge. She could speak, or she could be silent. They couldn't get it from her unless she chose. All this was in the air as the Inspector said,

'Well now, Mrs. Larkin, just cast your mind back. The beating is over. Nellie has gone to her room crying. Don't tell me you were there at your window and never looked to see what was happening to Flaxman.'

She said in a stubborn voice,

'He went off up the road. Cursing like I told you.'

'You could hear him whilst the beating was going on?'

'Every now and again.'

'And after the beating was over – where was he then?'

'I couldn't say.'

'Couldn't, or wouldn't?' He used a light tone with a laugh in it. 'You see, I don't believe you could miss anything if you tried – and you can take that for a compliment. Come along now, I don't mind betting you had your eye on Flaxman all the time you were listening to the row between Nellie and her father.'

Her lips tightened.

'That's just what you say.'

He changed his tone.

'Look here, this is a thing you can tell me. If you could hear all that banging and screaming from the Humphreys's cottage, Flaxman must have been able to hear it too. Do you mean to say he just walked away and left Nellie to it? Didn't he make the slightest attempt to protect her?'

She gave a scornful laugh.

'What – him! He'd got enough to do on his own account, I reckon! That shot was worrying him above a bit. He'd took most of it about the back and shoulders. He'd go a little

201

way and turn round and claw at himself, and go on a little more and stop dead and stand there cursing.' She gave that scornful laugh again. 'He'd got enough to worry about without Nellie!'

'And how far had he got by the time the beating was over?'

Mrs. Larkin capitulated. She would be a star witness and have her pictures in all the papers. She said,

'Just about halfway to that waste piece of ground.'

They looked together from the window. The road was plainly in sight.

'You went on watching him?'

She nodded.

'For a bit. Enough to make a cat laugh the way he'd keep clapping a hand first one place and then another and cursing all the time!'

'You could hear him?'

'Enough to know he was at it. And a good thing he'd got too far away for me to hear the language!' She rounded this off with a virtuous sniff.

'Did you see him get as far as the waste piece of ground?'

'Just about the beginning of it.'

'And there was no one on the road behind him?'

'Well, no, there wasn't.'

'You'll swear to that? You may have to, you know.'

The tip of the sharp ferrety nose went an angry pink.

'Anything I've said is all the same as if I was on my oath! I haven't said nothing that isn't true! Nor nothing but what I'm willing to stand up in court and take my Bible oath on!'

'So there was no one on the road behind him — ' Frank used a meditative tone. Then, with an abrupt change of manner, 'Or in front of him, Mrs. Larkin? On the road from the village?'

She didn't answer. He said insistently,

'Was there anyone on the road in front of him, coming from the village?'

She backed away.

'Well then, there was.'

'Man, or woman?'

202

She shook her head.

'I couldn't see — nobody couldn't have seen. It was gone ten o'clock and more.'

'There was a moon.'

'It never come through the cloud. All I could tell was there was someone coming along the road. So I reckoned whoever it was would give Flaxman a hand. And I shut my window.'

'Sure about that?'

'Of course I'm sure! Nellie, she'd stopped crying — least-ways she'd stopped bawling out loud. And it was too dark and too far to bother any longer with that Flaxman, so I gave up. I was as cold as a stone. I made myself a good hot cup of tea and went to my bed. And that's the gospel truth.'

Frank came away with the strong conviction that it was.

'And if it is,' he observed to Grayson a little later, 'it lets Tom Humphreys out.'

Inspector Grayson said he thought so too.

CHAPTER XXXV

During the rest of the day everyone in the village was asked where he or she had been between half past nine, and half past ten on the night of Flaxman's murder. There was apparently a collective alibi for the men who remained in the Falcon after Tom Humphreys had gone out. They had left together at ten o'clock, and since, as it happened, all lived on the side of Bleake nearest to Wraydon and farthest from the waste piece of ground where the body had lain, they went home in a bunch, calling out cheerful good nights as each disappeared into his own dwelling. And all their wives were prepared not only to say but to swear that they had not gone out again. This left a number of people whom there was no reason for suspecting, and who were for the most part asleep in bed. And the women – wives, mothers, sisters and grandmothers of Bleake – who had no possible reason for setting foot outside at such an hour.

Grayson had worked solidly through the lot, when he encountered Miss Silver coming out of the village shop. She bowed, and was about to pass on, when he fell into step beside her.

'Abbott tells me it was you who put him up to the idea that Mrs. Larkin might have seen someone coming from the direction of the village. Well, I've been through the place with a toothcomb, and there isn't anyone who will so much as admit to having been out at the time.'

Miss Silver did not consider this at all surprising. Inspector Grayson was doubtless an excellent officer, but not perhaps endowed with the finer shades of tact. Put as he had just put it, his questioning of the local inhabitant could only have sounded like an invitation to confess. With a slight preliminary cough she enquired.

'Did you, perhaps, make it sufficiently clear that you were seeking for the co-operation of a witness, and not preparing the way for an arrest?'

He stared.

'They had got the wind up, the whole lot of them. If anyone was out, he wasn't going to admit it – you could see that.'

Miss Silver smiled in the dusk.

'Did you have any conversation with old Mrs. Pease?'

She was aware of his perk of surprise.

'Granny Pease? Why, no! She was in bed with the rheumatics, and as to going out in the dark, why she wouldn't think of such of a thing. She must be well up in her eighties anyhow.'

'Nevertheless I think you will find that she did go out on the night of the murder.'

'What makes you think so, madam?'

His tone expressed an obstinate disbelief. Miss Silver ignored it.

'Her daughter, Mrs. Bowyer, works for Miss Falconer. She arrived as usual on the morning after the murder, and before

it had become public property. In the course of a cast
conversation with Miss Falconer she deplored the fact that
Granny, as she called her, was so venturesome – "Slipping
out last night when everyone's back was turned, and not a
word where she was going. Said she'd remembered a very
particular cough mixture from her great-grandmother's
recipe, and finding she'd got a bottle of it by her, she'd gone
down the street with it to Mrs. Miller's where they hadn't
been able to sleep for nights on account of Stanley's cough.
And after ten before she came home!" '

'You heard this yourself?'

'No, Inspector, it was said to Miss Falconer, who only
spoke of it to me about half an hour ago. She had heard
that you were anxious to find anyone who might have seen
the murderer, and her conscience would not allow her to
keep silence. If I had not met you just now I would have
rung up the police station at Wraydon.'

He was frowning in the darkness, a fact which Miss Silver
was very well able to deduce from the tone of his voice.

'It is most unlikely that she saw anything at all, but anyhow she can't very well be suspected of the murder, so
perhaps she'll be willing to talk. I'll say good night, Miss
Silver.'

He went striding on past Miss Falconer's cottage. He
would have to see the old woman, but he told himself that
he expected nothing from the interview. On the other hand
she had been out until after ten, and Mrs. Miller's house
was the last in the village. Coming and going she would pass
the entrance to the Ladies' House. There were possibilities,
but of course no use to build on them. He stood knocking on
the cottage door, and wondered who would come to it. It was
not the least of his surprises that it was Granny Pease herself,
in a large black shawl and slippers of crimson wool. There
was nothing on her head but its own sparse white hair, and
she immediately complained of the draught and told him to
come in and be quick about it. By virtue of some attenuated
relationship to his wife she addressed him as Johnny.

'Come to have a nice little chat with me, have you? Time
was when young men would come visiting me evenings – and

never too late to start again! Sit you down by the fire. I've a nice strong cup of tea in the pot.'

The tea was stewed and bitter, but he took it, repressed a shudder over his first sip, and said in a good-humoured bantering tone,

'Well, Granny, I'm glad to see you up and about. Aggie told me this afternoon that you couldn't move out of your bed with the rheumatics.'

Her cup looked blacker and must have tasted worse than his own, but she seemed to be enjoying it. Her face twisted in a malicious smile.

'Didn't want me to see you – didn't want you to see me! Keeping of us apart, that's what Aggie was a-doing! Jealous of my new young man, I shouldn't wonder, and thinking I wouldn't know nothing about your coming because of me having my forty winks! But her Ernie let it out. "What's that Johnny Grayson want, coming here?" he says. And I give it to Aggie proper! And now that you're here, I'll arst the same as what he did. What do you want, Johnny Grayson? You'd better look lively, or Aggie will be home, and maybe she'll pack you off.'

As he told her, she began to laugh, shaking and rocking herself backwards and forwards till her tea spilled over and she had to set down her cup on the top of the stove.

'Well, I never!' she gasped. 'Think I went after that Flaxman and got him with Mr. Humphreys's pruning-knife? I daresay there's been women might have had cause to do him in. A bad lot, that's what he was, and that Nellie Humphreys not much better! But I didn't take a knife to either of 'em.'

He laughed too.

'I didn't think you did, Granny.' He allowed a pause to lengthen. 'I thought you might have seen something.'

'And if I did?' Her tone had sharpened. There was no laughter in it now.

'Then I hope you will tell me.'

She considered. Her tea must have been cold now as well as bitter, but she finished it before she said,

'Will I have to come into court and swear to what I seen?'

'That depends on what it was.'

'Well then, it wasn't much. I come along to Mrs. Miller's with the cough mixture for her Stanley –'

'What time would that be?'

'Half past nine when I slipped out the back door. Listening to the wireless they was, and I went quiet.'

'Did you see anything then?'

She shook her head.

'I went along on, and I got to Miller's and I give her the mixture.'

'How long were you there?'

She screwed up her face.

'I don't rightly know. She was talking about Stanley's cough and how they couldn't none of 'em sleep nights for it. And I was telling her about my old great-gran. Better than all your doctors and chemists and National Health she was! Made up stuff for man and beast, and what she couldn't cure nobody could, and no use trying!'

Grayson could see that this kind of conversation might have lasted quite a long time. He gave up trying to measure it and said,

'It was past ten when you got home.'

'Who says it was?'

'Aggie does.'

She made a grimace.

'Well, I daresay.'

'And now, Granny, you saw something when you were going home. What did you see?'

' 'Tweren't nothing to make a song and dance about.'

'What was it?'

'I'd got my shawl over my head and my slippers on my feet. The street were as dry as a bone. I'd got outside of Millers', and I'd gone a little way, when I stubbed my toe on a stone, right through the wool of my slipper. It hurt something cruel, and I took and stood still under the big holly right over the way from the Ladies' House. I didn't feel like walking on that foot till I'd got it eased off a bit. So there I stood, leaning up against Bessie Turner's front gate and thinking whether I'd be able to get home alone.

No one couldn't see me on account of that big holly what she won't never have clipped.'

'Well?'

'Now, Johnny Grayson, don't you go trying to hustle me! Cruel bad, my toe was, and if I could ha' stood on one leg I'd ha' done it.' She screwed up her face reminiscently and then opened a winking eye. 'Time was I could! Egg race, hop-skip-and-jump – I'd win 'em all!'

He laughed.

'Some time ago, Granny!'

She nodded vigorously.

'Not but what I can't do a thing or two when I've got to! You'd be surprised!' Her eyes sparkled with malice. 'Well, I was just seeing if I could get my foot off of the ground by leaning on Bessie's gate, when someone comes out atween the gate-posts of the Ladies' House.'

'Who was it?'

She gave an odd cackle of laughter.

'And wouldn't you like to know that!'

'Yes, I should.'

'Then want must be your master, Johnny, my boy.'

'You couldn't see?'

She tossed her head.

'Nobody could ha' seen! There's the trees hanging over, and a shadow as black as you please. All I could see was there was someone moving out atween the gate-posts and along under the trees.'

'Which way?' said Grayson quickly.

She wagged her head at him.

'Just the way you would like it to be, Johnny – round to the left and along the road to Tom Humphreys's. And if you want to know what I thought at the time, well, I thought it was that Flaxman going after Nellie.'

He could get no more from her than that. She had taken it to be Flaxman at the time, but she couldn't swear to any distinguishing mark of man or woman. What she had seen was someone moving in the shadows, and she would swear to that. But it certainly wasn't Flaxman, because the time would be somewhere after ten, when, according to Mrs.

Larkin, he had had his peppering and was making his painful and interrupted way towards the waste piece of ground where he was to be stabbed. Grayson could have no doubt in his own mind that she had seen the person who had stabbed him, but as to who that person might be his guess was as good as another's. It went no farther than that.

CHAPTER XXXVI

They were having coffee that evening in the drawing-room of the Ladies' House, when Ione said,

'I'm going up to town tomorrow, Geoffrey. I may stay a night or two – I'm not sure.'

Allegra put in a fretful,

'How sudden of you! I might have wanted to come too, but I can't all in a hurry like that.'

'Why, Ally, I told you this morning!'

'Yes, I know, but that wouldn't have given me time.' She shut her eyes and leaned back in her chair. Her voice faded out.

Ione found herself glancing at Geoffrey. He was frowning. Perhaps the same thought was in both their minds. Why must Allegra have time before she could go to town? To let someone know that she was coming, so that she could get more of the drug which had been destroying her? She said quickly,

'I heard from Louisa Blunt this morning from Paris. She has actually left the flat, so I can take it over at any moment, and I think I had better go up and see to the business side of it. She is the most casual creature in the world, and I shall feel happier when I have taken over the keys. She seems to have left them with a Mrs. Robinson who is the ground floor tenant. I don't know her, and she doesn't know me, but I've sent her a wire to say I'll call for them in the morning. I don't want to find she has gone out.'

Allegra opened her eyes and began to talk very quickly.

'It's going to cost an absolute fortune if you are really going to have new curtains everywhere. That pale yellow stuff with the feathers on it would be nice for your bedroom. You could lie in the dark and think of them coming down like snow, couldn't you?'

Jacqueline Delauny said in a vexed voice,

'I didn't know you were going to be away, Miss Muir, or I wouldn't have arranged to go out for the day, and now I am afraid it is too late to put it off. My friend has been ill, and it would upset her very much. I do wish I had known!'

Geoffrey showed some impatience.

'There isn't the slightest need for all this! I suppose I can look after Ally!'

Allegra half opened her eyes and said with a kind of absent sweetness,

'Better than anyone, darling – can't you?'

'I hope so.' He had a smile for her whether she saw it or not. Then he turned to Jacqueline Delauny.

'You're taking the Alvis, Jacky? I suppose you'll be back for dinner?'

'Oh, yes – I'm only so sorry –'

'There's no need.' Finality in the tone and in the gesture with which he set down his cup and went out of the room.

Jacqueline's eyes followed him. All the muscles of her face were taut, but the eyes gave her away. It occurred to Ione, and not for the first time, that she was heading for a breakdown. When the door was shut behind Geoffrey Trent she drew a long breath and turned back again. She said with an unusual agitation in her manner,

'I really am vexed, you know. Both of us to be away all day like this – I really wouldn't have had it happen! I thought everyone knew I was having the day to go and see my friend.'

Allegra looked through her lashes.

'I didn't. And Geoffrey didn't seem to.'

A quick flush coloured Jacqueline's cheek-bones.

'But of course he knew! He was letting me have the Alvis.'

The lashes closed down. Allegra put up a hand to hide a yawn. She said in an indifferent tone,

'Oh, was he? I thought – it sounded – as if he was asking you – if you were taking it. You don't generally wait for him to say you can – do you?' This time there was no attempt to suppress the yawn. She pulled a cushion down and snuggled up against it. 'So sleepy – ' she murmured, and appeared to all intents and purposes to be asleep.

Ione found herself saying, 'It doesn't really matter in the least, Miss Delauny. Allegra will be quite happy with Geoffrey, and it will do you good to get away.'

She tried to make her voice cordial, but even to herself it sounded cold. They had all been living in an atmosphere of strain, and it wasn't only Jacqueline who would be the better for getting out of it, even if it were only for a day.

It was a little before ten when they separated for the night. Ione went to her room and packed the very few things she was taking. As she went to and fro, as she bent over her suitcase, she had a most uneasy feeling that she was being watched. It was not for the first time. Every now and then when she was in her room there would come that feeling of alien eyes upon her. In the beginning she had thought of Margot, hiding somewhere in the room and ready to jump out. She would open wardrobe and cupboard and look under the bed, but there was never anybody there. And just lately she had found herself wondering whether the spy-hole that gave access to the study was the only contrivance of its kind in the Ladies' House. The thought was not a pleasant one.

She completed her preparations with relief, drew back the curtains, opened a window, and climbed into the four-post bed. It was stupid to start thinking about that sort of thing! Now, with the darkness covering her, she could tell herself just how stupid it was. Thought wandered a little way, and came back. There was something about being watched, spied on – it shook you. The house was too old. Too many people had lived their lives and thought their thoughts there. When you lay quiet like this they pressed about you and did not give you room. She fell into a most uneasy sleep. Afterwards she knew that she had dreamed. But the dream was gone. Nothing left of it but a shuddering sense that it had come out of one of the dark places of fear.

Her train was an early one. She was glad of the need to get up and dress. A lowering morning, but not wet. She put on her town clothes – neat black suit, fur coat, little hat with an edge of veiling – and was particular about make-up and nail-polish.

It was when she had turned back to take a used handkerchief out from under her pillow that the thing happened. It might have happened any day or at any time, this way or another way – what did it matter? But it had to happen now. The bed-head was carved in bold relief – flowers and leaves, an archer shooting at a deer, initials twined together and caught up in a lovers' knot. As she straightened up with the handkerchief in her hand, her hat pulled sideways. The veiling had caught in one of the carved initials. She felt it tear, put up a hand to the place, and jerked it free. The thought went through her mind that a pin would settle the damage, and that it would never show.

And then she saw the hole in the bed-head. The jerk that had freed her veil had opened a tiny panel. The shield which bore the initials and the lovers' knot stood out like an open door. A crumpled fold of paper stuck out. Without any conscious volition her hand took hold of it and pulled. The torn-out sheets of Margot's diary were there under her eyes. Crumpled sheets, and a scrawl in a childish hand. She saw Geoffrey's name. Her hand stiffened. There was no time, no place for thought, only one dominant impulse – to get away from the place where this poor child had been tricked out of her life.

She folded the sheets without feeling them and pushed them down the front of her blouse. The used handkerchief had fallen on the bed. She picked it up, took it over to the soiled linen-basket, and dropped it in. Then she shut the little panel in the head of the bed and went down to her waiting taxi.

The Alvis was ahead of them, storming down the drive, turning away to the left where they turned to the right.

CHAPTER XXXVII

Ione sat in the train with her eyes shut. She was in a carriage full of people, and every time the train stopped, which it did at every station, someone got out or got in. It was borne in upon her that in her hurry to get away she had caught the slow train by Marbury, which certainly did reach London in the end but not until it had picked up the inhabitants of a dozen villages bound for Marbury market. If she had not been so blinded by impatience she would have waited for the fast London train which left a quarter of an hour later and arrived a good half hour before the wretched contraption in which she was now being jogged along. Impossible to read the torn-out pages of Margot Trent's diary under the eyes of all these country people packed round her with their string bags, their baskets, their spreading coats, and the large feet which seemed to take up rather more room than there was.

At Marbury there was an exodus. She was left alone except for an elderly lady who appeared to be deep in a woman's magazine. The train would not stop again until they were near London. As it gained speed, she slipped her hand inside her blouse and brought out the folded sheets. When she had read them through she went back to the beginning and read them again. She had arrived with a kind of horrified amazement at the last scrawled line, when the elderly lady addressed her.

'If I do not interrupt you – you seem so very much interested – but I was wondering whether you would object to having the window very slightly open at the top.'

Ione gazed at her rather blankly. She had not really seen her before. There had been just an impression of someone drab in the corner. She now saw a long nose, a tight mouth, and a pair of very inquisitive eyes. She made haste to say,

'Oh, the window – no, of course – please do anything you like about it.'

'Just a couple of inches then. I cannot consider it hygienic to travel in a compartment to which no air is admitted. My invariable rule at home is two inches at the top and two inches at the bottom for every window in the house.'

It sounded frightfully bleak. Not feeling called upon to make any comment, Ione re-folded the sheets of Margot's diary and put them away in her handbag. What was she going to do with them? What could she do? She must have time to think.

She was not to have it. Those inquisitive eyes had followed her every movement. The rather high, precise voice addressed her again.

'Allow me to introduce myself – Miss Wotherspoon – 21 Marling Road, Marbury. A very pleasant locality – quiet, and yet close to a shopping centre. Perhaps I may know your name?'

Short of being rude to a chance-met stranger, a lapse for which Cousin Eleanor's training had completely unfitted her, she must give her name with as good a grace as she could contrive.

Miss Wotherspoon remarked that it was Scotch, had some general observations to make on that country, and came back to her starting point.

'I do hope that I have not disturbed you. I always think conversation makes a journey pass more pleasantly. But you did seem so much interested in what you were reading. Not a private letter of course, or I should not be remarking upon it. More like the pages from a child's exercise-book – very untidy writing. And of course a child of that age could hardly produce what would be of interest to a grown-up person.'

Ione said nothing.

But Miss Wotherspoon had not done. She gave a small hard laugh, and proceeded in a manner which was obviously intended to be arch.

'And you know, that was what made me just a teeny bit

curious – a child's exercise, and your deep interest. You did say, *Miss* Muir, did you not? But perhaps some niece? Or nephew?'

Ione found herself saying,

'Miss Wotherspoon, the child who wrote those pages is dead. And now perhaps you will not mind if I shut my eyes and do not talk any more. I have rather a headache.'

She leaned back into her corner and closed her mind to a number of small ejaculations such as, '*Oh, really!*'. 'I had no idea!', 'I'm sure I wouldn't for the world!'. Cousin Eleanor or no Cousin Eleanor, she could not have endured Miss Wotherspoon's catechism for another moment. That it would have gone on all the way to town, she had no doubt. And everything else apart, she must think – she must think – she must think.

Just how much legal weight would those scrawled pages carry? Would they be admitted as evidence? She just didn't know. What came to her more and more clearly was that she couldn't take the responsibility of knocking about London with them. They might be valueless, or they might be of an absolutely crucial importance. It wasn't her responsibility to say or to judge. She held on to her bag with both hands and knew what she must do. She couldn't carry this sort of burden alone, nor did she want to be alone with it any more at all. Something like the cold that glances back from ice sent a shudder through mind and body at the thought of it. She was taking no more responsibility, and following no more lonely paths. As soon as they arrived at the terminus she was going to put those torn-out sheets in a registered envelope and post them to Inspector Abbott at Scotland Yard. And she was going to ring up Jim Severn and ask him to meet her at Louisa's flat. She felt a most extraordinary sense of relief.

CHAPTER XXXVIII

Mrs. Robinson opened the door of her ground floor flat and beamed at Ione. She was one of those large shapeless women who must have been quite ravishingly pretty at seventeen before the apple-blossom colour had deepened to a universal flush and spread with all that spreading fat. She had on a short-sleeved overall, and the skin on the inside of the arm above the elbow was still as white as milk. And her eyes as blue as a baby's. Straw-coloured hair in a kind of demented haycock completed the picture.

'Miss Muir?' she said in a slow, pleasant voice. 'Pleased to meet you, I'm sure. And a good thing you sent that wire, or I'd have been out as sure as anything. And you needn't to bother about the key, because the other lady has just gone up with it.'

'The other lady?'

Mrs. Robinson nodded.

'Miss Blunt's cousin – elderly lady. Said Miss Blunt asked her to meet you here and explain about one or two things she was to look after for her.'

Really Louisa was too inconsequent! 'An elderly cousin' sounded like Lucy Heming, and if ever there was a bore and a person you couldn't get rid of, it was Lucy.

She took herself up in the automatic lift with the feeling that Lucy Heming on the top of Miss Wotherspoon was just about the last straw. She would expect to be provided with cups of tea, and she would cling. Useless optimism to imagine that she would vanish from the scene when Jim Severn walked in.

The door of the flat was ajar. She closed it behind her, slipping up the safety catch so that Jim would not have to ring. Four doors opened upon the little hall – bathroom and kitchenette straight ahead, each of them just a slip, bedroom to the left, and sitting-room to the right. The sitting-room door stood half way open. It disclosed Louisa's rather oddly assorted furniture. She was at the moment devoted to peasant arts and crafts, but had not gone so far as to divest herself of inherited Chippendale and Dresden. A tall grey-haired woman in old-fashioned clothes was looking out of the farther window. She turned as Ione came in, and she was not Lucy Heming.

There was a moment of bewilderment. Then, as the dark eyes met hers, Ione knew. A bare right hand came up out of a ramshackle old bag, and it held a revolver. Incredibly, but as it seemed actually, the revolver was pointed at Ione's head. The grey-haired woman said,

'Stay just where you are and put up your hands, or I shall shoot!'

The voice was, without any disguise, the voice of Jacqueline Delauny. It was all quite unbelievable, but it was happening. You can't argue with a revolver at point-blank range. Ione put up her hands.

'That's better!'

'I can't keep them like this for very long, you know.'

'It won't be for long – you needn't worry. Throw your bag over on to that sofa! Not anywhere in my direction now, or this little toy will go off!'

The bag was in her left hand. She threw it on to the sofa and saw Jacqueline Delauny edge round until she could reach it. The catch was a stiff one, and she could only use the fingers of her left hand, but she got it open, backed with it to her original position, and turned the contents out upon a small table without for a moment changing her steady aim. Purse, compact, handkerchief, shopping-list – she could only afford the swiftest glance, but she knew at once that what she wanted was not there.

'What have you done with them?'

'What have I done with what?'

'As if you didn't know!' Jacqueline's voice was deadly.

'Perhaps if you were to tell me –'

'I tell you you know – you know – you know! Pages from that damned diary! You found them!'

'Yes, I found them.'

With the first shock over, thought had steadied. She must play for time. Jacqueline would not shoot her whilst there was something she wanted to find out. She went on in just her ordinary voice.

'How did you know that I had found them?'

Jacqueline's voice dropped.

'Do you think I didn't watch you? Every night when you went to bed – every morning when you got up. There's a very good spyhole in that room – you'd never notice it was there. They knew how to hide things in those days. And I saw you find the diary. I always knew it was somewhere in the room, but I never thought of there being a hiding-place in the bed. I saw your veil catch and the door fly open. And I couldn't do anything about it – there wasn't time. I had to take the long way round to Wraydon, and change into these things, and catch the fast train up. A bit of luck your getting into the slow one. That's what you did, wasn't it? But you wouldn't have given me a second's thought if you had seen me on the platform like this – now would you? I had it all planned before you found the diary. You had to go because of the money for Geoffrey.' Her voice changed again. 'Where are those papers?'

Something very heavy was passing along the road. There was so much noise that it was useless to speak until it had gone by. As the rumbling died away, Jacqueline laughed and nodded.

'That is when I shall shoot you, my dear Ione – when something like that is passing. And I shall go away and tell Mrs. Robinson how frightened I am about lifts – I walked down the stairs, and there was such a very odd-looking man coming up – I was quite glad when I got past him.'

Ione wasn't sure – she couldn't be sure – but she had an odd sense of not being alone any more. She couldn't say that she had heard a sound from the hall – no one could have heard anything while that great lorry went by. But Jim could have opened the outer door on its safety catch and walked in. He could be standing behind her now in the little hall with no more than the slant of the door between them. It had been half open when she came into the flat, but she had begun to close it before she recognised Jacqueline Delauny. Nobody in the hall could now be seen from where Jacqueline stood.

Into these thoughts there thrust with harsh insistence,

'What have you done with those torn-out leaves?'

Ione allowed her voice to waver.

'Jacqueline, I really can't go on standing with my hands above my head like this. If you want me to answer your questions you'll just have to let me sit down.'

There was a small gimcrack chair with a brocade seat about a yard away on the left. Jacqueline considered it. Nothing within throwing distance. She nodded briefly.

'You can sit on that chair until I've finished with you. Keep your hands in your lap, and don't try anything on, or you'll be dead before you know what is happening!'

It was a relief to sit down, and she was clear of the door. She didn't quite know why, but that seemed important. If Jim was there in the hall . . . She began to wonder why she had thought that he might be there. If he was, then it could be very important indeed. They mustn't be in the same line of fire. Yes, that was the thing that was eluding her. She must hold on to it. Jacqueline must not be able to hold them both up at once. If she showed any sign of firing at one, the other must be able to rush her. That was it – keep taut, be ready to spring and spoil the aim. And meanwhile time – time – time –

If she could be sure about Jim.

She wasn't sure. When she had rung him up from the station there had been a kind of leaping gladness in his 'Ione!' She had kept her own voice quiet.

'I'm in a call-box on my way to Louisa Blunt's flat. She's really gone at last, and I've got to measure things up. I suppose you couldn't –'

'But of course I could! Just give me the address, and I'll be right along!'

That was the way it had gone. And if 'right along' meant

what it sounded like, he could have been here by now. But was that the reason why she had thought there was someone in the hall? He could have been there. It mattered so much – but was he –

It was no more than the faintest of faint hopes.

Out in the hall Jim Severn was standing within touching distance of the partly open sitting-room door. He had walked in whilst the heavy lorry was passing, checked at the sudden rush of noise, and as it died down heard Jacqueline Delauny laugh and say, 'That is when I shall shoot you, my dear Ione – when something like that is passing.' The words were quite incredible, but they froze him where he stood. He listened to Ione saying that she could not go on standing with her hands above her head. He listened to Jacqueline telling her that she might sit. As she moved to do so, he was aware that she was no longer in a direct line between him and Jacqueline. If he couldn't think of anything better before another of those heavy lorries came by, he could try what a sudden rush would do. The chances were that Jacqueline would swing round, and that meant she would swing away from Ione.

She might not – she might fire first – the revolver might just go off – he might have to take that risk. An agony like cramp took hold upon his mind. He would have to take a chance, and the thing with which he would have to take that chance was Ione's life.

In this moment, and once and for all, he knew just what it meant to him. He faced it as people do face unescapable danger, and with that the thing that was like cramp let go. He heard the women's voices and what they said. He would be able to repeat what they said. But it did not take up all his mind. Thoughts and plans came and went there. He thought about standing at the front door and ringing the bell. But Jacqueline had gone too far. She had said what could never be taken back. There would be no way out for her except by shooting, and she would shoot Ione first. No, his original idea of a desperate rush was better than that. Better still, something that could be thrown.

He looked about him. An umbrella-stand – an oak chest – a thin salver of pseudo-oriental brass . . . With infinite caution he began to move in the direction of the bedroom.

Inside the sitting-room Ione sat with her hands in her lap and thought about time – how it galloped – how it lagged –

Jacqueline's voice broke in.

'Where are those papers? Have you got them pushed down inside your things? Pull open your shirt and let me see!'

Ione undid the soft white bow at her neck and pulled the shirt away on either side. Even from across the room it was obvious that no pages from a schoolgirl's exercise-book were concealed there.

Jacqueline spoke angrily.

'Then where are they?'

Ione was doing up her shirt, tying the bow again.

'They're not here.'

'What have you done with them?'

'They are in a safe place. You won't really expect me to tell you where, will you? But I can tell you what is in them if you like.'

Jacqueline stamped her foot.

'You read them?'

'Oh, yes.'

'In the taxi – in the train? There wasn't time before you left the house! What did you *do* with them?'

Ione kept her voice level.

'Don't you want to know what Margot said?'

The foot was stamped again.

'What did she say?'

'That you told her Geoffrey said she could have one of the old ropes from the potting-shed. I don't wonder you were anxious to find those torn-out pages.'

'Where are they?' The words came quick and panting.

'I told you – in a safe place. If you shoot me, the police will have them.'

Jacqueline came a step nearer – a step – and another step. Under the grey wig and old-fashioned bonnet her eyes flared. Then with an unbelievable effort she controlled herself and took two slow paces back again. Her mind worked on the things which Ione could have done with those pages. Cloakroom at Wraydon – at the terminus – she could have made them up in a packet. Or she could have bought an envelope and posted them – to herself – to Geoffrey. If it was the cloakroom, there would be a ticket – it would be in her bag – she could use it when Ione was dead. She said,

'The cloakroom – you put them in the cloakroom!'

'Oh, no.'

'Then you posted them! You wouldn't let a weapon like that right out of your hand, would you? You posted them to yourself! Or to Geoffrey! Yes, to Geoffrey, so that you could make him send me away! Very clever, but not quite clever enough, because I shall see to it that the letter never reaches him! And even if it did – even if it did – I shall have done too much for him – a great, great deal too much! He can never do without me now!'

Ione's hands held one another. They must not shake. Her voice sounded cool and sceptical as she said,

'That sounds very grand, but what exactly have you done besides telling Margot she could take that rope? And supplying Allegra with morphia?'

For a moment she thought that the revolver would go off – there was such a blazing fury in Jacqueline's eyes. And then quite suddenly she laughed.

'Margot put that down? She had been hinting about it on and off for quite a time, but I wasn't sure how much she knew until just at the end. She would have had to go some time, but that meant I had to get on with it. You see, she was threatening to go to you. Oh, you can look at me, but if you knew how sick I was of the creature – her tricks, her slyness, the way she came between us! I tell you it was she who made Geoffrey break off with me! He was afraid she might notice something! As if I cared!'

Ione said,

'He was fond of her.'

Jacqueline laughed scornfully.

'That's Geoffrey to a T! Don't you know him yet? He is fond of people. It makes life so easy and pleasant. He was fond of Margot – he was fond of Allegra. He was getting quite fond of you. He was even kind enough to be fond of me!'

'Yes – he told me so.'

Under the elderly make-up Jacqueline had turned quite white. The effect was rather dreadful.

'I've done everything for him!' she said. 'Just everything! He couldn't have settled up Edgar's affairs without me. I knew them inside out. I could have done more if I had gone out with him to Alex. He wouldn't take me – because of Margot. But I got him to put in Muller as manager, and we were able to carry on with the dope business without Geoffrey knowing. Of course Muller had to go slow and watch his p's and q's, and there wasn't much for me to do on the receiving end for a bit, but we were getting going again, and Geoffrey thought his affairs were looking up. And then that fool Muller had to go and get himself arrested!'

Ione looked at her and said,

'Why did you meddle with Allegra? What harm had she done you?'

'What harm! She had taken Geoffrey, hadn't she! But that wasn't the reason. I may have my emotions, but I don't let them interfere with business. We had to have money. And then it turned out that there was not so much as we thought, and that Allegra couldn't even leave her share to Geoffrey whilst you were alive. So you came into it. She had to have your money, and then Geoffrey would have it all.'

'When Allegra had been got out of the way?'

'Oh, yes. An overdose – so easy with a morphia addict.'

'And me? That push in the back on the island at Wraydon – that wasn't really meant for Allegra, was it? It was meant for me.'

'Clever, aren't you!' said Jacqueline Delauny. Her whole voice and manner had coarsened. 'But I wasn't on the island, you know.'

'The Professor was,' said Ione – 'Professor Regulus Mactavish – the Great Prospero. And now I will tell you something you don't know. I heard him talking in a London fog. He had his foot in a half-open door, and he was saying that he wouldn't risk his neck for less than two thousand pounds.'

It was a shot in the dark, but when Jacqueline caught her breath and came out with 'Where – where were you?' she knew that it had come off. She said,

'I followed him – we met Jim Severn. You gave the Professor his orders, but he wasn't very good at carrying them out, was he?'

'He's a fool!' Jacqueline's voice was full of scorn. 'I was born in the show business, and he has been useful once or twice. His daughter can't do without our stuff, and he'll do most things to get it for her. But when the island business didn't come off he wouldn't go on – said it wouldn't be lucky for any of us.' Her voice went down into sombre depths. There was a silence before she said in quite a casual tone. 'So I had to take it on myself. And meanwhile Flaxman started in to blackmail Geoffrey. He heard Margot say that he had said she could have the rope. Well, he had to be got out of the way before I could deal with you. Child's play of course. The fool was running after Nellie Humphreys – I knew he slipped out to see her most nights. Easy enough to get word to her father – of course he never knew it came from me. After that I only had to watch my opportunity. Actually it fell out better than even I could have planned. The violent row and the charge of shot – well, they were just plain gifts from the gods. I'm born lucky, you know. Whatever Prospero may say! So that finished up the Flaxman business, and I was ready to deal with you.'

Ione had become less and less able to feel anything at all, but at this moment she felt a crawling horror. It might have been the matter-of-fact way in which Jacqueline spoke of Flaxman's death as a slight but necessary preliminary to her own murder, or it might have been that the shock which she had received was passing, and with it the merciful numbness it had induced. She said,

'You can't reckon up your luck till the end – and the Professor warned you.'

Jacqueline had a sudden startled look. There was angry protest in her voice.

'Prospero! I tell you he had cold feet! Him and his Scotch second sight! He can't come that sort of stuff over me – I've known him too long! I tell you I was born in the show business! And I'd have been there still if I hadn't had the wits to climb out of it! Prospero's my uncle – do you hear? He's my mother's brother, and that poor girl his daughter is what I might have been if I hadn't got out! Fell from the high wire when she was no more than a kid! And a cripple for life! That's why she has to have the dope! You and your smug complacency, what do you know about the way people live? You've always had money – background – security, where I've only had what I could get for myself! And what I'm going to get is everything that you have always had! And I'm going to enjoy shooting you to get it! There's something heavy coming now – as soon as it is right under the window I shall shoot! I hope you're ready –' The jeering note slackened on the last word and petered out.

Through the noise of the approaching lorry Ione was aware of movement in the hall. She did not hear Jim Severn's hurried tread, but she felt it. All lesser sounds were lost in the approaching roar, but under her foot the floorboards shook.

Things take so long to tell, and they happen so quickly. What had reached Ione reached Jacqueline a bare second later. Her voice failed. The door, already partly open, was kicked aside. A large bright green earthenware jug came hurtling through the air to send Jacqueline Delauny crashing back against the wall. The noise of the breaking china with all the weight of a full jug of water behind it was joined with the appalling racket outside. The solitary shot which missed everything except a hideous Majorcan vase was hardly noticeable in the general din.

Jim Severn, having swung his missile, followed it. Jacqueline lay crumpled up at the foot of the wall with shreds of green pottery scattered about her and a copious flood of water soaking into everything within reach. The revolver had flown out of her hand and lay between the windows. Jim Severn went across and picked it up. He remembered to use a handkerchief to wrap it in.

Ione got to her feet and went slowly across to where Jacqueline lay. She had not known whether her legs would carry her. They did, but she couldn't feel them. First she was sitting on Louisa's little upright chair whilst Louisa's bedroom jug flew past her and the shot which was meant to put an end to Ione Muir went off harmlessly and only broke a vase. Then she was standing looking down at Jacqueline and wondering if she was dead. Wig and bonnet had slipped. A strand of wet black hair hung down on the old fashioned coat. There was blood from a deep fast-bleeding cut. It crossed an outflung wrist, and the blood ran down into Jacqueline's hand. Did people bleed when they were dead? She didn't think they did. She went down on her knees in the wet and began to knot her handkerchief round the arm above the cut.

Jim Severn was ringing up the police.

CHAPTER XXXIX

It was late enough when Jim and Ione were free to go. Looking back to the time before the police arrived, it seemed as if it had lagged endlessly. Water and blood upon the floor, water and blood upon their hands. All that hatred and passionate feeling which had so horribly impended quite mute, quite still, as if it had never been. Jacqueline Delauny was alive. There was a pulse in the wrist and breath between the pallid lips, but it was like being in the room with a dead person. Presently they were not so sure that she was unconscious. Jim Severn kept himself between her and the windows. He had no intention of letting the police arrive to find them with a suicide on their hands.

After the police took over time moved into its second phase, a kind of dreadful hurry. Coming and going of the police surgeon – an ambulance – the removal of Jacqueline Delauny

– the taking of fingerprints – the taking of statements from Jim, from Ione, from Mrs. Robinson.

'You're sure she said that she was Miss Blunt's cousin?'

'Now what do you take me for, Inspector? Do you suppose I'd have let her have the key to go up if I hadn't thought it was all right? Half took a letter out of her bag and said Miss Blunt had asked her to meet the other lady here – got her name pat and all. "I suppose Miss Muir hasn't come yet?" she said. "I'm a little early. I'll just go up and open the flat." Very pleasant spoken she was, and how was I to think of there being anything wrong? There'd be an elderly lady here to see Miss Blunt every so often. Not that I ever had a real look at her, but you know how it is – these old things in their black clothes, why you don't take any particular notice of how they look.'

A very voluble witness. It took time to confine her statement to matters of fact.

Ione's statement swam in her head. Describing what had happened only made it seem less like anything real. She was here, in Louisa's room, and a policeman was writing down what she said, but it did not seem to be one of the things you can believe. The policeman looked at her rather oddly once or twice. Presently he said, 'Are you all right, miss?' and she found herself saying very slowly and carefully,

'Yes – I – think – so –'

She shut her eyes while he read her statement over to her, and heard the words go by. They were her words, but they meant less than ever now. She wrote her name, and the pen fell out of her hand upon the floor.

After that there was a fuss. Jim seemed to be angry, and Mrs. Robinson had made her a cup of tea. She was lying on Louisa's tight, hard sofa. Someone was saying that there was a taxi waiting. Jim Severn took her home in it. She thought of it that way. He might have been a properly married husband taking her home and scolding her most of the way because she had given him the fright of his life. In between he said things like 'Darling, are you all *right*? Are you quite *sure* you're all right?' – all incoherent and emoted. And she lay back against his arm and felt his shoulder warm and strong under her cheek.

It was Jim's turn to be scolded when they got to the flat. Nannie took charge with a will.

'I never heard of such goings on! And hours past her lunch – no wonder she's faint! But I've got a good drop of soup won't take a minute to warm, and a nice dish of cheese and egg all ready to put in the oven for tonight. And then into Miss Barbara's bed you go, Miss Ione, for there's nothing like a good sleep when you've had an upset!'

It was late when Ione woke. Barbara's room was dark except for the square of a window. The curtains had not been drawn. They hung straight and black on either side, and between them there was light reflected from a lamp in the street below. As she rose on her elbow, the door was very gently opened. In the sort of voice which would not wake the lightest sleeper Nannie spoke her name.

Ione sat right up.

'Is it frightfully late? I feel as if I'd slept for hours.'

'And so you have, my dear.'

The light was switched on and Nannie came over to draw the curtains.

'Eight o'clock, and time you had something more inside you – going without your lunch the way you did! I'm sure I haven't patience with Mr. Jim, and so I told him! And I was to ask whether you would have something on a tray, or if you would feel equal to coming in on the sofa and having your supper with him. There's a nice housecoat of Miss Barbara's you can slip on and not trouble to dress. And it's no use your saying a word, because she'd be giving it to you with both hands if she was here. Loving and giving, that's Miss Barbara from a child. So you take and put it on, my dear, same as she'd want you to.'

Barbara's housecoat was dark blue velvet, the softest, warmest thing in the world, and the most comfortable. It made her eyes look dark and her skin very white. It was nice not to have to put on the black suit again. Getting away from it seemed to lengthen the distance on the other side of which Jacqueline Delauny had talked about murder.

She said in a sudden startled voice,

'There won't be anybody coming round – from the police?'

Nannie looked grim.

'Only over Mr. Jim's dead body is what he said he told them. So I shouldn't think nothing about it.'

Ione turned tragic eyes on her.

'But, Nannie, I oughtn't to be here. There's my sister – Allegra! I ought to have gone down to her at once! I don't know what happened to me –'

Nannie sniffed.

'Clear wore out and no lunch,' she said. 'To say nothing of shootings and all sorts. And you needn't to worry about Mrs. Trent, because there's a Miss Silver rang up to say she was going over to stay with her until you came down, and you wasn't to worry, because she was quite all right. Not taking a lot of notice was what she said.'

No, Allegra was still in her dream. Things didn't really reach her yet – only if it was anything to do with Geoffrey – That seemed to get through. She would be all right with Miss Silver.

She went into the sitting-room to meet Jim, and he took both her hands and kissed them. And then Nannie came in with the soup.

She kept on coming in and out. Sometimes she stayed and talked – about Barbara, and about Barbara's husband and her children – about Jim when he was a little boy. 'And that obstinate, I never knew a child to touch him!' And whatever she said it was all as if Ione was part of the family and it was proper and right that she should know these things.

When she had finished clearing away Jim came and sat down on the sofa beside Ione.

'No one can stop Nannie talking,' he said. 'But she doesn't generally talk so much – about Barbara and me. I think perhaps she thinks you ought to know the worst.'

'She said you never changed.'

'I don't think I do – much. Would you find it dull?'

'I don't think so. I'm not very changeable myself – I mean about my friends.'

'I wasn't talking about friends. I was talking about us.'

She said rather faintly,

'It's too soon, Jim.'

He looked surprised.

'I don't know what there is soon about it. I knew at once – well anyhow the second time for certain. And then I tested that by staying away, and it only got stronger. You did say once that you felt as if you had known me a long time.'

She looked up, began a smile, felt it tremble, and looked down again.

He said, 'You see?' and put his arm round her. 'And when I was waiting in the hall in that blasted flat and I didn't know whether we were going to bring it off or not – well, I'm not going to tell you what I felt like then, but things don't hurt as much as that unless they are for always. Of course you can have as much time as you want – if you really want it, but I hope you don't. You see, you won't want to go and live in that flat of Louisa's now – at least I shouldn't think you would.'

Ione was unable to repress a shudder.

'Oh, no!'

'Well, I supposed you would feel like that, so I thought it would be a good plan to get married, and then you could come and live here.'

She looked up again, this time with spirit.

'Darling, people will do most things for a flat, but I draw the line at marriage.'

His arm tightened.

'You are to be serious! How did you feel when you knew I was bringing you here?'

Ione said, 'Safe.'

'I felt as if I was bringing you home. I want to know whether you felt that way too.'

Ione had one of her impulses. What did it matter how long they had known each other in the stupid measurements of time? What did it matter what people thought, or what people said? This was the place where she belonged.

Jim's voice was insistent.

'Ione, didn't you feel like that – *didn't* you?'

With something between a laugh and a sob she put her head down on his shoulder as she had done in the taxi and said,

'Yes, I did.'

CHAPTER XL

'Did you think it was the woman?' said Frank Abbott. 'In the end it lay between her and Trent, with quite a good chance that they were in it together. It's a bit of luck for him that the Delauny couldn't resist crowing over Ione Muir and making out how clever she was. And that there were two witnesses to what she said. Curious how the criminal must crow to someone. In this case, of course, she thought she was perfectly safe. Ione wasn't going to live to give anything away, so she could have a good time getting it off her chest and no harm done. If she hadn't been so explicit, Trent might have found it hard to clear himself. Which brings me back to where I started. Honest now – when it became clear that it must be one of them, which of them did you think it was?'

Miss Silver looked at him across the last stocking of the set which she was knitting for Roger, the youngest of her niece Ethel Burkett's three boys. Three pairs for Johnny and three pairs for Derek had already been despatched, and by tomorrow this set also would be in the post and she would be able to turn her attention to something pretty for little Josephine. She said gravely,

'I have tried to keep a perfectly open mind, but there was something about Jacqueline Delauny which arrested my attention. First impressions are of great importance, and both in her case and in that of Mr. Trent I received them during the inquest upon that poor girl Margot. It was plain that

231

both were under the influence of some very strong feeling. In Mr. Trent's case it really did appear to be grief, bearing out what I had heard of his affection for his ward. Miss Falconer talked about him a good deal, you know. From what she told me, and from my own observation, he appeared to me to be of a simple and affectionate disposition. I had, of course, to be on my guard against being too much influenced by her partiality. But it was not only in Miss Falconer's opinion that he stood high. Even sour old Humphreys had to some extent attached himself. My own impression deepened continually. Simplicity, kindness, a mind neither subtle nor clever – such people have few qualifications for a criminal career.'

Frank did not allow himself to laugh.

'And the Delauny? You got the impression that she might qualify?'

A slight cough reproved this levity.

'Owing to the position of my seat, I was able to observe her closely during the progress of the inquest. The first thing that struck me was that she was dramatising the occasion. All that dead black, where the two ladies of the family had been content with something quite simple and unobtrusive. But to dramatise a situation does not necessarily imply guilt. There are quite well-meaning people who have this habit, but they are as a rule self-centred and unstable. Miss Delauny appeared to me to be under the influence of some very strong emotion. Such a feeling is extremely difficult to hide, and though in this case it might be supposed that it was connected with the dead girl, I did not get the impression that the emotion was grief. It seemed to me to be linked with Miss Delauny's awareness of Mr. Trent, and to be susceptible of a very personal interpretation. I also felt sure that she was afraid. She was being very careful about her face, but as she held her hands together in her lap they strained until I expected every moment that a seam of her glove would start. In the witness-box she was calm. There was a rush of tears to the eyes when she was asked whether Margot had been reproved or punished for the tricks which she so often played. In what seemed like a genuine burst of affection and grief she

232

said, 'Oh, never!' and went on to explain that in such cases punishment only served to confuse the abnormal mind. The Coroner was, I discerned, a good deal irritated by these remarks. But the desired impression had been made. If there was anything to find fault with in the girl's treatment, it was on the side of too much indulgence. Later, when we were all leaving the hall, I had the opportunity of watching Miss Delauny. She had a handkerchief clenched in her gloved hand. She put it suddenly to her lips and held it there. At the same time she became aware that I was watching her. She looked down, but not quite in time. There had been a certain expression in her eyes, and the more I thought about it, the more convinced I became that what I had seen was a momentary unguarded spark of triumph.'

'Triumph?' said Frank in a meditative voice.

Miss Silver inclined her head.

'I became increasingly certain that it was something more than relief. Even the latter would have seemed inappropriate. In someone genuinely fond of the poor girl the mood one would expect was one of gentle sadness and regret, sympathy with Geoffrey Trent, and relief only to the extent that a painful ordeal was now over. But I was aware of feelings more intense than these, and without having any definite ideas upon the subject of foul play, I began to wonder whether an obstacle had not been removed. Miss Josepha Bowden had commissioned me to come down here with a view to setting her mind at rest upon the subject of Mrs. Trent. I had nothing reassuring to report. The poor girl was a drug-addict, and I had to consider whether her husband was in any way responsible for her state. I found myself unable to believe that this was the case. Especially as the plan of the projected crime developed. It was Miss Muir's life which was primarily aimed at. It was she who was to be pushed off the island at Wraydon in order that her very considerable fortune should pass to her sister. Mrs. Trent would then, but not until then, be able to make a will in her husband's favour. If she herself were to die first, her fortune would merely pass to Ione Muir. In the absence of a child, Mr. Trent could inherit nothing as long as his sister-in-law lived.'

Frank raised those very fair eyebrows.

'And with so strong a profit motive for Geoffrey Trent, you decided against him as a suspect?'

'I found it difficult to believe that he would engage in so subtle a plan. I did not think it would be within his competence, and he appeared to me to be genuinely fond of his wife. I may say that this has been amply borne out by the experience of the last few days when I was staying at the Ladies' House. Mr. Trent, though obviously suffering from shock and grief, was always to be relied on to show consideration and affection for his wife. The disclosures with regard to Miss Delauny, the part she played in Margot's death and in the murder of Flaxman, together with the discovery that she and Muller had not only been using the business which he had inherited as a screen for illicit drug traffic, but that she had been secretly supplying his wife with morphia – these things might have unbalanced any man to the extent of making him indifferent to the welfare of others. Yet during all the time of my stay Mr. Trent was in constant concern not only for his wife but for Mrs. Flaxman. The scornful accusation brought against him by Miss Delauny is a true one. He is a man of warm domestic affections. He becomes fond of people – his family, his employees, the people whom he meets. This is a quality very difficult to simulate. I found myself believing it to be genuine.'

Frank lifted a hand and let it fall again.

'As far as you are concerned the race is glass-fronted – you just look through and see what is going on. If I were to let myself think about it, it would terrify me!'

Miss Silver knitted placidly.

'I have cultivated the habit of observation. These things are not really difficult to perceive. In the case of Jacqueline Delauny there was an obvious strong emotion. I did not need Miss Muir to tell me what that emotion was. I was only surprised that it was not the talk of the village.'

Frank said quickly,

'It wasn't? How do you account for that? I thought villages knew everything.'

Miss Silver coughed.

'Miss Delauny was very discreet in her manner. She dressed as if she was in mourning. She devoted herself to her charge and to Mrs. Trent. In these circumstances a certain amount of devotion to Geoffrey Trent would be only suitable and becoming.'

'But you decided that it was more than that?'

Miss Silver said gravely,

'I thought it was one of those passions which bring disaster. As Lord Tennyson puts it, "The crime of sense" becomes "the crime of passion". When I came to see you I was feeling very anxious indeed. I believed Miss Muir's life to be in danger, but there was no evidence upon which it would be possible to take effective action. I was indeed thankful when, after Flaxman's death, a connection with the illicit drug traffic brought Scotland Yard into the case.'

Frank nodded.

'Geoffrey Trent is lucky to have been able to clear himself. Muller and the Delauny woman have tumbled over themselves to give each other away. But they both say Geoffrey didn't know. He was the ornamental figurehead, and a very useful one he must have been. Something likeable about the fellow in spite of his film star looks. Well, as I say, he's lucky though he doesn't think so at the moment. I never saw anyone so knocked over as he was by the torn-out pages of that girl's diary. No wonder the Delauny was ready to pull the house down to find them. I never saw anything so damning. The girl had watched and spied until there was very little she didn't know. "Jackie has let Allegra have some more of the white powder. I wish she wouldn't, but if I tell her I know, she'll let me do anything I want. I shall only have to say I'm going to tell Geoffrey and she'll eat out of my hand." That sort of thing, all in the most frightful scrawl and with every kind of spelling mistake. And at the end, "Jackie says Geoffrey told her I could have one of the old ropes out of the potting-shed. I don't suppose he did, because he jawed me so last night, but it'll do to tell old Humpy if he's cross." Poor Trent broke down and cried like a child. The girl must have written that sentence the last thing before going out and getting the crazy rope that killed her. And Jacqueline

Delauny told her he said she could have it. Well, as I say, he mightn't have been able to clear himself, so he's lucky.'

Miss Silver laid down Roger's last stocking for a moment.

'And Professor Regulus Mactavish?'

Frank's lip twisted.

'He may have been born to be hanged, but it won't be this time. There isn't as much evidence as you could balance on the point of a needle. Miss Muir heard him say he wouldn't risk his neck for less than two thousand pounds, and he says he was discussing a dangerous stunt in connection with one of his illusionist tricks. No one saw him push those two girls on the island at Wraydon, but half a dozen people, including yourself, saw him hook his stick round Allegra Trent's arm and jerk her back when she was almost under the bus. No, he's lucky too, but like Trent he doesn't think so just now. Do you know how I found him? Sitting with a bottle of whisky before him and trying to get drunk! He was just back from his daughter's funeral – the one he used to get the dope for. He'd a black muffler round his neck and the tears running down his face. And he couldn't get drunk! I came away and left him to it, but just about then he wouldn't have cared if I'd charged him with murder. The more people you meet, the odder they come, don't you think?'

After her own manner Miss Silver agreed.

'A study of increasing interest. I must always feel grateful that it has fallen to my lot. If I may quote again from Lord Tennyson:

> "To search through all I felt or saw,
> The springs of life, the depths of awe,
> And reach the law within the law." '

She laid down the completed stocking and smiled at him.

'There is a warning in an earlier verse. I forget just how it occurs, but it is worth remembering. It is: "Not to lose the good of life." '

He could have been moved to laughter. Perhaps he was. Maudie and her Moralities! Three quotations from Lord

Tennyson, Rogers' stockings finished, and a number of ends neatly and firmly tied! Deep down beside the laughter there was another spring. He took her hand and kissed it.

'Revered preceptress!' he said.

THE END

PATRICIA WENTWORTH

OUT OF THE PAST

Carmona Hardwick was spending the Summer entertaining friends and relatives in the huge, ugly old house left to her husband by Uncle Octavius. Their seaside reverie was rudely interrupted by the sudden arrival of Alan Field, a very murky figure indeed from Carmona's past

Co-incident with his arrival was a marked rising of tension in and around the house. When that tension exploded into murder, it was only the fortuitous presence of Miss Silver which enabled this highly complex business to be sorted out. Indeed, if her wisdom had not intervened, virtually anyone *but* the murderer might have been arrested.

'Miss Wentworth's plot is ingenious, her characterization acute, her solution satisfying.'
The Scotsman

CORONET BOOKS

OTHER TITLES
BY PATRICIA WENTWORTH

All these books are available at your local bookshop or newsagent, or can be ordered direct from the publisher. Just tick the titles you want and fill in the form below.

Prices and availability subject to change without notice.

CORONET BOOKS, P.O. Box 11, Falmouth, Cornwall.

Please send cheque or postal order, and allow the following for postage and packing:

U.K. – 40p for one book, plus 18p for the second book, and 13p for each additional book ordered up to a £1.49 maximum.

B.F.P.O. and EIRE – 40p for the first book, plus 18p for the second book, and 13p per copy for the next 7 books, 7p per book thereafter.

OTHER OVERSEAS CUSTOMERS – 60p for the first book, plus 18p per copy for each additional book.

Name ....

Address ....

....